A Montrose Valley Romance

COMING HOME FOR CHRISTMAS

Karen Baugh Menuhin
& Jo Baugh

Copyright © 2024
by Little Cat Publishing Ltd

Published by Little Cat Publishing Ltd

All rights reserved. No part of this book may be reproduced or used in any manner without written permission of the copyright owner except for the use of quotations in a book review.

This is a work of fiction. Names, places and incidents either are the product of the author's imagination or are used fictitiously. Any resemblance to actual persons, living or dead, events, or locales is entirely coincidental.

NO AI TRAINING: Without in any way limiting the author's [and publisher's] exclusive rights under copyright, any use of this publication to "train" generative artificial intelligence (AI) technologies to generate text is expressly prohibited. The author reserves all rights to license uses of this work for generative AI training and development of machine learning language models.

First paperback edition.

ISBN 979-8-3338491-1-3

*Dedication to Stuart, Alex, Evie and Beth
who are simply the best*

CHAPTER 1

Only forty minutes to go! She'd been lost in a daydream, but the huge modernistic clock up on the slate paneled wall caught her eye. She double checked her watch — the meeting was meant to be quick, but the guy from accounts was still droning on. What was his name again? Dickie? Rickie? Forty minutes was enough time, wasn't it? She wouldn't miss the train…

The bean counter held a sheaf of notes in his hand. He turned another page — there were even more to go — and she still had work to finish. A frisson of panic caught her breath. Should she do something? Ideas ran through her mind — *I could faint? Don't be ridiculous, who faints nowadays? I could knock my water glass over my horrible gray skirt? Nope, finished my water twenty minutes ago. Knock a whole jugful of water all over the conference table?…No Jessica, don't you dare…*Not that she ever would, conscientiousness and duty had always defined her, and it had been reinforced from an early age. Mom's mantra rang in her mind. *'Don't rock the* *boat; Jessica, if it's you or a man to go, you can guarantee it'll be you.'*

It's 1992, Mom, times have changed, she'd objected, but the mantra had been repeated too many times.

She covered her watch with her hand and turned her gaze to the world outside. Enormous floor-to-ceiling windows overlooked the Manhattan skyline, she could just make out the top of the spectacular Christmas tree at Rockefeller Plaza through a swirl of snow flurries. This time of year, the city was blazing with color — lights everywhere, Santas ringing handbells in the street, dazzling window displays in all the department stores, and merry music blaring from every shop doorway. New York certainly put on a show, but all the lights and holiday cheer only served to make her homesick — if you could be homesick for a place you've never lived.

The flurries thickened. Would the trains be running on time? The lines got dicey up past Albany this time of year. Maybe they'd be late? Or early, so as not to be late? Her pulse quickened. Only one overnight train ride on the Montrealer and then she'd be in her favorite place in the world: Montrose, the town at the heart of Montrose Valley, Vermont.

"Jessica?" Her boss, Frank, startled her. She snapped upright, brown eyes blinking. "Could you stay for a couple more hours this evening? We might be able to knock out that new section of code by seven. What d'you say?"

She looked round at her colleagues — whose eyes widened in alarm, as though they might be his next victim.

She opened and closed her lips, quelling a stammer. "I'm leaving for vacation right after this meeting. Remember?" She tried an upbeat note and a smile.

The smile achieved nothing. Frank's frown deepened, his sandy brows almost touching. "What, already? Did I approve that?"

Jessica took a breath. There was no way she was going to miss out on Montrose. "Yes, but I'll be back on the 31st for the New Year's Eve launch." And a great New Year's Eve that was going to be — testing and fixing errors all night to ensure their new platform launched right on the stroke of midnight.

Frank continued to look dubious, as though this was news to him. "There's plenty to do between now and then."

Jessica's shoulders dropped. "But we talked about it at the start of the year." *Then again in August. And again last month, when it came time for him to sign the final forms.* It had even been logged into the wretched accounting system for the past three weeks. She'd saved up her entire annual vacation days for this — two whole weeks of freedom over Christmas.

Frank scratched the back of his bald head. "With the launch coming up, we really need the whole team…I'm not sure we can spare you.…"

Around the table, Jessica's colleagues shifted uncomfortably in their ultra-modern chairs, trying to avoid getting dragged in. Frank's lectures all ran around the same track, which was why Jessica had been careful to do this by the book. "I'm really sorry, but I just can't change my plans this last minute." She held her breath, forcing herself not to break eye contact.

After what felt like an eternity, Frank's gaze slid away. He stood up. "No, no, of course not," he sounded peeved. "But don't you forget about that Team Leader role. You're in with a chance, but there's plenty more wanna take a shot at it." He nodded at her colleagues, watching every move. "You have a great vacation, Jessica." He made it sound almost like a threat.

"And you too," she replied, flashing another determined smile.

The carrot and the stick — Frank was good with those. She let her breath go slowly, then sat up, back straight, trying to focus as Rickie ran through more accounts stuff. There were just a few more lines of code and one last test run waiting for her at her workstation and then she'd be free! Bags packed and waiting under her desk, she was all ready to go — no reason to go by her cramped Queens apartment.

The meeting finally ended and everyone filed out into the corridor, no-one talking, faces set and serious. She reached her desk to find the red light on her phone flashing. Two new voicemails. *If this is Frank telling me off, I swear…*Jessica picked up the phone, a lock of chestnut hair falling to curl against her cheek, she pushed it back behind her ear as she straightened up and braced herself for another argument.

"Are you on your way yet?" The moment the chipper voice filled her ear, Jessica broke into a huge grin. Lily never

bothered with trivialities like hello or goodbye. She just launched straight into whatever thought she was currently nursing. *"I hope you packed good boots. And extra gloves — but if you forget, we can pick up more at the Christmas market. It's opening tomorrow! Did I tell you I signed up for a couple of volunteer slots?"*

Jessica stifled a laugh. Lily had indeed informed her of the Christmas market plans. Along with at least a half dozen more activities: carol singing, the Santa parade, festive dinners and tours... Not that Jessica was a tourist. She'd been visiting Montrose since she and Lily first met at Montrose Valley summer camp as preteens. But she'd only ever visited the valley in summer — long, beautiful, sun-drenched summers that she missed dearly, even now.

The last time she'd been in Montrose was for Lily and Grant's wedding the previous July — a whole eighteen months ago. Lily was always talking about how Montrose came alive for Christmas. It sounded like a real life snow-globe scene. The tiny town (population 800, last Jessica checked) swelled to more than double its size over the holidays. Tourists came from all over, because everyone wanted that picture-perfect Vermont Christmas experience.

Jessica included.

"I hope the trains are behaving," Lily was speaking too fast as usual. *"This snow's only getting heavier anyway, but that's not why I called! I just wanted to warn you that I may have gotten myself into a bit of a pickle... I'll explain more when*

you're here. Grant and I will pick you up at the station in the morning. Can't wait to see you!" She almost sang.

The beep sounded, leaving Jessica beaming. A pickle? Knowing Lily, that could mean just about anything.

Jessica hit play for the next voicemail, and her smile wavered. *"Hello, Jessica dear, it's your Mom."* Her mother's soft voice. *"Just calling to say have a safe trip. Could you call me when you get in?"*

The line went dead and Jessica exhaled, anxiety knotting in her chest. She tucked the phone back into its cradle, feeling grateful her mother hadn't tried to change her mind again. Her brother had invited her and their mom to his fancy penthouse apartment in Central Park West. Simon was the real high flier in the family. Something in finance, he talked about hedge funds a lot. Fine, he was the golden boy, and Pop had always said Jess was just as clever, but she was a girl and a very pretty girl at that... Simon called his little sister Beanpole because she was tall and thin and without curves, and mostly still was...She sighed. Simon hadn't been exactly thrilled about her decision to spend Christmas in Montrose Valley. If he was upset about Jessica missing the holiday at home, she'd understand, but that wasn't his problem — he kept talking about how unprofessional and inappropriate it was to take time off just before the big launch. "You're the one saying that you're as good as anyone and you'll show us all," he'd teased her, although there was an undertone there. She understood why, after Pop died, Mom had cleaved closer to her smart son, and he'd helped her out, and Jessica had tried the same. But she was still building her way into a career. Simon was older, more established, he could take time off and Jessica just couldn't.

You're just starting out, honey, her mother had said in support. *You're so lucky to have landed such an amazing job, and in that big fancy building, too. It's such a great opportunity. You need to put in your dues now, while you're still young enough to climb the ladder.*

While Jessica understood where the concern stemmed from—growing up, she'd witnessed firsthand how her mother's abandoned career still haunted her, even though being a stay home mom was normal back then. But it was 1992 now; Jessica was twenty-six and yearned for a life of her own; time and freedom to do the things she loved, like going to Montrose to spend Christmas with her closest friend.

The clock was ticking. As her computer sighed to a close, she tugged her canvas bag out from under her desk, then weaved her way out between cramped workstations. Nobody waved, or even looked up, they were all bent over their keyboards, fingers tapping furiously, eyes glued to their screens. Frank watched her from his gleaming glass and chrome corner office, the stark overhead lighting reflecting off his bald head; she felt a twinge of guilt — was she being a bad team player? Leaving everybody in the lurch?

No! She told herself. I'm not going to let him browbeat me. She'd worked overtime for weeks to get ahead of her project and delivered everything she'd promised and been assigned. She'd even sacrificed her summer trip to Montrose and spent the whole year working. It's the first chance she'd had to spend Christmas in Vermont, and it might be the last for years…maybe ever, she thought to herself.

Ned's desk was at the very back of the room. Poor guy, if he could climb inside his computer, she'd swear he would. She gave him a big smile as she walked by. His pallid cheeks flushed pink, then he held out a piece of paper torn from a pad. *Happy Christmas Jessica* was written in tiny neat letters. She stopped, turned about, and bent to kiss him on the cheek. He turned beetroot red.

"Happy Christmas Ned," she said, softly.

The ladies' room was deadly quiet. Locking the door, she tugged nearly new jeans and an overlarge cream cable sweater from her bag. The sweater was brand new, and she stopped to hold it up, smelling the wool and feeling the softness against her cheek. Then she quickly changed out of her drab work clothes and sensible shoes, pushed slim feet into fur-lined snow boots and finally shrugged into her long red winter coat. There was just one more thing to add — a red bobble hat with snowflakes embroidered around the rim. A bubble of excitement burst into a dazzling smile — now she was 'Holiday girl!'

No one said a word in the elevator, although there were a few sideways glances as she stood with brown eyes sparkling among her gray-suited colleagues. She was largely oblivious to the admiring glances. Tall and willowy with lithe limbs, gleaming chestnut hair falling in soft waves, flawless skin and molded lips always ready with a smile. She'd been pretty as a girl and had grown into an alluring young woman. Not that she thought much of it. It's what's inside that counts! Her mother had taught her that, too.

"Happy holidays, Miss Jessica," Peter the porter called from his desk with a grin.

"And to you, too, Peter!" she called back gaily.

The glass doors swished aside as she hesitated on the threshold. Swirling flurries had turned into something closer to sleet, and heavy, leaden skies rolled over the tops of the towering office buildings. Heavy traffic had already churned the fresh snow into grim, gray sludge. Heaps of it lined the sidewalk with only a narrow walking path in the center, replete with ankle-deep puddles.

Only five blocks to Grand Central, then she was on the home stretch. She took a deep breath and stepped out onto the crowded sidewalk to thread through the hunched commuters trudging home.

The train was already in the station. She breathed a sigh of relief as she climbed aboard. There was a seat left next to the window. She stowed the bag, took out her book, and tried to suppress her smile. She was on her way!

CHAPTER 2

Dawn broke in long rays of pink and pale gold just as the Montrealer coasted the last miles toward Montrose Valley. Jessica was already sitting up in her plush red seat, nursing a cup of coffee from the dining car. She nestled closer to the window, ignoring the snoring man slumped across from her, and leaned her tired forehead against the cold glass. This view, the first glimpse as you entered the Valley, was her favorite in the summer, and now she watched in wonder as the breathtaking panorama unfolded in winter white.

The train had climbed the snow-glazed mountain pass and snaked through the spectacular mountain range surrounding the valley. Below them, so far down it looked like a model Christmas village in a Fifth Avenue window, Montrose sparkled as the long rays of dawn spread across white blanketed meadows, lighting up the valley.

Jessica drank in the familiar sights: the river — now a frozen skein of ice — that wound through the valley bottom. The diamond-shaped lake off in the distance, where she and Lily used to canoe with their fellow summer campers. Including Lily's cousin, Luke…

The town lay in the center, a collection of roofs, spires, houses…there was the town square, its huge Christmas tree only a speck from this distance. Next to it, the main church, with its slender white steeple, surrounded by the historic district with its stately Greek Revival and Federal style homes. Further afield, farmhouses with board and batten sidings dotted the tree-lined slopes around town, and if she looked hard enough, she could just make out the cluster of Dutch barns and wooden cabins of the summer camp.

Memories of her last year there lingered, especially that final going away weekend. Luke had taken her hand, and they'd slipped out of the movie show and while the rest of the camp was still engrossed in E.T., they'd walked up to the long jetty jutting out into the lake.

Jessica and Luke had danced around each other all summer — a glance here, a brush of fingers there, a late-night dare jumping into the lake clad only in their underwear… But that last night, she'd finally realized she wasn't imagining things. That he felt the same way about her.

She'd never forget that first brush of his lips. The taste of her cherry lip gloss mingling with the Coke he'd been drinking, the beating of her heart so loud she was certain he could hear it.

Then she'd returned to finish High School, and he'd gone away to veterinary college, returning years later to join the local practice, which he now ran himself.

She'd probably see him around town...

She sighed so heavily it fogged the train window. They were little more than children back then. It was 10 years ago and her first ever kiss — of course she romanticized it. And last she'd heard, Luke had a girlfriend. He was off-limits, and she'd been working too hard. All work and no play had her pining for memories of a romance long since gone.

Although she could have sworn there had been something there at Lily's wedding, but they had both been so busy with their bridesmaid and groomsman's responsibilities that she'd barely had time to eat dinner, let alone dance with anyone — Luke included.

Rolling her eyes at herself, she abandoned the view to start organizing her bags. She always spread out on trains, and last night had been no exception. Tugging her coat back on first, she collected the book she'd been reading. A family saga stretching over generations, love and loss amid the struggle to survive. She gazed at the illustrated cover, then tucked it into her handbag.

As the train screeched slowly into Montrose station. Jessica was already at the door, red bobble hat pulled low over 'sleepy head' hair, handbag over one shoulder, case gripped tight. She was practically bouncing on tiptoes as she waited for the train to stop.

Through the door window, she spotted the petite figure in a pink coat with the telltale shock of strawberry blonde hair scanning every window of the train. Lily saw her a second later, and jumped up and down, waving with her entire body. Next to her, Thor, her enormous sweetheart of a husky, barked frantically, with Lily's ever-patient husband, Grant, keeping a firm grip on his leash.

Husband — that sounded so strange, Jessica was still adjusting to the term. For most of the years she'd been coming up here, Lily had simply called Grant "the doctor" or "the man." No need to get more specific, because Jessica always knew who she meant, no matter how many times the pair of them will-they-or-won't-they'ed.

When they'd finally gotten together, a little over two years ago now, they'd speed-walked through fiancés and straight into a blissfully happy marriage.

The wedding had sealed their happiness. Lily had never seemed more content, or Grant, for that matter. Every time Jessica phoned, they were laughing over something or other, cooking cozy dinners at home, or figuring out what to fix up next in their old farmhouse.

The train juddered and squealed to a halt and after an interminable wait, the doors wheezed open. As the stationmaster shouted "Montrose Station, change here for Montrose Valley," Jessica was already halfway down the steps, and by the time she reached the platform, Lily had nearly bowled her over.

"You're here!" Lily cried, face buried somewhere around Jessica's shoulder. "I can't believe it."

Jessica dropped her bag and wrapped her arms around her friend. "I made it! I finally made it!" She laughed in delight, both of them hugging and smiling like crazy. "I've been dreaming of this for so long!" Jessica exclaimed and stepped back the same time Lily did.

"Still the same lovely Jessica," Lily said and dashed a tear from her eye. "I was so worried they'd find a way to hold you back."

"So was I," Jessica replied. "But I'm not missing this Christmas with you guys."

Grant was still restraining Thor, who was whining in excitement, tail wagging furiously. "I'd come hug you too, but Thor might flatten you in the process."

"Let him go. I'll be fine," Jessica said.

Grant eyed her dubiously, his eyes dark below black brows. "You sure? You might wanna brace yourself." He spoke in his usual steady, reassuring tone.

Jessica dropped to one knee. Only then did Grant drop Thor's leash and the dog bolted straight into Jessica's arms, wriggling all over like a kid who'd just eaten his entire sack of Halloween candy at once, his snow wet paws soaking her jeans in an instant. Struggling to keep herself upright, she couldn't quite dodge the tongue on her nose — how did Thor always manage to aim straight for that?

Laughing and wiping her face, she struggled back to standing while the dog raced circles around the three of them. "This is just so wonderful," Jessica said.

"You have no idea." Lily grabbed her arm, tucking it into hers, while Grant picked up Jessica's abandoned bag from the platform. "I've been dying here without you. A whole Montrose summer with no Jessica."

"You came to visit me just before fall." Jessica reminded her.

"I know, but it's not the same," Lily countered, then grinned again. "It'd be best if we could have you for all seasons."

"I know, but let's be real," Jessica said. "So, what's on the agenda? I heard something about a market?"

"Now you've done it." Grant grinned, showing white teeth in a tanned face, the morning sun catching his thick black hair. Tall, strong, with Greek good looks from his mother's side; Dr. Grant Ellis was a calm foil to Lily's fizzing energy, and a firm favorite at the local hospital.

Lily's blue eyes lit up in her heart-shaped face. A spatter of freckles across a small nose, pale skin and lips painted frosted pink. She was as pretty as a porcelain doll. "Okay, so, yes. We're volunteering at the Christmas market tomorrow — I figured you might need a bit of a rest day, although, you know, not too much of a… well, you'll see." She breezed ahead of them, leading the way along the platform, dry under cover of the canopied roof, its red and yellow painted beams redolent of steam, coal, and days of old. Behind them, the train eased its way out of the station, continuing on its journey.

They walked out onto Main Street.

Jessica's breath caught.

Unlike the gray sludge in New York, the deep snow here was pristine, its smooth surface sparkling with tiny crystals of ice catching the sunshine. Christmas lights strung across the streets, evergreen garlands tied with red ribbons framed the windows of stores and offices. A magnificent blue spruce stood in the center of the square, strung with hundreds of tiny bulbs, and beautifully decorated in baubles of red, green, and gold.

They turned left onto Main Street, chattering gaily along the snow-bound path. The postwoman spotted them and waved a gloved hand. "Lily, I've got a real heavy package in the back for you."

"Oh, thank you, can you drop it at Mom's?" Lily called back. "We're headed over there now."

"Sure can. I've a pile of mail for her anyhow. Oh, and happy hunting!"

"Oh, not you too, Janie!" she said in mock horror as the smiling postwoman climbed into the USPS van.

Jessica looked puzzled, although she was more surprised by the news that they weren't going straight to Lily's. "We're going to your parents?" She'd been counting on a hot shower and brush up.

"Just a quick welcome home," Lily promised. "Seriously, you'll love it! And we left our car there, so no more walking afterwards."

"Right, OK…" At least Lily's parents were only a five-minute walk from the train station — as opposed to Lily and Grant, who lived on the outskirts of town.

"I take no responsibility for any of this," Grant said.

Before she could ask for more details about this 'quick welcome home,' Lily elbowed her side.

"Did you get my voicemail?"

"Yes." Jessica glanced over. "What's this about a pickle?"

Lily heaved another sigh and threw her hands in the air. "It's all Caitlin's fault."

"Ugh," they chorused. Caitlin and Grant broke up three years ago, yet somehow she always found an excuse to try and worm her way in between Grant and Lily.

"I thought she'd give up the ghost now that you're, you know, married," Jessica went on.

Lily glanced over her shoulder at her husband. "Funny you should say ghost. Remember how I told you about my new business idea?" she asked, turning back to Jessica.

Nodding, Jessica said, "Sure. You want to digitalize genealogical records so you can help more people find their ancestors or connect with relatives they've lost touch with." It was a great idea, and right in line with Lily's joint passions: helping people and delving into history.

"Yes! Well, Grant suggested I talk to Ed about advertising the business — you remember Ed Stanton, right? He runs the Post."

The Montrose Valley Post, the biggest newspaper in the valley. "Sounds like a good idea," she said slowly, sensing a catch. Especially when Grant started laughing.

Lily aimed a swat in his general direction. "Be quiet, you," she ordered. "The thing is, Caitlin's working for Ed now. He sent her to write the story, which was really uncomfortable, you know. Anyway, I was explaining the business, how it's kind of like hunting for ghosts, since you can only find traces of some people…"

Grant started laughing louder. Thor barked excitedly, always eager to be included.

"No sympathy in my own family, I swear," Lily grumbled. She fished in her pocket. "Well, Caitlin took my quote totally out of context. Look." She thrust a crumpled page of newspaper under Jessica's nose.

Jessica took it, stopping to smooth the paper until she could read the headline. *Local Entrepreneur Lily Ellis Starts Ghost-Hunting Business.* She took one look at Grant and burst out laughing.

"It's not funny!" Lily protested with a pretend pout. "She included my phone number and everything."

"So that's what Janie meant about 'happy hunting'." Jessica was still laughing.

"Yes, and I'm just mortified. Half the town is calling me 'ghost-buster' after that film. I spoke to Ed. He's going to pull the ad before the next edition, but everyone already knows, and someone telephoned, asking me to help find out why her house is being haunted."

"No, seriously?" Jessica's eyes rounded. "That's got to be a prank."

"That's what I said," Grant called. He'd fallen behind as Thor paused at almost every lamppost, his black nose sprinkled with snow.

"I don't know, maybe not. It was a lady called Mrs Clara Ryan. She's quite elderly and lives up at High Meadows House and… well…" Lily's expression melted from annoyance into worried sympathy. "She claims she's seen her late husband around the place and wants me to investigate. What should I do, Jess? I don't know anything about ghosts."

Jessica wrapped an arm around Lily's shoulder and gave her a quick squeeze. "Don't worry. We'll go talk to her together and figure it out. How hard can it be?"

"Okay." Lily said, but still fretted. "But if she wants us to mess around with an Ouija board or something, I'm out. Those things give me the creeps."

They swung left at the flower shop, already bustling with preparations for the day's deliveries and holiday orders, and onto Lily's parents' street. The houses here were smaller than on the outskirts of town, and older. But Jessica had always appreciated their history. There was something picturesque about the clapboard cottages, trimmed in white, each with its own unique story. Lily's parents' place stood out, the lone red brick structure with a huge arched window in the front. It used to be the old schoolmaster's house, before the school moved to a bigger location on the outskirts of town.

The house was set back from the sidewalk with a low, white-painted picket fence. May to October saw it burgeoning with flowers, but come winter it was holly, red berries and neatly trimmed pines all frosted in snow.

Lily swung open the gate and darted up the neatly shoveled walkway ahead of Jessica and Grant. Jessica glanced sideways at him. "What am I getting into?"

Grant flashed her a sympathetic smile. "I tried to talk her into a later start-time, but you know how excited Lily gets. And, to be honest, Estelle couldn't wait to see you either."

Jessica turned at the sound of the front door opening. Lily's mother, Estelle, rushed out, arms wide. "Jessie-bear!" Jessica submitted to another round of hugs, laughing as Estelle tried to drag her indoors.

"Come on now, out of the freezing cold." Estelle insisted, her round face pink from baking.

Lily and her mother looked so alike — despite the 26-year age gap. Estelle had acquired gray in her red-blonde hair and her figure had softened and filled — but they shared the same sweet smile and bubbly nature. She was barely taller than her daughter, wearing a simple button up dress in tan with a linen apron tied around her waist. "You must be starving. Goodness knows they don't serve anything edible on that train. Come on, we've fixed you up something special — Thor, leave it!" Estelle said as the dog gleefully snatched a slipper from under the hall stand. "Lily, that dog of yours. You should enroll him in the next behavior training session. The vet's clinic are running them in the evenings."

"Technically, it's not until next month," a masculine voice called from upstairs. "But I can ask the trainer if she's available for private sessions. That's if you're not too busy busting ghosts."

"It's ghost hunting and I'm not doing that either," Lily called back in pretend indignation.

Jessica turned slowly, even though she already knew who must be standing on the upper landing. She'd recognize that warm, resonant voice anywhere.

Sure enough, Luke Jensen leaned over the second-story banister, grinning down at them. "Hey Jess," he said, fixing her with his gaze. Even from down here, she could tell his eyes were as blue as she remembered. That, coupled with the blond hair, early morning stubble and angular

Nordic features that ran in this family, made for a dangerous combination. Without realizing it, Jessica's hands flew to snatch off her hat and scrabbled to straighten her mussed-up hair.

"I'm guessing, by the look on your face, that dear cousin Lily didn't warn you about the welcome-back breakfast. Be honest, have you missed this style of chaos?"

"Don't be silly, of course she misses it," Estelle shouted as she took off toward the kitchen.

Luke headed downstairs, looking relaxed and right at home in a blue crewneck sweater and jeans. He crossed the polished wood floor to where she stood frozen to the welcome mat and reached out to hug her. Only a light hug, not a huge, encompassing embrace like Lily or Estelle's, but it still sent shock waves through her. The sensation of his arm around her shoulders, his warm, musky scent mingled with cedar from his cologne.

"That true?" he gazed down at her, his face inches from hers.

Jessica suddenly laughed, feeling almost lightheaded.

"Yes." She leaned back just far enough to catch his eye. "She's right. I've missed you all so much."

CHAPTER 3

Once Jessica got over the whole ambush aspect of the breakfast party, it was a perfect morning. Lily's father, Jakob, regaled them with the town gossip Jessica had missed over the past year and a half since her last visit. This was much embellished and exaggerated by all of them and had her laughing over her French toast and creamy coffee. She'd forgotten how much fun they were. Jakob, white-haired and still lean despite having retired from his job as town police officer, had always had a soft spot for her.

Talk turned to Lily and Grant's recent renovation projects on their old farmhouse: they'd finished the stonework over the fireplace, and new weatherboard covering the porch. Grant had started fitting out the reading room of Lily's dreams, and Lily had planted a new garden out back. She was trying to talk Grant into just a "teeny tiny" chicken coop, but everyone unanimously agreed that would be a terrible idea until Thor grew out of his puppy phase. Something that seemed unlikely, given he was already two and as boisterous as the day they'd brought him home.

And Luke, well… Jessica couldn't miss the hints Estelle was lathering on thicker than the syrup she poured over Jess's second helping of French toast.

"It must be difficult to keep up at the clinic when you've got that whole house to yourself to look after, Luke," Estelle kept saying. Or, "How've you been holding up, Luke? Any new prospects on the horizon?"

"I've got a new veterinary partner starting in the new year, that'll take the weight off," he spoke unhurriedly, easily deflecting his aunt's teasing. Jessica caught his attention long enough to share a commiserating grimace, and he gave her that crooked grin that had set her heart jumping ever since they'd caught each other's eye over the campfire all those years ago.

So, Luke's single now. That was… interesting. Not that she was happy about it of course — breakups were awful, and Luke was her friend, she told herself firmly. Although they were once nearly more…a small voice said, which she instantly dismissed.

She also couldn't help but notice how Luke had seated himself right next to her, voluntarily. Or how often he stole glances at her from the corner of his eye when he thought she wasn't looking. As everyone finished eating, he leaned back and casually stretched his arm across the back of her chair. Jessica stiffened, holding herself upright, her hands in her lap, not wanting to give herself away in front of the family— not that there was anything to give away.

Lily announced they should go home and let Jessica rest, which was a blessed relief. There were goodbye hugs all round; Luke's was as brief as the hello had been and she told herself that was just fine. Then just as she was turning to go he caught her eye, a gleam of curiosity in those sky blue irises — as though he were suddenly seeing her as the woman she was, and not the girl she had been. She held his gaze for a second.

"See you around, Jess," he said, the smile lifting his lips once more.

"Sure, that would be…um…" she said, her voice catching in her throat. She cursed herself for being an idiot, then turned to follow Lily out to the car, feeling like she was walking three feet above the ground.

Grant drove them across town, Jess tucked in the backseat of the Jeep Grand Cherokee with Thor, who flopped straight across her lap. Jessica's heart was still singing, but the rest of her was sinking into sleep even as they motored slowly out into the snow covered road.

They arrived at the farmhouse a few minutes later, swinging into the snowy driveway and parking right outside the front door.

Grant took Jessica's bag as she turned to Lily.

"I have to phone Mom. She'll rest easier when she knows I'm here."

"Sure." Lily took her to the telephone in the hallway, in a niche under the stairs with a built-in bench to sit on. "I know what my Mom's like, and after losing your Dad like that, she must be pretty anxious."

Sorrow pulled at Jessica's face. "It was just out of the blue. It still doesn't seem real." Lily knew the story. He'd had a heart attack leaving the house for the office. Her Mom saw him collapse and did everything she could, but he was gone before the ambulance arrived.

She reassured her mother that she was fine and would see her as soon as she got back, then Lily took her straight up to the cozy third-floor attic suite.

A two-hour nap later, and a long hot shower, she went down to find Lily and Grant in the spacious living room, blazing log fire crackling in the hearth as they quibbled over a game of Scrabble. Thor's white tail thumped on the ground as Jessica came in.

"So we didn't completely wreck you on day one," Grant joked.

Lily ignored him. "How're you feeling?" She'd changed into a fluffy pink sweater that added soft color to her cheeks.

"Reborn." She dropped cross-legged onto the brown leather sofa beside Grant.

Lily sat on the other side of the chunky coffee table from them on a sheepskin rug — she always eschewed chairs whenever possible, which was why nearly every room in the farmhouse sported thick, fluffy rugs on its wide planked floors. She'd even hung colorful woven rugs on the white painted walls — it suited the simplistic, uncluttered décor; a perfect balance of tradition and comfort, breathing new life into the beautiful old house.

"Good." Lily grinned. "Because I've got more plans for

us later this afternoon." Grant shot her a pointed look, and Lily raised both hands in surrender. "If you have the energy, of course. No pressure. But Grant's on nights at the hospital and Mrs. Ryan called again, and I'd love some backup for this whole ghost situation."

"Going ghost-hunting, hey?" She fixed a straight face. "Well, I can't let you get cursed or possessed, or whatever by yourself, can I?"

"Wouldn't you rather wait until tomorrow?" Grant suggested.

"Don't be silly. Ghosts don't come out in the daytime," Lily said. "She asked if I could come over around four and I agreed."

"Fine by me," Jessica shrugged with a smile.

"On your head be it," Grant conceded.

They had a late lunch of pumpkin soup and fresh bread before Grant left for the hospital. Then they settled down for a cup of milky coffee in front of the fire.

"How're you doing, Jess?" Lily asked the question that had probably been on her lips since they'd picked her up.

"Just so happy to be here," Jessica's reply was noncommittal.

"What about work? Driving you crazy?" Lily sipped her drink from an over large mug, both hands wrapped around its warmth.

Jessica laughed. "No more than usual, I'm climbing the career ladder — I figure I'm up on the second rung now."

Lily laughed at that, then fixed her gaze. "What about romance? Any city slickers caught your eye?"

Jessica grimaced. "Argh, don't go there."

"That bad?"

Lights suddenly winking into life across the meadow diverted Jessica's attention. The neighbor had turned on exterior lights; icicle-shaped bulbs dripping from the porch, and a group of snow-coated pine trees flickered into life, complete with little stars perched on top. Jessica wondered who had risked life and limb to climb up and plant the stars so high.

"Jess?" Lily wasn't giving up.

"I just don't have time, and I'm too tired after work." She made the usual excuses.

"Isn't there anyone in the office? It seemed like a pretty big place,' Lily said. She and Grant had been there when they joined her in New York for a long weekend that summer, just to spend some time with her, as there was no chance Jessica could escape.

"It's seriously disapproved of, and anyway, they're all into their computers." Jessica sipped her coffee. It always tasted better here, something about the water probably.

"They should be fighting over someone as amazing as you, not staring at stupid screens."

"Yeah, sure." Jessica gave a low laugh.

"And you always preferred real men," Lily teased her.

"And you're no different." Jessica threw back.

"How's your mom doing now?" Lily changed direction.

Jessica took another sip of coffee. "She's adjusting. You know how hard it hit her when Pop died…." Jessica hadn't wanted to enter this territory, but Lily deserved to know and they'd always shared their problems. "She still has the apartment, but she's happier when she stays with Simon. Trouble is, he's got a life to lead, too. We talked about her moving into a community, and she's keen, but Pop's investments didn't do as well as they'd expected. It's all kind of difficult." She shrugged, her face falling.

Dusk darkened the room and Lily reached to switch on a lamp next to her. "Luke's single again."

Jessica directed a gaze at her. "Your Mom made that pretty clear."

"He got badly burned," Lily said quietly. "He thought she was the love of his life."

"Have I met her?" Jessica asked.

Lily shook her head, strawberry blonde strands catching on her fluffy jumper. "She was working with him, but she couldn't settle, she needed something more — more than Montrose has to offer anyhow. She wanted a career in the horse racing world. Glitzy, you know. She asked him to go with her, he refused." She looked away. "It was a while back. He's kinda got over it, or it seems that way. He's dated a couple of times, but I don't know if he's truly ready to move on." She glanced up, a sparkle in her eyes. "But it would be perfect if…you know!"

"Don't push fate, Lily," Jessica told her firmly, then fell silent as she absorbed the news. She should hang back from Luke; if he was interested, he'd make a move. An image suddenly flashed into her mind, the two of them standing by a picket fence, a house in the background, a life in the valley…don't be ridiculous, she dismissed the nonsense. Dreams don't come true.

She put her cup on the coffee table. "You'll be late if you don't get a move on," she reminded Lily.

"You're coming, you said you would!"

"Did you tell Mrs Ryan that? Because I'm not going unless she knows."

"Of course she knows." Lily jumped to her feet. "Come on!"

They bundled up in hats, boots, gloves and jackets, and the pick of scarves knitted by Estelle over the years. Suitably armored against the crisp cold, they set off under a clear starlit sky to walk the fifteen minutes across town to High Meadows House.

As they walked and chatted, Jessica breathed in the charm and beauty of Montrose in winter. All the houses had been decorated for the holidays; twinkling lights outside, porches decked with garlands. Some of the front yards had cheery snowmen sporting woolen hats, carrot noses and mittens on their stick arms; each one its own design, gleefully wrought by the children of the house. The scent of wood smoke lingered on the still night air, mingling with fresh pine and cedar and that special Montrose Valley smell. Jessica inhaled deeply, wanting to remember this scent, to be able to recall it whenever New York felt particularly grimy and soulless.

She and Lily had walked the historic district of Montrose countless times, but had never actually been inside any of the manor houses — originally built for the wealthy local landowners. Many of the same families still owned them.

Jessica adored old homes steeped in history. Imagining what it was like to live in one was a daydream that got her through the stickier months at work — during the build-ups to launch days or the frantic weeks after launching a new product, when they needed all hands on deck to make sure whatever new piece of software they'd inevitably oversold didn't crash and burn.

This is the new world. Tech is the future; put your time in, learn the business, and soon they'll be throwing money at you. That was the mantra; it kept Jessica and her coworkers burning the hours away on too little reward. *One day it will all pay off…*

She felt a pinch of nerves and suppressed them, shaking her shoulders to dispel the thought of work. I'm on vacation, she reminded herself. Lily, mistaking her shudder for shivers, looped her arm through Jessica's and leaned in close to walk the last few hundred yards.

"Have you met Mrs Ryan before?" Jessica asked.

"No, but she's well respected in town. One of the old families, or her husband was anyway. I was amazed when she called me."

Wrought-iron gates guarding High Meadow House were wide open, leading them between two stone pillars and up an elegant curving driveway to the house itself. The driveway snow was criss-crossed by footsteps; the rest of the grounds were untouched and flawless. Towering trees bordered extensive lawns, dotted with shrubs, bushes and arbors, all shrouded in a blanket of white.

The house looked more like a mansion to Jessica's mind

— rising three stories tall, topped by gabled roofs. Tiny white lights twinkled along the eaves, the sash windows framed with boxwood garlands finished with satin red ribbons. The wraparound porch trimmed with brightly lit bulbs, and a huge wreath hung on the gleaming front door. The entire place resembled a Hallmark card; something that might be titled *Christmas in Vermont*.

Lily surged up the steps and pushed hard on the doorbell.

CHAPTER 4

"Coming!" called a voice from inside. A second later, the door opened inward to reveal a plump-cheeked woman with thick gray hair piled on top of her head in a bun. "You must be Lily." she smiled. "And you must be Jessica. Come in, come in, Mrs. Ryan is expecting you." She spoke kindly in a New England accent. "I'm Bethany, the Housekeeper."

Jessica and Lily slipped off their snow covered boots, leaving them on the inside mat and padded in thick winter socks behind Bethany into the grand foyer. They both stopped in their tracks and gasped at the magnificent staircase rising gracefully to the upper floor; a curving mahogany bannister with wide steps covered with a damask carpet runner attached with brass rods. The hardwood floor was inlaid with intricately patterned parquetry, which was repeated along the wide corridor leading into the house itself.

Bethany waited for them to remove their coats and hung them up. As they laid their mittens and hats onto a gleaming mahogany hall table, Jessica couldn't help but notice an assortment of walking canes tucked into the corner in a large jar alongside multiple horn-handled umbrellas.

"Onwards we go." Bethany almost sang the words. She led them past a few formal rooms, all set with fine period furniture, lamps, clocks, and ornaments.

Whilst Lily chattered happily to Bethany about the upcoming holiday festivities, Jessica's eyes widened with amazement at the sheer volume and variety of beautiful pieces everywhere she looked. But the house itself seemed rather careworn. It was clean and polished but fraying at the edges — bare spots on the silk rugs and sofa arms, old scuffs and scratches on the floors. One of the crystal chandeliers was missing an entire arm, and Jessica spotted water damage on some of the faded wallpaper covering the walls.

Jessica understood why. Repairs for a house like this must cost a fortune, not to mention all the things that you couldn't see — the roof, heating, plumbing, and so on. Still, it hurt to see such a grand home suffering the ravages of time. A real sleeping beauty, she thought, her mind racing with all the possibilities of what it could be again.

At the end of the hallway, Bethany led them into the busiest room yet. A mishmash of styles created a cozy, welcoming atmosphere. Settees, sofas, and fainting couches all gathered around a double-wide fireplace with a roaring fire. Heavy curtains pulled tight against the night, and multiple lamps created pools of light on every side table, illuminating collections of porcelain trinkets, silver photo frames, and a multitude of books and magazines. A large mirror set over the marble mantle reflected the light and warmth back into the room, further enhancing the snug effect. Evidently, this was the room where living was done.

Only when they stepped into the toasty warmth did Jessica realize that the rest of the house had felt drafty indeed. Beside her, Lily exhaled a deep sigh of happiness. This was her kind of room, utterly without pretense, and welcoming to all.

"Lily and her friend Jessica are here, Mrs. Ryan," Bethany said.

"Girls! How delightful to see you. Thank you so much for coming." Mrs. Ryan spread her hands in welcome. "It's such a bitter cold evening. Can I offer you something to drink? We have coffee, tea, hot cocoa…we even have sherry." She gave them both a sweet smile.

Jessica reckoned Mrs Ryan to be in her late seventies and rather too thin. Dressed in a long tawny wool frock that looked as though it was a size too large, and a paisley shawl around thin shoulders. The firelight loaned her cheeks color, lines etched around her eyes and lips spoke of a life filled with laughter.

"Oh, hot cocoa for me please," Lily said, moving towards the fire, her hands outstretched to its warmth. "Jess?"

"Tea would be great, thank you." Jessica hesitated, moving aside to let Bethany pass on her way to the kitchen. Mrs. Ryan gestured to the sofas.

"Sit, sit! Feel free to push anything out of the way. I apologize for the clutter, I like to have my favorite things around me," she spoke gaily as if excited by having company.

Jessica moved a stack of National Geographic magazines to an end table and slid onto the far end of the sofa, its down-filled cushions softly compressing beneath her. Lily sat next to Mrs. Ryan, then startled up and drew a leather-bound photo album out from under her.

"Oh, how silly of me. I brought it so I could show you…" Mrs. Ryan extended a hand and Lily passed the album over to her. But she didn't open it. For a moment, she fell silent, her eyes on the dulled brown cover, her finger gently tracing the gold embossed letters — 'Joe and Clara'.

When she exhaled again, it was a slow, uncertain sound, her voice softer, almost hesitating as she spoke. "I feel a bit silly, I have to admit. I wasn't going to talk to anybody about this, and poor Bethany has enough to fret about as it is."

"Don't be silly," said Bethany, bustling back in with a silver tray of drinks. "I'm not the fretful type as you well know."

She put a mug of cocoa on the table in front of Lily and a cup of black tea for Jessica. Mrs. Ryan had the same black tea with a wafer-thin slice of lemon floating on top.

"Cream? Milk? Sugar?" Bethany asked, her hand hovering over the tray of pretty porcelain pots.

"No, thank you. It's just fine the way it is." Jessica smiled as she picked up the cup.

Lily stirred her cocoa, the scent of which made Jessica wonder if she'd made the wrong choice. But the tea was very tasty, some smooth brand, much better than the type she usually drank.

"Heavenly," she murmured.

"It's Earl Grey, from Harrods," Mrs. Ryan said, her eyes sparkling. "Joe fell in love with it during the war. We always treated ourselves to a hamper from Fortnum's every Christmas." Her face fell. "I still drink it. It always makes me think of him."

"Well, it's delicious," Jessica said, her chest tightening at the sight of Mrs. Ryan's sorrow.

For a moment, the only sounds were the faint tinkle of china as Bethany set down plates of iced cookies. Then she left, closing the sitting room doors behind her. Silence fell once again, save for the crackling fire, and a clock ticking on the mantle shelf. Mrs. Ryan had watched Bethany go, a distant expression on her face. Then she blinked and brightened again.

"Right, let's see now. When I saw your notice in the paper, Lily, I felt much better about things. After all, I should be able to talk about this. If you're brave enough to advertise yourself in public as a… well, what would you call it, a paranormal investigator? Is that the proper term?"

Jessica's eyes began to dance, and she lowered them so as not to give herself away.

"I guess so?" Lily replied warily. "I'm pretty new to this, too." She fidgeted in her seat, and Jessica could tell she was feeling guilty for the misunderstanding. But it was too late to back out now, and the elderly lady was clearly comforted by their presence. Lily cleared her throat and continued. "Would you like to tell me why you called me, Mrs. Ryan? You said something about your husband on the phone?"

"Oh, please, call me Clara." Mrs. Ryan — Clara — smiled again. "And yes, that's right. My Joe…" She turned back to the album of black and white photos in her lap and opened it to the first page. "Right here," she said, rotating the book so Jess and Lily could see.

A handsome young man grinned up at them from the page. He wore a U.S. Air Force uniform, medals on his chest and one arm wrapped around the narrow waist of a gorgeous young woman in a wedding gown. Jessica would've recognized that smile anywhere, even having only known Mrs. Ryan for a few minutes.

"Wow," exclaimed Lily, leaning in for a closer look at the photograph.

"You look beautiful," Jessica said, and Clara laughed.

"Flattery will get you everywhere, my dear. But if you ask me, he was the looker between us. All eyes were on my Joe wherever we went. I was the lucky one."

Lily and Jessica both protested. But Joe Ryan really had cut a handsome figure in his prime. Dark hair, dark eyes, and sculpted cheekbones that highlighted his sharp jawline and arresting smile. His strong, broad shoulders and height emphasized the lithe curves of the young Clara, and it was obvious they would have cut quite the dash together.

"We met a few months after the war ended. Joe had stayed behind to help with some of the re-building efforts in Germany once he'd had medical clearance." Clara paused, then passed the album to Lily so she could flip through it. Jessica moved next to her to lean against her shoulder, looking at the photographs as Clara's story unfolded. "Joe had an awful time of it. He'd been stationed in England with the Royal Air Force. He was a bomber pilot."

Lily turned the page, and she and Jessica both sighed at a larger photo of Clara and Joe, clearly taken a few years after their wedding. They were at a beach somewhere, the sun full on their faces, arms around one another's waists.

"Sounds brave," Jessica said.

"He was. But…" Clara sighed. "His plane was shot down over enemy territory. The Germans captured him and held him as a prisoner of war for almost a year until the camp was liberated."

"Oh, how awful," Lily breathed. "That must have been terrifying."

"Joe never talked much about that year," Clara went on. "Or about what he did during the war. He told me the basics of course, but overall, he thought it didn't matter. He always said that his life started over the day we met." Her eyes glazed for a moment. "I was working at the time, on the men's accessories counter of a department store in Burlington. Joe was one of my customers. He asked me out the day we met. I told him I didn't believe he was serious. So he came back every day for a month, buying something new each time." Clara chuckled. "He probably had 10 pocket squares by the time I said yes! My boss loved him."

"What finally changed your mind?" Lily asked, grinning.

"Well, those beautiful eyes didn't hurt. Or his broad shoulders." They all laughed, and Clara glanced at the album again. "I just realized that I was only putting him off because I was scared we might not work out. And I decided not to make my life decisions from a place of fear anymore."

"Words to live by," Lily said softly.

Jessica nodded and suppressed another sigh. *I want that someday.* The kind of love that made you feel new, like your whole life had been rebooted, like you were the center of someone's whole world. Her parents had found it with each other, but so far, she'd only managed to find a string of failures. Each New York finance-or-tech-obsessed guy she had dated seemed worse than the last. Either they were money-obsessed, ego-centric and career-focused, or introverted, nerdy types that couldn't speak to anything beyond the latest tech developments. Often, she had felt like a third wheel to their other interests.

"That's lovely, Mrs — Clara," Lily caught herself.

Clara pressed her lips together, frowning. "But now, of course, I wonder whether that might be the problem. If something happened, something he never fully came to terms with. Maybe that's why he never really talked about it, and why he can't rest…"

Lily and Jessica traded another glance. "What makes you think he's not resting?" Jessica asked carefully.

Clara's gaze drifted from the photo album to the window. Jessica followed her eye-line, but all she could see outside was the distant sparkle of the town, the church steeple and the top of the library tower just visible beyond the high garden wall.

"I saw him," Clara said, her voice pitched so quietly that Jessica and Lily had to lean in to hear. "Out in front. I wasn't sure at first; it was growing dark, and I was half-asleep, just woken from a nap. Bethany had left for the day, and a sound woke me. I went to the window, and I saw him…he was wearing his flying jacket and everything. I cried out, and stepped back, and then when I looked again, he was gone."

Lily and Jessica traded another look. "Are you sure it was him?" Lily asked gently, placing her hand over Clara's.

Clara took Lily's hand in both of hers.

"Trust me. I'd never forget my husband's stance." Clara sighed, gazing at the fireplace. It crackled, one of the logs snapping in half and throwing sparks up the flue.

They sat for a moment, digesting that. Lily shot Jessica another look, one that Jessica recognized from their camp days as *help I'm in over my head*.

Jessica gently cleared her throat. "Well, if he is, er… not resting because of something from his past, maybe we should take a look at his history again. Do you have any more photo albums? Or perhaps some of his things?"

Clara brightened. "What a lovely idea. Of course. There's a whole trunk up in the attic. Would you like to look through it? Oh, but…" Clara glanced at the grandfather clock on the far side of the room. "Bethany's already stayed later than usual. I should really let her get home for the evening."

"That's alright," Lily said quickly. "I've kept poor Jessica up late too — it's her first night here. Why don't we come back tomorrow morning?"

"You wouldn't mind?" Clara's eyes brightened.

"Not at all," Jessica said, unable to resist the older woman's expression filled with hope.

"Wonderful. Let me see if Bethany can help you find your things…" Clara turned to reach for a bell she kept on the side table next to her.

As Clara turned away, Lily leaned in close to Jess and whispered. "What are we getting ourselves into?"

CHAPTER 5

Where…? Oh…Lily's guest bedroom… Jessica woke, momentarily disoriented. She lay on her back, trying to focus on the sloping roof and crisscross of wooden beams.

Long rays of pastel pinks and orange filtered through frost etched windows. She'd forgotten to close the curtains last night — which was a huge plus, she thought, because the sunrise lit the room with color and the promise of a beautiful winter's day.

She stretched her arms wide, luxuriating in the old-fashioned bed, with its tall newel posts and blue and yellow patchwork quilt covering the warmest down duvet. The walls matched the blue, a cream wool carpet on the floor, along with the inevitable fluffy rug. Furniture was simple country style, white painted and oak trimmed and picture frames to match. Lily had a habit of buying local art from wherever she could find it and paintings of mountains, meadows, covered bridges and old farm houses arrayed on the walls.

Charming as it all was, there was still a distinct chill in the air. She wriggled out from under the covers with a brief pang of regret and quickly pushed her bare feet into the pink slippers Lily had thoughtfully provided to pad to the bathroom and run the shower till it steamed.

Twenty minutes later, dressed in a chunky red sweater and the same jeans of yesterday; her still damp hair loosely pinned, she headed for the stairs.

The scent of bacon filled the house, along with the distant sound of Lily singing. Jessica smiled and entered the kitchen to find Lily and Thor dancing together to her out-of-tune rendition of "Winter Wonderland."

The dog woofed a greeting, Lily grinned, then dropped Thor's paws to grab the spatula next to the stovetop.

"Don't burn, please don't burn." She switched the gas off and quickly maneuvered the bacon onto a plate. "Did you sleep?" She turned her head briefly, strands of strawberry blonde hair escaping a hastily tied bun. Pale pink sweater, blue jeans and no makeup; just fresh faced, lightly freckled and a big smile. Lily still looked like the teenager Jessica knew from camp.

"Like a baby."

"Breakfast's nearly ready — you still like your pancakes with cinnamon on top?"

"You bet!" Jessica poured two cups of strong coffee from the pot on the white-tiled countertop, then perched on one of the leather high stools, hands cradling the steaming mug. "How was Grant this morning?"

"Oh, the usual after a night shift." Lily pouted in sympathy. "Just going to bed as I was getting up. He'll probably be out of it until late afternoon. But!" She brightened.

"That gives us plenty of time to check out Mrs. Ryan's attic before our market shift in town."

"This ghost hunting is all go!"

Lily gave her a look and Jessica laughed, then took a contemplative sip of coffee, sleepy eyes on the simple farmhouse table and mismatched wooden chairs gathered round it. "Seriously though, what do you make of Mrs Ryan's whole ghost situation?"

"I don't know… I mean, I can see how it'd be easy to get startled, all alone in that house. And it's obvious she misses her husband." Lily paused between flipping pancakes to gaze out at the cloudless blue sky beyond the window. "Grant and I have only been married a year and a half and I already can't imagine how it'd feel to lose him." She gave a shake of her head. "It must be so hard after a whole lifetime together — adjusting to being on your own again."

"Yeah, my mom's been going through the same thing." Jessica murmured, guilt fretting at her. This trip had been planned at Lily's wedding and she'd been dreaming of it ever since. Her father had died unexpectedly late last year and sent an earthquake through her family. Fourteen months on, they were still reconciling to it.

Lily held out a hand for Jessica's plate and heaped three pancakes and a half-dozen thin strips of bacon onto it.

Beside them, Thor whined, then thumped his tail on the yellow pine floor.

"Are we fueling up for an Arctic trek here or what?" Jessica joked. Though she couldn't complain too much

— Lily's pancakes were heavenly, and she'd added her specialty, a sprinkling of cinnamon mixed with powdered sugar.

"Pretty much," Lily said. "It's twenty degrees out there, and we're due more snow tonight. So, eat up! You need fuel to stay warm."

Laughing, Jessica poured an amber trail of maple syrup over the stack of pancakes. "Let's hope Mrs. Ryan heats her attic." She waited until Lily was distracted, then broke off a piece of bacon and dropped it under the table to the waiting dog.

"That dog's going to love you forever," Lily lectured as Thor ate it in a single bite then gazed up with sapphire blue eyes, his black nose twitching.

"I sure hope so!" Jessica dug in. "Don't worry." She grinned. "I have a feeling today's going to be a good one." Although maybe that was the pancakes talking.

* * *

Jessica and Lily peered up the rickety stairs into what appeared to be a cavernous attic space. A frigid breeze whistled down, making them shiver.

"Would you like me to grab your coats and scarves?" Bethany asked, her face creasing in concern. "It's pretty drafty on these upper floors, and the attic is … well, Mrs. Ryan hasn't been able to get the insulation upgraded in a while."

"Thank you so much Bethany, but I'm sure we'll be okay," Lily said, nudging Jessica's side. "Right, Jess?"

Despite the thick thermals under her sweater, Jessica seriously debated whether she ought to take Bethany up on the offer. But Lily had fixed her most determined expression, so she figured to soldier on. "All good here, Bethany, thank you."

"The sooner into the breach, the sooner back out again," Lily called as she placed a boot onto the first step and began to climb upwards.

"That's not the quote," Jessica grumbled, following quickly behind her.

Mrs. Ryan had been so excited to see them again that morning. They'd dawdled in the living room for an hour already, chatting about things Clara and Joe had done over the years, drinking tea and listening to stories and anecdotes. Jessica wondered how often Mrs. Ryan had visitors. It was sad to think of the older woman all alone in this rambling house — aside from Bethany, of course, who had seemed as excited as Mrs. Ryan about their guests.

Sunlight seeped in through grimy dormer windows, their sills piled with snow. Shafts of light cut across dark shadows, and the wind whistled as it eddied around the shingles. Lily shone a flashlight this way and that, the beam sliding over furniture-shaped forms under gray blankets.

A cobweb brushed Jessica's cheek. She stifled a cry before sweeping it off, then moved swiftly to catch up with Lily, her boots scuffing bare floorboards, disturbing more dust.

"Do you see a trunk?" she whispered, not sure why she was whispering. Something about the dark space made her feel like she ought to be quiet...*So as not to disturb any ghosts.* The thought jumped into her mind. She didn't believe in ghosts, not really, but up here, she could almost understand where Mrs. Ryan was coming from...

"There." Lily's flashlight alighted on a heavy steamer trunk. It looked like something straight out of a 1940s movie set. A full-length mirror stood next to it, and an old wicker chair beyond.

Lily fiddled with the latches, then pushed the lid back, causing a cloud of dust to billow up, making them both sneeze.

The bright beam revealed a neatly folded airman's uniform to one side, medal ribbons sewn onto the chest, the colors dulled and faded with age.

"It's the uniform Joe wore at his wedding," Jessica whispered.

"I know. Why are you whispering?"

"Same reason as you!"

They both laughed quietly, feeling strangely nervous in the dimly lit space.

Next to the uniform, several journals were piled up, their gray covers curled at the edges and spotted with damp.

Lily picked up the topmost book and wiped a hand across the cover. As she opened it, a pair of theater tickets slipped out. "Oh, darn. Hold this." She handed Jessica the flashlight and knelt to scoop them up.

Jessica focused the beam on the yellowed pages. "Look at this." The cramped handwriting was made in pencil, the letters smudged and barely legible. Each page held a different keepsake — a leaflet about how to affix a gas mask, another held a flyer advertising a night of dancing in the Officers' Mess. "This must be from when Joe was deployed in England," Jessica murmured.

"These are too," said Lily, holding up the ticket stubs. "For a show on the base, it looks like?"

"Wow. There must be so much history here." Jessica lowered herself cross-legged to the floorboards, too absorbed to think about the layers of grime, or the cold. The notebook transfixed her — she wished she could read Joe's writing — and that he'd written in ink.

Lily continued digging through the trunk. "Look at this," she pulled out a photo album bound in flaking tan leather, and opened it. "Oh… It's Joe during the war." He wore a flying suit under a leather jacket of a very different style from the formal outfit he'd worn to his wedding.

"Wait." Jessica reached for it. "Didn't Clara say that she saw his ghost wearing a jacket? Do you think it was this one?"

"Maybe! Let's show her this photo and see if she recognizes it." Lily said, her blue eyes shining with enthusiasm.

"Great, but just one more rummage," Jessica said. They lingered for minutes more, sifting through the trunk, making sure there weren't any more treasures to unearth.

A short time later, hugging their finds in their arms, they trekked back down the stairs to return to the bright, warm living room, tingling with cold, but full of excitement from their foray. Bethany brought in mugs of hot coffee to warm them up while they gleefully showed off the trove to Clara.

"They were with his uniform — the one he wore for your wedding," Jessica told her as they sat together on the sofa, slowly turning the pages of the notebooks. Some of the pages were brittle with age, and the mounts were coming unglued, but they were in remarkably good condition, despite not seeing the light of day for years.

Clara's smile turned soft and fond. "Joe's old diaries. He told me he kept them right from when he was posted, but he was such a pragmatist. Every entry was about what he ate during the day and how much he spent. He always included the weather for the day too, that was the airman in him, or maybe just the British obsession rubbing off on him," she chuckled. "He did save ticket stubs, though, and posters of events he went to, that kind of thing. But it would've been in England, of course. Before he was… well…" Her expression darkened.

Lily bit her lip, casting a worried glance towards Jessica. After a moment, she opened the photo album. "What about this jacket, Mrs. Ryan?"

"Lily, it's Clara, please," she scolded, clicking her tongue as she accepted the book. The moment she saw the photograph, her eyes widened. "Oh my word, that's it. The very jacket he was wearing the other night. Oh, girls." When she looked up again, her eyes shone a little too brightly around the rims. "What do you think it means?"

Jessica and Lily traded another look.

"I'm not sure," Jessica said cautiously, "But if I had to

guess, I'd think it means that wherever he is, he's thinking of you."

Clara pressed her lips together. "No," she replied softly. "It's more than that. I could've sworn he wanted something, or maybe needed something….. But he startled me, and I cried out, and then he was gone," she broke off with a sigh. "Well. I suppose I've scared him away — what do you think we should do now?" she asked with a smile of anticipation.

Lily squirmed in her seat. "Clara, I should tell you that actually — "

"We need to get to the Christmas market," Jessica interjected quickly. She couldn't bear the thought of letting Clara down by admitting that they actually had no idea about ghosts. She'd seemed so excited to have visitors, and Jessica loved listening to her stories — it was fascinating to hear about a time so different from the one they lived in. A time of deep human connections, in a deeply uncertain world. A time before computers like the one waiting in Jessica's office, ready to dominate her every waking minute the second she got back to the city.

What was the harm in visiting a lonely old lady and hearing her relive the past? Especially if it meant they could avoid hurting her feelings.

Lily raised her eyebrows at Jessica. But all she said was, "Yes, we really mustn't be late."

"If anything else happens, call us right away and we'll come over to see you," Jessica added. "Right, Lily?"

"Right," Lily repeated, a crease of worry on her forehead.

"Thank you again, girls. It's so good to have you here." Clara beamed at them both, so genuinely delighted that Jessica almost regretted the well-meant deception.

CHAPTER 6

It was noon by the time they left High Meadows House — nearly time for their volunteer shift at the market. Lily started the car. Their breath steamed as they waited for the engine to warm up, the windshield fogging from inside, casting shadows across their faces.

"You should've let me tell her," Lily objected, turning the heater up. The incoming blast of air was cold, and Jessica shivered in her red coat, wrapping her arms together tightly across her chest.

"It would only have upset her," Jessica argued. "And what would be the point? Either way, it's not like we're actually going to uncover a ghost. She's lonely, Lil. She wants company and the idea of a dream. We can go visit her, at least."

"Under false pretenses!" Lily wrinkled her nose. The window defrosted enough to see through, so she put the car in gear and turned around, heading back through the wrought-iron gates and towards the town square. "I don't know, it just doesn't sit right."

Jessica turned in her seat and gazed at High Meadows House. "Do you want to go back and tell her?"

Lily heaved a sigh. "No. Not now. But if she calls us again, we're confessing, okay?"

"Deal," Jessica agreed, leaning back in her seat. Turning toward Main Street, Montrose was in full swing — at least as busy as it ever got. Couples hand in hand, children in colorful boots and scarves, skipping in excitement, grandparents with arms linked, people stopping to take photographs — animated and smiling folk streaming towards the heart of town from every direction.

"Wow. It looks busier than in August!" Jessica exclaimed. She was used to the summer crowds, when hundreds of holiday makers from New York and Boston flocked to Montrose Valley.

"I told you!" Lily beamed as she pushed open the car door, grabbing her pink hat before climbing out. Jessica tugged her own snowflake hat firmly down over her ears and slid hands back into her leather gloves before she braced herself for the cold once again.

They scaled the heap of snow at the curb onto the sidewalk and melted into the crowd. Jessica couldn't help but catch her breath when they reached the center. One of her college classmates had lived in Germany, and she'd always talked about the big, beautiful Christmas markets held there every year. This one looked just how Jessica had always imagined them.

Wooden booths lined the square, each with its own pointed rooftop, fretted gables and porch awning, like miniature versions of the houses around them. And like the houses, their eaves had been strung with lights and garlands of evergreen held with red and tartan ribbons.

They continued past booths, all offering different wares — one displaying hand-carved ornaments, another with blown glass baubles and painted ceramic figures. Jessica hesitated over a pretty angel with a wonky halo and gilded wings.

"We can't be late, Jess," Lily reminded her.

"Ok…" Jessica walked slowly by the next booth. Locally made candles with scents like pine, cloves, cinnamon, and orange spice. The fragrances were so strong they filled the air to mingle with all the other delicious seasonal smells emanating from the surrounding stalls.

A make-your-own Christmas wreath stand had attracted a crowd of families. Jessica smiled delightedly at the sight of a little blonde-haired girl's completely over-the-top wreath. She'd covered it in so many pink bows and glittery stars that you couldn't even see the woven pine boughs beneath.

Lily grabbed Jessica's arm. "Right, I'm confiscating you now."

They headed through the crowds to the biggest booth, which was open on both sides and taking up almost the whole far end of the square. Circular high-top tables were set outside on the swept cobbled square and several patrons were already leaning on the tables, mugs of steaming drinks or spiced apple cider in hand, amiably passing the time of day or watching the throng.

The girls climbed the short step to the warm interior. Jessica gazed about and heaved a contented sigh as the outside chill faded in the warm fug.

A huge vat of bubbling apple cider was set over a burner surrounded by a four-sided counter. One section was dedicated to roasting chestnuts over an open grill with a large pot of milky hot chocolate simmering next to it. There were three busy servers working behind it, all dressed in matching candy cane-striped aprons over their warm winter clothes.

"Come on, we're in here!" Lily dragged Jessica over to a section of the counter and lifted it up so they could step inside. The moment they entered, heads swiveled in their direction and all three of them suddenly burst into tune.

"Nana-na-na-nana. Ghost busters!" They sang together as if they'd rehearsed it, then burst out laughing.

"Oh, you…you…" Lily turned pink, her hands flying to her cheeks, but she couldn't help laughing, nor could Jessica. "I am never going to live this down."

She shook her head and went to give them hugs.

Jessica recognized them from her visits over the years. Daniella Peyton came straight over. Curly brown hair and a round face, she had worked at the movie theater back when Lily and Jessica were campers in the Valley. "Jessica, you're a sight for sore eyes." She held out an apron. "Here you go, you're one of us now. We'll be swamped with customers again before you know it!"

Jessica grinned and slipped it on, wrapping the strings around her slim waist to tie in front.

The tall guy, Brett…something… gave her a wide grin and wave. She recalled he was a volunteer firefighter, she'd met him at Lily's wedding, but could not for the life of her remember his last name. She racked her brain because he really was rather a hunk and she should have taken more notice. There was a shorter, stockier man with him. He was called Colin and worked with Grant at the hospital.

"Lily! How wonderful to see you!" called a familiar voice. Jessica turned to see Miss Daisy Beddows, the owner of the most popular B&B and cafe in town, come bustling up. She was clutching a jar of miniature marshmallows, climbing the steps up to the booth, a big smile on her face. "Oh, my goodness, and Jessica, too. Now I know it's my lucky day." Miss Daisy made a beeline over to Jessica to give her a tight hug. "It's been too long, dear heart. Eighteen months, at the very least!"

Jessica's cheeks had taken a glow. "I know, it really has."

"And you've grown even more lovely than ever! And what a beautiful coat, the perfect red for you. I guess that's the advantage of city life, all those wonderful things to choose from!" Miss Daisy beamed, then let her go to hand the jar of marshmallows to Lily. "I thought you might need this, dear," she said with a bubble of laughter.

"Oh yeah, I'd forgotten about the ghost busters' marshmallows," Lily replied, frowning at the jar. The others laughed. She gave a mock pout, then grinned.

"I'm so glad you're both here. We need all the help we can get! We've had such a rush this morning, the lunch time lull was a blessing. I've already had to place extra orders for apple cider, and we'll be needing more milk and cream from Maplehurst Dairy." Miss Daisy's violet eyes shone with excitement, although there was a shrewd intelligence behind the open gaze. She wore a big red sweater patterned with little green Christmas trees layered overtop of a turtleneck. A striped wool hat with earflaps and red tassels covered her silvery-white hair, and she wore outrageous red and green tartan pants tucked into knee-high boots. She looked like a stylish Santa's little helper. Even her reading glasses had been chosen for the occasion — sparkly red frames, rather than her usual turquoise blue, which she was notorious for leaving all over her B&B. Miss Daisy was well known, and well loved in town, and whatever secrets she knew, and she knew most of them, you could be sure she'd never tell.

"It's the 'day one' excitement," Lily said. "Everyone's so excited that we're finally open." She'd pulled an apron on, and was wielding a black ladle in one hand, and holding another out for Jessica. "This is all yours. We're on hot chocolate duty!"

"It's two dollars a cup, and it's all going to charity." Miss Daisy went to stir the pot. "Now, I'm guessing you're still single." She leaned over and looked directly at Jessica's left hand. "We've still a few good men about town, you know," she teased, then threw a glance at Brett. "You could do worse…"

The pink in Jessica's cheeks warmed to red. "I…"

"And there's always our dashing young vet!" Miss Daisy said archly.

Lily called over. "Miss Daisy — are you match making again?"

"Well, and can you blame me?" Miss Daisy replied, laughter in her voice. "Oh, look, look, your first customer." Miss Daisy pointed excitedly over Jessica's shoulder.

Turning with some relief, Jessica saw Hugh Fellows, the owner of Montrose's one and only bookstore. He hovered by the vat of steaming chocolate on the countertop, peering suspiciously into it until the steam fogged his glasses. Unlike the colorful crowd, Hugh wore his usual buttoned up black winter coat, black trilby and gray scarf tucked tightly inside his collar. One might mistake him for a Grinch, with his wire-framed spectacles perched on his long nose and pinched, pale face, but Jessica knew that beneath his aloof exterior, Hugh's heart was in the right place. Providing that place involved books, of course. Give him a title, the more obscure the better, and he'd go out of his way to hunt it down, trawling his extensive network of bookstores in the state until he found a copy for a grateful customer.

Lily was poised to hand Hugh a mug of steaming chocolate. "Thank you, Lily, dear. And I would like to add my felicitations on your new enterprise."

"I'm not ghost hunting, Mr Fellows," Lily lowered her voice to a whisper.

"I am quite aware," Hugh replied in a low voice. "I spoke to Edward Stanton, and he explained the situation. I consider tracking ancestry to be far more impressive," Hugh added, and then gave a bow of the head, turned and walked off, mug held in gloved hands.

Mrs. O'Dowd from the flower shop was unashamedly eavesdropping. "There and that answers it, so it does. I said she wouldn't be chasing ghosts! How would you be catching them? Not with a net, that's for sure." She was wearing a green pixie hat and clapped matching gloves together in glee.

"It was a silly misunderstanding," Jessica replied as Lily gave the pot another stir. "Would you like Stay Puft Marshmallows or regular?"

"Oh Stay Puft for sure!" Mrs O'Dowd laughed, her broad Irish accent making Jessica smile. "Oh, this is such a delight. I'm having a day off from the store and having a fine time of it an' all."

Jessica put two extra spoonfuls of pink and white marshmallows on top of the steaming brew.

"And what about yourself, then?" Mrs O'Dowd carried on. "Estelle told me you were back. We've not seen you about this past…? Oh, how long is it now?"

"Eighteen months," Jessica said. "And I'm so happy to be here again."

"Well, we're thrilled to be having ye." Mrs. O'Dowd accepted her chocolate and blew on the liquid before taking a sip. "Now this is grand, so it is."

The line quickly began to swell — a mix of tourists and locals filing in, stamping snow from their boots, eager to sample the mulled cider, and everything else the stall had to offer.

Jessica's heart warmed — she'd missed this neighborliness. From the minute she arrived back in Montrose, it had felt like being enveloped in a cocoon. Back in New York, she could count on one hand the number of times she'd run into somebody she knew on the street. And aside from the bodega owner at her local corner store, nobody on her block, or in her building, would even recognize her, let alone enough to tell her they were happy to see her again, or that they'd missed her while she was gone.

The line of customers thinned after an hour.

"It's the Santa sleigh ride through town. It'll come by here," Lily said and took advantage of the brief lull to fill two steaming mugs for them both.

"I'll just rush and fetch more chestnuts and chocolate powder. I've got a pile stocked up back in the pantry," Miss Daisy told them and bustled off toward her B&B. The other three servers stopped working too and leaned on the counter to chat amiably.

Lily and Jessica took off their aprons and carried their drinks out front to one of the circular tables.

"Oh, I can hear them." Jessica's eyes lit up when the sound of sleigh bells filled the air. Excited chatter rose from the waiting crowd and Jessica looked eagerly as the throng parted to clear the way.

A horse-drawn sleigh was coming down the street toward the square, and their booth. From their vantage point, they had a perfect view of Santa sitting on the raised back seat of the crimson and gold sleigh. Dressed in the usual red and white, with a beaming smile behind his white whiskers, Santa waved and tossed candy to the kids on either side of the road.

"It's so wonderful how involved everyone gets in the community here," Jessica said, watching the stocky draft horse pulling the sleigh along. "I really miss that in the city. Here, everyone's so... connected." She knew just by looking at the horse that it belonged to old Mr. Gunter. He owned the farm and stables that butted up against their summer camp, and had a dozen riding horses, as well as a pair of percheron with the same tan coat, white fetlocks, and long, white-blonde manes and tails.

She'd learned to ride at camp and there'd been a horse and cart every summer to take the kids out on the longer trails. The cart had been pulled by a horse just like that. Heck, it might even be the same one — it was only ten years ago. How long did horses live? She wasn't sure, but figured it was quite a long time.

Steam swirled around Lily's face as she clasped her mug of chocolate. "It's nice. Well, most of the time. It's hard to get lonely around here."

"I'm so jealous," Jessica said, before she could stop herself. Then winced. "I mean, of course, it's just a different lifestyle. There are advantages to city life too. My career, for one thing, it's like working in the future, everything will be connected to computers one day. And then there's ... erm, going to Broadway shows, that's fun, and the art galleries, and the museums are amazing." She tried to sound upbeat.

"Uh huh." Lily side-eyed her, suppressing a smile. They sipped their drinks in companionable silence, watching the visitors.

The sound of cheering kids grew as the sleigh came

closer. It was only half a block from the booth — once it reached the square, the horse would have to turn left and continue around the market.

"If you like it here so much, why not move up permanently?" Lily asked innocently, her eyes fixed on the Christmas tree in the center of the square.

Jessica almost choked on a marshmallow. Lily patted her back as she coughed. "Fine, I'm fine." She waved a hand, then broke off at the sound of a frightened whinny and the sudden clattering of hooves. The horse was dancing sideways in its harness, its ears back, nostrils flared. It snorted loudly. The groom walking alongside tightened his hold, shortening its reins. He tried comforting words while a mother ordered her teenage son, his face flushed red, back onto the sidewalk.

Santa was calling out to the groom. The horse tossed its head high, suddenly tearing the reins from the groom's hands. He flailed, trying to grab them back, but too late, the horse reared then bolted into a headlong gallop with the sleigh, Santa and all, skewing behind it. Jessica gasped in shock, then she and Lily tried to scramble away as it careened straight for their booth, while the others shrieked and ducked behind the counter.

The horse charged on, fear in its bulging eyes, reins flying loose, adding to its panic. People leapt aside, out of its way, the air filled with screams. Seemingly from nowhere, a tall, dark-haired man stepped from the sidewalk, straight into the horse's path. He held his arms wide, his long black greatcoat making him appear even bigger and taller than he was. He calmly stood his ground without a word, looking straight at the frightened horse.

People shouted out, Santa was yelling, Jessica raked in a breath. The horse jerked its head, its hooves scrabbling on the snow packed ground, slipping as it tried to swerve away. The man stepped forward and deftly grabbed the loose reins as the horse veered, trying to stop as the sleigh skidded to a halt, pulling on the harness.

Gathering the reins in one hand, the stranger reached out to calm the bewildered animal. It reared up, then pranced, fighting to gain its balance on the slippery ground, its tail whipping the air. Murmuring in low, soothing tones, he reached to stroke the frightened animal's neck, keeping his feet well clear of its stamping hooves. Around the square, everyone went quiet, mesmerized by the scene playing out in front of them, holding their breath in case the horse bolted again.

Jessica was close enough to hear the gentle cadence of the stranger's voice, though not the actual words. He had his back to their booth, his focus on calming the horse, ignoring the gawking crowds and Santa, still sitting, shaken, in the sleigh, his hat now nowhere to be seen.

For a moment, it seemed as though the world stood still and there was just the man and the horse. He murmured to it, gently stroking its head until it settled to a standstill, calmed despite its heaving flanks and flaring nostrils. The shocked groom raced up to take the reins and let poor Santa climb shakily down, bringing his sack of candy with him.

As the man in the greatcoat turned, Jessica caught a glimpse of him, and her heart lurched. Classically handsome with a sculpted face straight out of a movie — something old-timey, black and white, like a Western, or a Cary Grant film. Thick dark hair spilling across sea-green eyes, which fixed for a second on Jessica's, before he turned back to the groom.

With her palm still pressed to her chest from the shock, Jessica could feel the rapid drumbeat of her heart against her ribcage. She forced herself to lower her hand and straighten, shaking off the fear that had seized her.

"Jess, are you ok?" Lily asked, her own voice trembling.

"Yes. Yes, I'm fine," she managed, throat still tight. From adrenaline, she told herself. Nothing more. "What about you?"

"Shaken," she admitted. "What a terrible thing to happen."

At that moment, a familiar blond head appeared, striding toward the throng of people forming a circle around the horse and sleigh.

"Let me through, let me see him." Luke's commanding voice quickly parted the flustered bystanders, his arms gesturing for them to step back, give the frightened animal some space. Jessica watched Luke lay a hand on the horse's flank, speaking soothingly to it as he stepped around, running his strong, expert hands down each leg, searching for any injury.

Jessica scanned the anxious faces for the stranger, the hero of the hour, but he'd already vanished back into the crowd — probably just another visiting tourist among the hundreds here today.

Talk and laughter slowly filled the square once more, tinged with relief, as everyone recovered from the shock.

Jessica moved forward without thinking and headed towards Luke.

"Poor thing, is he going to be ok?" Jessica asked Luke as she arrived in earshot.

Luke glanced up, his blue eyes clouded with concern. "Yeah, he was just panicked…weren't you, boy?" he spoke softly, patting the horse's neck. It lowered its nose to nuzzle his face. "Do you remember him from camp, he's called Harvey." He glanced at her.

"Pulling the cart? I wondered if it was him." Jessica smiled and their eyes locked for a moment.

"I telephoned last night, just thought I'd see how you were settling in," he said, his gaze still holding hers.

"Oh, we weren't in, we…um," she was about to blurt out where they'd been, but it suddenly seemed silly.

The groom had released the sleigh harness and called to Luke. "He's ready now. Thanks for checking him over. I'll sort out the sleigh."

"OK, I'm going to walk him home. It'll give him a chance to cool down, and I can see if there's anything strained," Luke told him, then turned back to Jessica. "You take care now, Jess."

"Sure," she replied, then stood back as he gently maneuvered the horse around to lead it away, back down main street.

Santa was already surrounded by young children eager to share their holiday wishes, but he called out a heartfelt thanks to Luke. Then he shouted *Ho-ho-ho*, raised a hand in the air and moved along the street, the colorful crowd following him like a red and white garbed pied piper.

Lily caught her up. "Thank goodness Luke was nearby."

"Yes…"

"Who was the guy who stood in front of the horse?" Lily was saying.

"I've no idea…"

"Well, it was a pretty darn brave thing to do. Or stupid. He could have been killed."

"Um…" Jessica's eyes were on the changing scene. She was trying to ignore the unsettled feeling in her stomach, a sensation she couldn't explain — like the excitement before Christmas, just waiting for something good to happen.

CHAPTER 7

French toast and coffee in the sunlit kitchen, followed by a half hour in the white blanketed meadow behind Lily's farmhouse throwing snowballs for Thor, made a blissful start to the day.

"I feel like a fraud," Lily had said at supper the night before.

"It's just a misunderstanding," Grant had replied, already dressed, ready to leave for his hospital shift the moment dinner was done.

"And it's made Mrs Ryan really happy," Jessica added. "She wouldn't have had anyone to talk it over with if it hadn't happened."

"The ghost may not be related to Joe Ryan at all," Grant had suggested between bites of the chicken pot pies he'd warmed for them while they were at their volunteer shift at the market. "Maybe it's been in that house for years, who knows. The place was built in the early 1800s; there could be all kinds of spooky stories in its past."

"You're not saying there's an actual ghost?" Lily had laughed.

Grant grinned at that. "No, I guess not, but why not check out the house's history in the library? It wouldn't do any harm, and you never know, you might end up researching Clara's family history for her."

"It would be Joe's family history, it was his folk's home," Lily reminded him.

"Let's do that, Lily," Jessica had said. "It's a fabulous idea."

So today was a visit to the library.

A short drive later, they approached the stone carved steps to the Montrose Township Library, established 1879. Standing in front was a bronze statue of George Montrose, the original founder of the town, his elegant frock coat and top hat dusted with snow. The building was handsome red brick with white colonnades in front, sash windows and two stories high. It stood between the post office and what passed for a police department in this small town — really just the sheriff, deputy and a couple of officers.

Colorful artwork decorated the central hall — fabric covered panels featuring pictures from the school kids in town, all drawn around the holiday theme: crayoned Santas carrying sacks of presents, reindeer pulling a flying sleigh, Christmas trees, plus a few dreidels and Hanukkah menorahs too. Jessica smiled at the signed names on the drawings; giant looped letters, wonky words falling off the page and those heavily accessorized with stickers, glitter and blobs of glue.

"How can I help you?" a pleasant voice interrupted. And then, a second later, "Oh, Lily! Hello! I haven't seen you for a while. How are you, and Grant, mustn't forget him," she added.

"Just fine — you remember Jessica?" Lily looped an arm through Jessica's and spun her around to face the librarian standing behind the plain oak counter. The name tag said Miss Collins, but the moment they locked eyes, Jessica blurted, "Matilda?"

Matilda Collins had been a regular staffer at the summer camp, and four years older than her and Lily. It had been almost a decade since Jessica had last seen her, but her soft voice and warm smile hadn't changed a bit. "Jess! How are you?" Matilda leaned in for a hug. "Gosh, you're way taller than me now," she joked. Most people were, except Lily — the two of them hovered around the 5' 3" mark, but Matilda's smart pump heels gave her the advantage today. Short and slim, she wore cat-eyed glasses, her dark brown hair tied back in a neat ponytail, and a warm wool dress under a matching navy jacket.

"I didn't know you lived in town," Jessica said.

"I didn't, not for a long time." Matilda smiled. "Went to library school in Boston, then stayed a few years after that to work in their system. But I was homesick, and my parents had been bugging me to move back for ages, so I thought… why not give it a go? It was pure luck the previous librarian was retiring, the timing was perfect and serendipity sealed the deal! I've been here almost three years now."

"Must have been a big change, coming from the city back here. Don't you miss it?" Jessica asked, curiosity in her voice.

"Definitely." Matilda laughed. "But it's a good job I'm kept busy because there's only about dozen eligible men in a twenty-mile radius, and I grew up with most of them. But Boston was getting a bit overwhelming." She shook her head. "Don't get me wrong, I loved being there during my twenties. Now I'm thirty, though, and I just don't have the same drive to go-go-go all the time. Country life suits me, you know?"

"I can imagine it," Jessica said, then quashed the latent longing.

"So what brings you girls in here today? Besides a catch-up, of course!" Matilda looked from Jessica to Lily inquiringly.

"We were actually looking for some information on High Meadows House," Lily said. "It's a… research project. For Mrs. Ryan."

"Oh really? Local history, Family Tree? What sort of research?" Matilda kept right on smiling at them, unaware of how ridiculous their answer was going to sound.

Trading a sidelong glance with Lily, Jessica said, "Um, sort of. We're interested in any events that happened at the house, any stories about, er… unusual occurrences."

Matilda blinked politely. "What do you mean?"

With a sigh, Lily replied, "Ghosts. Or creepy stories, anything like that."

To their surprise, Matilda didn't bat an eyelid. Thankfully, she must have missed the article about Lily's new enterprise in the Montrose Valley Post. "Is this for the Halloween tour next year?" Her smile turned mischievous.

"I always thought High Meadows House could give the Darby Estate a run for its money."

The Darby Estate was another large, stately historic home in Montrose Valley — Lily's parents had taken her and Jessica on a tour there one summer, during the week it opened to the general public. Jessica recalled the extensive lawns and beautiful walled gardens out back, complete with a hedge maze, and the cavernous rooms with high ceilings and glittering chandeliers.

"What do you mean? Darby Estate is haunted!" Jessica exclaimed.

Both Matilda and Lily laughed.

Then Lily murmured, "Maybe."

"No…well, who knows." Matilda shrugged. "The Darby Estate hosts a huge Halloween party every year to raise funds for the Children's hospital wards," Matilda explained. "It's mostly geared towards the local kids. They turn the place into a haunted house, with scarecrows and skeletons to spook the visitors on the way in. They've got apple bobbing, costume contests…"

"Creepy cocktails for the adults," Lily added, grinning. "The caramel apple rum last year was scrumptious."

"But the highlight of the party is when old Mr. Darby himself comes out in period costume to tell the story of the Lady in Red." Matilda picked up the story with a little shiver and leaned closer over the counter as Lily and Jessica did the same. "The Lady in Red haunts the Darby Estate. Supposedly she was married to a wealthy merchant in the late 1800s who often traveled abroad to bring home tea, silks, spices and other valuables. She used to pace the balcony on the roof of the manor, seeking any sign of her husband returning from his latest journey. She couldn't go up there on the last trip he took, there was a terrible storm. Several people died, including a man he'd been traveling with. She was told by mistake that it was her husband who'd perished, and she threw herself from the topmost floor down onto the marble hall, breaking her neck and dying instantly. Allegedly it was right where the crowd would gather to hear the story and everyone always stepped back as though the lady had just fallen at their feet."

"People claim to see her up there," Lily interjected, wrapping her arms around herself like she was trying to calm her goosebumps. "Or else wandering the grounds, her red dress all drenched in blood…"

"Yikes!" Jessica exclaimed, enjoying the story. "But how would anyone see the blood if her dress was red?"

"Jess will you stop with the sensible," Lily told her, then rolled her eyes. "You're always so practical."

"I am not," Jessica denied hotly.

"And city suspicious," Lily added.

"That's outrageous and totally untrue," Jessica retorted.

"You always were, Jess." Matilda cocked her head to one side.

Lily laughed. "There you have it!"

Matilda returned to the matter of their visit. "Now, is the Lady in Red the sort of thing you're looking for at High Meadows House?"

"Yes!" Lily nodded firmly. "I mean, hopefully not as gruesome, but…"

"Right. There should be some information over in the local history section. Let's see." Matilda led them through the main lobby to one of the smaller side rooms. The familiar scent of old leather bindings, foxed paper and beeswax met them on the threshold.

Shelf upon shelf of books, journals, ledgers and magazines filled the room, furnished with cozy-looking armchairs and cushioned reading nooks along the walls. Matilda showed them the local history sections, then left them to it with a cheery wave and an offer of help if needed. Lily selected an armful of reference books; notable townsfolk in the 1800s; the founding of Montrose in 1798; and a couple of hefty tomes on local architecture. Jessica found a few interesting-sounding titles herself: Legends of Montrose Valley, Haunted Vermont, and a book simply called Montrose: Past and Present.

Together, they stacked their hauls on the table in the center of the room and settled in leather chairs lit by green-shaded lamps. The next hour or so passed in companionable silence, leafing through books. Every so often, one or the other would break the quiet to read aloud an interesting tidbit, they found a lot of information on the town's founders, its notable figures, and several more spooky stories along the lines of the Lady in Red, but nothing about the history of High Meadows House.

That's when Matilda popped her head into the room. "Psst. Girls!" She beckoned them, keeping her voice low since a few other library patrons had trickled in. "Come along here…" They set aside their books and followed her to the back room. "I've been doing some digging of my own," Matilda explained, indicating microfiche reading machines. "And I thought you might want to see this. It's a list of newspaper articles that mention High Meadows House. There's quite a few microfiches, so it might take you a while to get through them all…"

"That's fantastic!" Lily clapped, then shot a guilty look around the echoing room. "Oh, sorry. I mean, but it is fantastic!" she stage-whispered. "We'd love to take a look. Thank you."

Cold linoleum and brash overhead lighting gave a glare to the workaday room, making them both blink. A row of chunky black microfiche readers stretched along one wood-paneled wall. Simple metal and wooden chairs were set in front of each, reminding Jessica of grade school.

"I haven't used one of these since I graduated," Jessica joked, slipping onto the nearest seat. "I used to think they were so high-tech…" She laughed under her breath.

"Right?" Grinning, Lily inserted herself at the next reader while Matilda quickly reminded them how to load the fiche plates and operate the viewing screen.

"I know you'll know how it's done, but I'm supposed to instruct you," she said lightly. "Slide the fiche upside down onto the glass lens and then you can see them through the viewer…here, like this," she pushed the flimsy film onto a flat glass plate, backlit with a bulb. "Then the screen magnifies it for you." She waved a hand at the large screen rather like an old black and white TV. "Then you can move around using these dials."

They'd only been skimming newspaper articles for ten minutes when Lily let out an excited squeal. "I found him!"

"Who?" Jessica leaned back from her own reader, blinking as her eyes readjusted.

"Our ghost. Take a look!" Lily scooted aside so Jessica could lean over to read the screen on her machine. It was an article from a 1912 edition of the Montrose Valley Post.

"Wow, I didn't realize the newspaper was that old," Jessica murmured.

"Look at the third paragraph!" Lily hissed, impatient.

Quickly, Jessica scanned the article. It was an article about High Meadows House itself: how it had been built, and an interview with the current inhabitants, the Ryans. Jessica's eyebrows rose. Apparently, the house had been in Joe's family for a long time.

Finally, she reached the paragraph Lily was talking about. Miss Victoria Ryan claimed that her great-granduncle, Lewis T. Ryan, continued to haunt the house "even now, forty-eight years after his death." She went on to say that she'd recognized him by his uniform, "a private U.S. Infantry uniform like the Bluecoats wore."

"She must be talking about the Civil War, right?" Jessica murmured.

"It fits, don't you think? A war uniform… and this guy is even Joe's relative!" Lily was on the edge of her seat, positively bubbling with excitement. "What if Clara really saw him?"

"I don't know." Jessica worried at her lower lip. "I suppose it's a funny coincidence, but…"

Lily wasn't listening. She'd already hurried off to the lobby to fetch Matilda.

After Matilda skimmed the article too, she nodded thoughtfully. "I haven't heard the story before, but we do have records of everyone in town who fought in the Civil War, plus lists of all the men who were killed. Let me fetch them."

It didn't take long to confirm that Lewis T. Ryan had indeed fought for the Yankees in the U.S. Civil War. "He'd been injured in the Battle of the Wilderness in Northern Virginia, 1864," Matilda read out. "He was put on the transport cart to take him home and died just before they entered the back gates of the house…Oh, so that's why he haunts it, he was trying to reach home."

"That's so sad," Jessica said.

"It was tragic, wasn't it?" Matilda said and continued reading. "His younger brother, Thomas M. Ryan, also fought, but he returned safely, and went on to live a happy family life, married, and five living children. He died aged 69."

"Wow! I guess that was considered old back then," Lily said, her eyes widening.

From him, they found it easy to trace a line from Thomas's eldest son, Benjamin, all the way to Joe Ryan in the present day.

"We've got to tell Clara!" Lily practically bounced out of her chair, dropping her coat and mittens on the floor in her haste to get going. Shooting Lily a wry look, Jessica said, "Let's grab a bite to eat first and think about how to position this history to her." She really wasn't sure that she bought this new theory, and wanted some time to consider before they took it to Mrs Ryan.

After thanking Matilda yet again, Jessica and Lily wandered back out onto the street. The market was in full swing, but Jessica needed something a little more substantial than gingerbread cookies and hot pretzels.

It being almost lunchtime, the café attached to Miss Daisy's B&B was now open, and gearing up for the rush, its freshly chalked menu board sitting on the sidewalk. Lily paused to peruse it as Jessica reached for the front door; it swung open, and a tall man in a black greatcoat and fedora hat pulled low over his eyes stepped out. He locked eyes with Jessica and for a split second, she caught her breath.

The stranger! The man from the market the day before, the man who'd leapt in front of the charging horse. She'd recognize those cut-glass cheekbones anywhere — not to mention the sea-green eyes glinting in the shadow beneath the fedora.

From the way those eyes looked into hers, Jessica could've sworn he recognized her too. But just as she opened her mouth to say something — thank you for saving our lives, maybe? — he sidestepped and hurried up the street without a word, neck hunched into his raised collar and hands plunged deep into his pockets. In his wake, Jessica shivered, the light flurry of snowflakes falling suddenly feeling colder than before, then remembered to close her mouth again.

Classic tourist, always hurrying around, not taking time to say hello or be friendly with the locals. Jessica shook herself. Ignore him.

As Lily and Jessica stepped inside and closed the door, the bell overhead tinkled merrily to announce their presence. Warmth enveloped them at once, along with the scents of fresh-baked scones and melted cheese, and a low rumble of conversation. They stamped their boots on the mat, and shook off their coats, nobody paying them much mind, too immersed in their own and each other's company.

Behind the counter, Ellie-May, Miss Daisy's assistant, was busy chatting to another customer. Ellie-May was fresh-faced pretty, with blond curls tumbled about her face. The same age as Jessica and Lily, her mother had been Miss Daisy's housekeeper for years. Ellie-May was sweet, but according to Lily, who knew all the town happenings, Miss Daisy only let her work in the café, because Ellie-May had accidentally ruined three loads of linens in a row while 'helping out' in the B&B. Kind and willing, she could be more than a little ditsy.

"The sandwich of the day?" Ellie-May was asking the man in front of them. "Hold on, I wrote it down so I wouldn't forget, let me just find what I did with it…" She looked behind the old-fashioned cash register, then moved a couple of cake plates under the display counter, then a strawberry cheesecake aside. "Erm…" she gazed up at the man with wide-eyed innocence. "How about cheese and ham?"

Lily turned to face Jessica again, eyes still bright with excitement. "What do you think he looked like? The Civil War soldier. I wish cameras were more common back then. Do you think there would be any pictures anywhere? Do you think he looked like Joe?" She was almost on tiptoe, with a million questions just waiting to burst out — and she was doing really well just to contain it to three.

Biting her lip to keep from laughing, Jessica peered over Lily's head at the board mounted on the wall which listed the specials for the day. The quibbling man in front of them was finally finishing, and they were next in line. Jessica quickly debated: the broccoli cheddar soup sounded good. Or maybe the tomato soup with a grilled cheese sandwich? "Do you seriously believe in ghosts, Lil?" she asked while she skimmed the options.

"I didn't think so," Lily mused, following Jessica's gaze and considering the board herself. "But hey, now that I'm a ghost hunter, I've got to believe in them, right?"

Both of them burst into laughter. They didn't notice the previous customer had moved aside until Ellie-May called out, "Is it true, then?" She was wide eyed. "You're really a ghost-hunter? I saw the ad in the paper last week, but I didn't believe it. That's so cool!" Ellie-May beamed at Lily.

Before Lily could reply, however, someone behind them scoffed loudly. Jessica spun around and froze.

Right behind them in line, blonde hair permed into perfect waves, bright lipstick and full eyeshadow incongruous on a casual weekday morning, stood Caitlin Johnson. She wore a pencil skirt, tight blazer, and spike heels despite the half a foot of snow outside, and her shoulder pads added at least an extra six inches beyond where her arms were. "I knew it," Caitlin snapped, mascaraed eyes narrowed at Lily. She leaned towards her, pointing an accusing red-tipped finger. "You told Ed that article was a lie, but here you are declaring yourself a ghost-hunter. You tried to sabotage me."

Lily's cheeks turned even pinker than usual. "I said it as a joke, Caitlin," her voice held a note of irritation. "You took it completely out of context, just like you always — "

"Like I always do?" Caitlin's voice rose, her eyes glittering. She threw her hands up in a gesture of disbelief. "That's always your story. You're always so right, playing the innocent, just waiting to be rescued. And they all fall for it. Well, I'm a career girl, and I don't play stupid for anyone. And I don't like anyone playing stupid with me either. Running to Ed was a low trick and I know why. You're so jealous, it's pathetic."

Talk about the pot calling the kettle black. This feud had been simmering ever since Grant and Caitlin broke up. Shortly afterward, it became obvious to anyone with eyes that he was interested in Lily, and Caitlin began the smear campaign to end all smear campaigns.

What made it even more ironic was that Lily might've been the only person in the whole of Montrose Valley who didn't realize Grant had feelings for her. It took far too long, and some blunt talking from Jessica, before

Lily finally noticed what had been right in front of her all along.

Now that the two of them were happily married, Caitlin's spite had kicked into a whole new gear.

The cafe's busy hum had stilled, and from the corner of her eye, Jessica noticed the entire room was watching them, whilst trying to look like they really weren't. Pulling herself up to her full height, she took a deep breath. "Caitlin, I'm a career girl from New York City. It doesn't mean we have to elbow our way through life, and it doesn't mean we have to be jealous of those who have taken their own path either." Jessica spoke her words slowly and calmly to ensure they were heard. "Trust me, Lily is perfectly content. You can tell, because she doesn't try to destroy other people's happiness."

Caitlin's eyes flashed as the barb landed, and she rocked backwards on her heels. She opened her mouth to retort, but then caught herself and cast a glance around the crowded café, including Ellie-May, who was gaping at the scene. With one last huff, Caitlin spun around and stormed out into the cold, the ridiculous shoulder pads making her look like a footballer leaving the field.

Watching her go, Lily heaved a deep sigh, her own shoulders slumping downwards. "I thought time was meant to heal all wounds," she murmured. Even now, after those insults, Jessica spotted compassion in her gaze as Lily watched Caitlin cross the street, and felt waves of empathy for her sweet natured friend.

"Normally it does," Jessica replied softly. "But not if you let them fester."

CHAPTER 8

Awkward confrontations aside, lunch at the café hit the spot. Lily chose the sandwiches, while Jessica tucked into a steaming bowl of tomato and red pepper soup, with a grilled cheese sandwich made with sharp Vermont cheddar to dunk in it. They'd almost finished eating when the side door of the café, the one that led upstairs into the adjacent B&B, opened.

Miss Daisy poked her head inside and quickly scanned the room. Her eyes finally landed on the girls. "Oh good, you're here." She beckoned Lily and Jessica hurriedly. They exchanged confused looks, but stood to follow her into the adjacent B&B lobby. "Grant called looking for you," Miss Daisy explained. "He says Mrs. Ryan had been in touch. She wants you to call her as soon as you can; it sounded urgent. Is everything alright?"

"How funny. We just found something we need to talk to her about actually." Lily glanced at Jessica. "We've been doing some research for her. But… maybe some new information came to light her end too."

From the expression on Lily's face, Jessica could guess what she was thinking. They'd told Mrs. Ryan to call them if anything else happened. Had she seen the ghost again?

"What sort of research?" Miss Daisy asked as she directed them to the phone table in the hallway, violet eyes bright with curiosity.

"Oh, um, about her house," Lily said absently, already scanning the phonebook for Mrs. Ryan's number. Then she pressed her ear to the phone and dialed the number.

Realizing there was no privacy to be had, Jessica lightly touched Miss Daisy's sleeve, who was leaning a little too close to Lily. "Is that poster for tomorrow evening?" Jessica asked, startling Miss Daisy.

Miss Daisy's focus followed Jessica's finger. "Ah, yes, it's the dinner I'm holding for the animal shelter, Lily has already bought tickets."

"She didn't mention it." Jessica moved closer to peer at the poster. "That's Luke!"

Big letters declared Charity Wine and Dine! All Donations Go to Montrose Valley Animal Shelter. The background was a snow covered building and the foreground showed a photo of a smiling Luke holding a puppy with a bandaged paw.

"Yes, and we've sold out all the tickets already," Miss Daisy smiled sweetly at Jessica then over to Lily, still talking on the telephone. "It must have slipped her mind."

Jessica frowned. "I'm sure it must have."

"It is quite informal, so don't think you have to dress up," Miss Daisy added gaily.

Lily put the phone down. "We've had a slight change of plans. Well, change of venue, actually."

Jessica's eyebrows rose. "Oh?"

"Mrs. Ryan has invited us to stay at High Meadows House tonight," Lily said, her smile wide, eyes sparkling with meaning. "Since Grant won't be home until morning anyway, I told her that'd be fine. If it's okay with you, Jess?"

"This is for tonight, is it?"

"Yes…" Lily answered slowly.

"Not tomorrow night?" Jessica continued, then pointed at the poster.

"Ah, now I was saving that as a surprise," Lily said, then grinned. "Come on." She hooked her arm under Jessica's and they quickly said their goodbyes to Miss Daisy, who was almost quivering with curiosity.

"You weren't planning another ambush, were you, Lily?" Jessica asked once they were outside on the sidewalk.

"It's a charity dinner to help out my favorite cousin," Lily raised big innocent eyes at Jessica. "In what way would it be an ambush?"

Jessica met that with a frown, but Lily plowed on in a low voice, "Clara says she saw him again, and asked if we could sleep there tonight, in case he comes back?"

"He's not coming back, Lily. It's just her imagination," Jessica said.

"I know, but…if we go and nothing happens, it would give us the chance to explain everything to her."

Jessica sighed. "Yes, and that really is what we should do now."

* * *

After dinner and Grant had left for the hospital, Jessica and Lily piled into the car and set off for High Meadows House with Thor in the back seat.

Wrapped in several layers of sweaters and a wool shawl, Clara let them inside herself, since Bethany had already left for the night. "I apologize for the lack of heating upstairs," she said. "These old houses are so drafty. But I asked Bethany to light the fire in the room you'll be using, so it shouldn't be too uncomfortable."

The enormous bedroom Clara showed them to still held a chill, but the fire in the hearth was doing its best to warm the high-ceilinged space. As for comfort, Jessica didn't think she'd ever stayed in such a sumptuous room. Against the far wall, facing the door stood a large canopied four poster bed, the mattress so high there was a tiny stool placed by the side to step up into it. The faded wallpaper reflected dancing flames from the fire and helped instill a feeling of warmth.

Against the other wall, a mahogany daybed laden with a mountain of pillows was freshly made up, and was easily larger than Jessica's bed in her apartment. Two wing chairs stood before the fire, with matching footstools, all in a dark red damask, and Bethany had stacked a pile of extra firewood into a large basket beside the hearth. The carpet, a Persian rug with an intricate pattern, covered most of the floor, and helped keep the drafts down. A cozy dog bed had been found for Thor, lined with a plaid wool blanket of his own.

"It's nice to have an animal in the house again," Clara said, ruffling Thor's fur after she'd shown them to their room. "Joe and I used to have greyhounds. High-energy, but so lovable. I couldn't handle one on my own, I'm afraid, though I miss waking up to their noses in my face…" She tweaked Thor's nose; he licked her palm in response.

Clara settled in one of the chairs by the fire while Lily and Jessica unpacked their overnight bags and treats and food for Thor.

Finally, once they were situated, Lily plopped down cross-legged on the carpet in front of Clara while Jessica settled in the other chair. "Tell us again what you saw?" she asked.

Clara paused, burying her fingers in Thor's scruff as though for support. "I was asleep in my room. It's on this floor." She pointed out the door to the hallway that curved around toward her bedroom. "I'm not sure what woke me. But I couldn't get back to sleep, so I went over to the window to look outside. The moon was so bright…" She paused, looking sheepish. "I'll admit, I haven't been sleeping very well since all this started happening. At first, I thought I was still dreaming, because I was thinking about him, and there he was! My Joe, right there in the front driveway. He was gazing toward the house, just like the last time I saw him. But as I watched, he lifted his head to look at me."

"What happened then?" Lily asked, almost breathless.

"I went downstairs. To see if it was really him, and..." Clara shook her head. "I don't know. I suppose I wanted to see if I could talk to him this time. Find out what he wanted. But by the time I got to the ground floor, he was gone. I'm not so fast on my feet as I used to be down the stairs now. I went through every room to look outside, but there was no sign of anyone. I scared him away again."

Despite herself, Jessica felt goosebumps rising along her forearms. She thought of the civil war soldier, dying just before he reached his home. Could it be him? Or even Joe?

As if sensing everyone else's moods, Thor let out a plaintive whine. Clara scratched his ear soothingly, while Jessica moved to sit closer to the fire, a small chill rippling down her back. It's just the cold draft from the window, that's all.

After a brief silence, Lily's cheery, upbeat tone brought them back to the moment. "We found something in the library that might interest you." As succinctly as she could, Lily summarized the article they'd found and the links to the family history. "The poor man died just before he reached home."

"Well, it's tragic, and I could understand his yearning, but I'd recognized Joe's jacket. It was his flying jacket, the same one he wore in the photos you saw that were taken of him during the war. It wasn't a Civil War uniform."

Lily's shoulders slumped. "Maybe the ghost changes outfits? To keep up with whatever era we're in?"

"I've never heard of a ghost doing that," Jessica said, then laughed at the ridiculousness of it. "Then again, I've never seen a real ghost either…"

"Haven't you?" Clara asked, her thin brows raised. "But I thought you were ghost hunters?"

Lily's cheeks turned pink and the words came tumbling out. "Oh, I just have to tell you. It was a mistake, I'm so sorry…"

"But it was a good mistake, because it brought us to you," Jessica quickly added as she saw Clara's mouth fall open.

They explained it all, including the long and stupid feud Caitlin had continued. Once they'd finished the tale, they waited nervously for Clara's reaction. She had closed her mouth firmly, her eyes growing rounder with every word of the telling.

Suddenly she let out a peel of delighted laughter.

"Oh what a scrape," she said as she tried to stop giggling. "Joe would have thought it so funny, and he'd have had something to say to me too." She took out a handkerchief and wiped her eyes. "Well, that proves fate really does move in mysterious ways…poor Lily, has anyone in town said anything about your new career?"

"One or two," Lily said dryly. "And my family are never going to let me forget it."

"And they won't be the only ones…" Jessica said, and they all looked at each other and burst out laughing again.

Thor had been watching, his ears waggling and head going from one side to the other as though trying to follow the conversation. He must have decided he'd waited enough and went over to push his nose into Lily's overnight bag.

"Someone smells the treats I brought," Lily said, jumping to her feet.

"I think we all need a treat after that!" Clara declared and insisted on making them hot cocoa (though she did capitulate and let Lily and Jessica carry it upstairs themselves).

They sat together for some while longer, still laughing and joking at the ghost hunting nonsense, until Clara excused herself to bed, leaving Lily and Jessica to themselves.

The fire crackled merrily in the grate now, and if Lily and Jessica sat close enough, it was possible to forget the wind that leaked around the windowsill or crept under the door from the hallway. Thor helped, leaning heavily against Jessica's side with Lily's toes tucked under his belly.

"You know, despite the shaky start to my ancestry research, it has been fun."

"It has," Jessica nodded. "And once people realize what you're really trying to do, I think you'll get lots of calls."

"Maybe you could do it with me? You know like partners?"

The smile died on Jessica's lips. "I'd love to, but I doubt you'll earn enough for two full-time jobs, Lil."

Lily bit her lip. "I know, but the offer's there."

Jessica sighed. "And I appreciate it."

"You always talk about how much you like interior design and doing up old stuff," Lily said. "Remember, you used to make those collages at camp from magazines. What about that?"

"I didn't study design in school. I'm not qualified."

"Well, what about something else? You could work in a coffee shop… I hear Mr. Fellows is looking for some part-time help in the bookstore."

Another laugh escaped Jessica. "Yeah, right. I'll just tell my Mom that all her and Pop's hard work and the money they saved to help pay for college has resulted in me getting a part-time job at a bookstore."

"If you're happy, isn't that what matters?" Lily replied.

"It's much more complicated after Pop died." Jessica took a deep breath. "And Mom doesn't want me to give up my career for a man, like she did. She loved my dad dearly, but she's always regretted not being able to work anymore. She was a chemist, and loved her work, but after taking time off to raise Simon and me, she couldn't get a place." Jessica lifted one shoulder in a half-hearted gesture. "Nobody wanted to hire a 40-something-year-old woman with an eighteen-year gap in her resume. Dad felt guilty for the fact that she wasn't able to go back to the work she loved, and it hit them financially too. They never felt really secure. They wanted me to have a better chance than they did — and I really get that. They worked so hard. I have to be able to support myself, secure my own future. I can't do that if I leave this job. And Simon would go berserk."

Lily took Jessica's hand and squeezed tightly. "I know. And I know they love you, Jessica, and want you to be successful. But it's your life, not your family's. You have to be happy too."

"It's reality, Lily, and all the goodwill and wishing in the world isn't going to change it," she said with a note of finality.

Those words kept circulating in Jessica's head as they got ready for bed. Snug and warm under the blankets, she mulled them over, watching the shadows grow as the fire died. *It's my life, not my mom's, not Simon's.* That was true. But her parents had brought her into this world. They'd sacrificed so much for her. The least she could do was keep her feet on the path they had laid out for her. But then another vision crept in, Luke, the house behind a picket fence, maybe an annex for Mom? What would she make of country living? She could skip between here and New York if it suited her…she smiled at herself, typical Jessica, so practical and yet always losing herself in a daydream.

Fatigue weighed and her eyelids fluttered closed. She was almost asleep when Thor started growling. It wasn't loud, more of a rumble somewhere deep in his chest.

"Hush now, good dog, go to sleep," she told him, but pricked up her own ears anyway. Nothing but the wind, or the creaks of this old house settling, she thought and burrowed deeper under the covers.

Then Thor growled again, louder this time. The hackles rose on the back of his neck, then he moved on stiff legs toward the window.

There was someone, or something, outside the house.

CHAPTER 9

Suddenly the shadows seemed darker than before. She sat up, straining to see in the faint moonlight filtering through a gap in the drapes. Outside the layers of down covers and knitted blankets, the room felt icy cold. She grabbed a hot water bottle Clara had given her earlier and held it close.

Thor was still staring at the window. He stood there, he'd stopped growling and was listening with his head cocked.

Jessica snuggled back down with a sigh of relief when Thor's lips drew back from sharp fangs and the rumbling growl reverberating in his chest grew even louder than before.

Every hair on Jessica's neck stood on end. "Lily," she whispered urgently.

Lily murmured in her sleep, nestling under the mountainous covers of the four poster bed, her strawberry-blonde head barely visible above the eiderdown. Jessica slipped out from under the covers, tiptoed over to the bed and gently nudged the spot she guessed to be Lily's shoulder.

"Lily!"

"Huh…wha?" Lily blinked, then moaned and squeezed the covers around her face. "'S too early, Grant. Still dark."

"It's me," Jessica hissed. "We're at High Meadows House, remember? Thor heard something."

For a beat, nothing. Then Lily inhaled deeply, slowly letting her breath out in a haze of white. She flung the covers back and sat up, rubbing her arms. "What's going on? I was having the nicest dream. Summer…we were out on the lake in the canoe…Luke was there, close to you…" She shivered and scowled at the dying fire.

"Listen," Jessica replied, putting her hand on Lily's arm to quieten her. Thor's gaze was still fixed on the window, his bared teeth visible in the half light.

Lily fell silent, her eyes widening. Just as she opened her mouth, Thor growled again, lower and more menacing this time, raising slightly off his haunches, ready to spring into action if needed.

Lily spun to catch Jessica's eye. "It — it could be the twigs touching the window?"

"It's too far away to touch." Jessica could see that the tree wasn't close enough. "I'm going to look." She was shivering, but grateful for the silence of her sock-clad feet. Padding quickly across the room, she leaned closer to the window and pushed the curtain aside to peer out.

The snow lay deep; a smooth and perfect surface reflecting the moon in a myriad of glittering crystals. Jessica traced the ridges of the back yard — shrubs and bushes in smooth mounds, a bump there that was probably a bench seat, another shrouded mass near the back of the yard, that must be an arbor.

Then she froze. A shadow near the gateway…it might be a shadow, it moved didn't it? She watched, Thor growled again, he was standing right next to her and sounded really loud in the silence of the room.

"Can you see anything strange?" Jessica whispered.

Behind her, Lily sighed. Rustling, followed by the patter of bare feet, then she joined her to gaze down. "I don't know." Her breath fogged the glass as she spoke. "We didn't exactly get a whole yard tour. Maybe Clara was out there?"

"In the dark?" Jessica looked at her. Lily stared back, reading the determination on Jessica's face.

"I am so not cut out for this ghost-hunting business," Lily grumbled, but shuffled back to the bed and shrugged on the fuzzy pink robe she'd brought with her, complete with matching fluffy slippers. "Alright. Let's go have a look."

Jessica grabbed her Merino sweater to tug on over her pajamas, then stuffed her feet into the pair of slightly-too-large slippers Clara had loaned her. She paused to toss another log onto the fire to catch while they were gone, and followed Lily out of the bedroom.

Thor paced alongside them, a big furry reassuring presence. Not that Thor had an aggressive bone in his body, but Jessica figured any potential intruders wouldn't know that. The sight of the thickset husky would make anyone think twice.

Her heartbeat quickened as they walked the long hallway around to the staircase. The house seemed to creak and groan with every step they took, and as the wind picked up, a howling and beating battered at a windowpane somewhere up in the attic.

Silently, Lily reached for Jessica's arm and slipped her hand through.

At the top of the staircase, they held their breath, listening, not that they could hear much over the gusting wind. They exchanged a sideways look, shrugged, and started carefully down the stairs, the darkness almost total without the faint moonlight to help. Thor trailed behind them, hackles still raised, the growl rising and falling in his chest.

At the bottom step, they paused again. Downstairs looked different in the gloom, less ornate and more foreboding. The grand furniture threw threatening shadows, spacious rooms and stately hallways offered more corners to conceal a prowler.

"I don't hear anything. Do you?" Lily whispered.

Jessica shook her head. "Let's do a loop? Just to make sure."

"Okay. But we're stopping in the kitchen for cookies," Lily replied. "If I'm awake at this hour, I require a reward."

Stifling a laugh, Jessica led the way along the hallway, Thor still on their heels. She itched to turn the lights on, but held back the impulse — if someone was out there, she wanted to find out, not scare them away.

At every doorway, they paused to peer around the doorframe, checking inside. The first couple of rooms were silent and still. By the third room, Jessica was beginning to think maybe it really was just the wind, and her pounding heart began to return to normal.

At the fourth room, a dining room with a table big enough to seat at least twenty guests, Jessica paused. Tall French windows looked out over the backyard, right at ground level, and the drapes were wide open. She could see trees in the distance. The mounds of snow she'd glimpsed from above were definitely a bench seat and an arbor.

Her shoulders relaxed, tense muscles letting go. Nothing there. She was about to turn around and head back to the hallway, where Lily was, when a dark shadow moved somewhere outside, it was man sized, she was sure of it.

So was Thor, he hurtled past her toward the windows, barking furiously, then pounded his paws up against the glass.

Jessica dashed after him and raised her hands around her eyes for a better look. There was nothing, whatever was there was gone. The yard was empty, though Thor didn't let up growling, his hackles raised.

"What the heck was that?" Lily cried, her eyes wide.

"I don't know…" Jessica shook her head. Her pulse was going wild now, a rapid thrum against her ribcage, adrenaline racing through her veins.

"Didn't you see what it was?" Lily moved past Jessica to peer out.

"I don't know. A shadow, but…" Squeezing her eyes

shut, Jessica tried to make sense of it. "Bears wouldn't come into a yard, would they?" Jessica tried rationalizing.

Lily chewed her lower lip. "Not usually, no. Anyway, they should be hibernating now. Maybe if one was around and someone left a trash can open by accident, or spilled something… They get a bit bolder when they are hungry."

"Hello?" Clara's voice, quivering, no doubt she'd been woken by their racket. "Who is it?" Her call from upstairs startled them back to the present.

"I'll go up and tell her what happened," Lily said. "Are you okay down here? Want to come up, or…?"

"I'm fine. You go and reassure Clara. Make sure she's ok, and I'll grab those cookies," Jessica said, because she needed a treat at this point too. They all deserved one.

Lily pointed to Thor. "Thor, you stay with Auntie Jess, okay? Take good care of her."

Thor whined in acknowledgment, thumping his tail as Lily exited the room. Jessica reached down to scratch his ears, unable to tear her eyes from the snow-covered yard. *What is going on in this house?*

* * *

They returned with Clara to gather round the fire in their room.

"But was it him?" Clara insisted. "What did you see?"

"A shadow, really that's all it was," Lily insisted.

"But Thor sensed something," Jessica countered. "And his senses are way stronger than ours."

Clara stroked the big dog's head, he was concentrating on the biscuits, but he closed his eyes in response anyway. "Joe would have loved him," Clara murmured. "And there was something there, dogs know more than we do about this sort of thing."

"Maybe you should advertise Thor as a ghost hunter?" Jessica grinned at Lily.

She laughed. "He'd be better than me any day."

"First thing in the morning we call the police," Jessica declared.

"Oh no, that's not necessary," Clara replied. "They'll just think I'm a silly old lady seeing things that aren't there."

"We saw something," Jessica insisted, "and it's their job to investigate."

"Fine," Lily agreed, then covered a yawn. "Just so long as nobody mentions ghost hunters."

She woke to the scent of frying bacon. Lily and Thor were already absent — having snuck out without disturbing her. The fire was burning merrily, piled with fresh logs and Jessica hurriedly pulled on jeans and sweater and swapped fuzzy bed-socks for slightly less fuzzy woolen ones before heading downstairs.

Clara, Bethany, and Lily were all in the kitchen, nursing steaming cups of coffee while Thor sat next to Clara's chair, his eyes fixed on her hands. It immediately became obvious why as Clara broke off pieces of bacon to feed him under the table.

"How do you like your eggs?" Bethany asked as Jessica entered, rubbing sleep from her eyes.

"Sunny side up, please." Jessica slid into the chair opposite Lily, as Clara shot them both sympathetic looks.

"It must have been him, I couldn't sleep for thinking about it, but I do feel better knowing I'm not the only one."

Across the table, Lily shot Jessica a worried frown. "Honestly, I don't know what we saw."

"Has anyone called the police?" Jessica said.

"I really think we shouldn't —" Clara began another objection.

"Now, I don't agree." Bethany clicked her tongue as she scooped several slices of bacon onto a plate for Jessica. "It's not right, Mrs. Ryan. You shouldn't be here all alone with who-knows-what creeping around your property. It was the middle of the night! No-one in their right mind is out at that time, with snow this deep too. I'll call Jeremiah, tell him I'm needed overnight here — "

"You'll do no such thing," Clara scolded. "I already keep you away from your husband all day, I'll not monopolize your nights too."

"But if it's dangerous, then we have to —"

"I'll go call the police right now." Jessica didn't believe in ghosts, but she'd definitely seen something last night, and Thor had heard it too. Something solid and real — it had to be, and if it was, it must have left some kind of trace behind. The police might find something.

"Oh no, you just stay right there." Bethany wouldn't hear of them leaving the table until they'd eaten — "Cold eggs are the worst way to start a day" — so they finished breakfast and Lily declared she would go call the police, given that her father was a retired officer and she knew them all.

"We could go out and take a look while we're waiting for them to arrive," Jessica said when Lily came back.

"Good idea," Lily agreed.

"Now what's the point in that," Bethany put her hands on her hips. "And the police officer won't thank you for it."

"We'll be careful not to mess any evidence up. Come on Jess," Lily said.

"So now you're taking ghost hunting seriously?" Jessica teased her.

They both laughed as they went to get togged up.

Bethany gave up her objections and led them through the warm kitchen into the laundry room and showed them the door out into the yard.

"Thor," Lily called back to the dog, who was more interested in table scraps. He came after the second call.

"Good boy," Jessica told him. "Let's go see what's out there."

The snow was glittering in the strengthening sunlight, and the wind had died right down. Today was off to a warmer start than the previous couple of days.

"We only need access to the wood pile every so often," Bethany explained, pointing out another lump buried under the snow. "My Jeremiah comes and brings in a big stack once a month so we don't have to be out here in all sorts of weather. Other than that, nobody comes into the yard until spring."

Jeremiah must have taken wood in before the latest snowfall because there was no sign of any tracks going out of the door to the wood pile. In fact, there weren't any tracks at all in the smooth surface of the snow.

Jessica headed off, Lily just behind her and Thor some way at the rear, exploring his own new world of scents. They trudged through the snowy expanse and made their way to the dining room windows.

"It was right up there," Jessica said, pointing up to an open gateway set between a group of tall trees, drifts built up against their thick trunks. It was beautiful in daylight, not spooky in the slightest.

"That must be the rear drive," Lily said.

The snow got deeper and deeper as they neared the gateway, Jessica's steps slowed, so did Lily's. Thor tried to plough through but the drift was actually above his head and only his black nose stuck out.

"We can't get through this way," Jessica finally admitted.

"And no-one's been here," Lily said.

"They might have come down from the road."

"Maybe…" Lily sounded dubious. "Come on, let's go indoors. I told the deputy the intruder was out back, he'll go looking that way, even if we can't."

CHAPTER 10

They were in the morning room, watching through the window as a police car pulled up. Almost an hour had passed, by which point everyone in the house was growing jumpy with nerves.

"Oh good, it's Troy!" Lily jumped up when she spotted the deputy exiting his car and hurried to the front door, where Bethany was already waving the officer into the spacious hall.

Lily knew everybody on the police force, as well as the officers in the surrounding towns. She had mentioned Troy to Jessica before — he was around their age and married to a pretty woman from Georgia, who everyone jokingly referred to as "his Southern belle."

"Lily!" Troy grinned. "You're mixed up in all this! It's not a ghost is it, because I heard —"

"No!" Lily exclaimed, then looked sheepish. "Mrs Ryan thought there's been someone around and we were helping listen out."

It wasn't quite an outright lie.

He gave her a quizzical look, then turned to Jessica. Short brown hair beneath his cap, gray eyes and a friendly smile despite the uniform and weapon he wore strapped to one hip. "Don't know that we've met." He nodded to her in the way of police officers.

"Jessica Brooks," she said. "Up from New York for the holiday."

"My best friend," Lily said. "She's going to move here someday, mark my words. I just need to find her a good enough job to keep her in town... or a man."

Jessica rolled her eyes at Lily, which made Troy laugh.

"I'm fresh out of eligible brothers, but I'll keep a lookout," he grinned. "Now, what seems to be the problem here?"

"The girls heard noises last night," Bethany spoke up from behind them. "They saw something in the backyard, but nobody's been out there in weeks, not since my husband last came to check the wood pile."

"I already took a look out back," Troy said.

"What?" They all said at once.

"The report stated the intruder was out back, so that's where I went," Troy repeated. "It's the kind of thing police do." He eyed them sideways.

"You drove to the rear gate?" Lily could hardly believe him.

"No, I drove along the track until the snow got too deep to go any further. There wasn't so much as a bird print, never mind anything bigger," Troy continued. "But I did find something out front."

"What?" They all asked again.

"Tire tracks from a sedan," Troy said and took his notebook out of his top pocket. "It wasn't from any of the cars parked out there, and we don't get many locals driving sedans. It was most likely a visitor got lost, or mistook this place for their hotel."

"But High Meadows House is a long way from the nearest guest property," Jessica tried to counter.

"Maybe," he replied.

"Could you show us?" Jessica asked. She saw the dubious look in his eyes, but she was certain there was something going on and she wasn't going to back down.

"OK, if that's what you want, come with me," Troy offered and moved toward the door.

Stuffing her hands in the pockets of her red coat, she and Lily followed him out to the front.

Thor had run all the way around the house, totally unfazed by last night's adventures. The moment he spotted them he raced across the snow covered lawn to greet Troy like a long-lost friend, then dashed off again with all the joy of a husky in his element.

Troy stopped when they reached a set of tire tracks some distance from where Lily's and Bethany's cars were parked.

"The car pulled off the road here, and there are footprints going toward the front gates." He pointed to them.

They stared. The footsteps were slightly blurred, as though made a night ago, but they definitely left the car and walked as far as the center of the tall gate posts and then returned to the car, which had obviously turned and driven away. They hadn't seen them because they'd arrived in the dark last night.

"You're sure you don't know anyone who drives a sedan?" Troy asked again.

"No, I don't think so," Lily said.

"Mrs Ryan has seen someone out here," Jessica told him.

"Jess, we promised…" Lily reminded her, but Jessica's blood was up. The tire tracks were proof, and so were the footprints.

"I don't believe this was just someone lost," Jessica insisted. "And Mrs Ryan is a vulnerable old lady in a big house all on her own."

The implications weren't lost on the officer. "I can take a couple of photos?" Troy fished out a camera from inside his jacket.

"Go ahead," Jessica said. "Whoever this is shouldn't be snooping around private property. They gave Mrs. Ryan the fright of her life!"

"If it's the same person," Lily pointed out.

"What are the chances of Clara seeing someone in the yard, and then us seeing something the next night?" Jessica argued.

"Either way, we'll look into it," Troy replied, calmly tucking the camera away. "More than likely it's some teenagers goofing around. Daring each other to peek into the haunted house."

"Haunted?" Jessica and Lily echoed.

Troy laughed. "Just a story that made the rounds when I was in school. Hey, maybe you should be investigating after all," he laughed, then stopped when he saw their faces. "Look, there's been no attempted entry, nothing broken or missing. But — if anyone sees anything unusual again, call us straightaway, alright?"

Lily nodded, her lips closed tight.

"Could we get a copy of those photos?" Jessica asked. "Just in case we see a sedan around here."

Troy gave her a bemused look, but shrugged. "Sure thing. Come by the station this afternoon and I'll have an extra set printed for you."

Which was how, after dropping Thor back home and grabbing a bite of lunch, they found themselves outside Mr. Russell's auto repair shop, clutching an envelope.

"This is silly," Lily said, adjusting her pink bobble hat more firmly over her ears. "You heard Troy. It was probably just some teenagers."

"Probably." Jessica nodded. "But what if it isn't? What if it's something more serious and we all ignore it and leave poor Mrs. Ryan undefended in that big old house?" When Lily still seemed unconvinced, Jessica forged ahead. "You can wait outside. This will only take a minute."

Lily huffed. "Obviously I'm still coming with you." Together, they entered the garage's shop area, a swirl of wind chasing them inside.

The tentative warmth and calm of earlier in the day had been blown away by another Vermont squall. The forecast was predicting snow again and Jessica was grateful they'd got these photographs before another fall erased all the evidence.

Evidence of what? Her mind kept asking if she was being paranoid, listening to her city instincts over Troy's more likely explanation. But something about the whole situation just didn't sit right with her. If it had been a one-time occurrence, that'd be one thing. Jessica could brush it off, like Troy clearly wanted to. But for someone to show up around High Meadows House multiple nights in a row…and what had been out back last night? Troy had explained he hadn't been able to get all the way down the rear driveway and they'd all decided it must have been an animal of some sort. But maybe that was just too convenient.

"One minute!" a cheerful voice shouted from the back of the shop. The shop was a glass-paneled front just off Main Street, with a workshop extending out back. Some attempts at Christmas decor had been made, tinsel dangled haphazardly from the corners of the shop desk and random points in the drop-ceiling.

A metallic crash sounded in the distance, followed by a muffled curse.

"Everything okay?" Lily called, a crease of worry on her brow. Mr. Russell pushed his way through from the workshop door, wiping greasy palms on his jean overalls and shaking his head ruefully.

"Really need to stop leaving the toolbox lying around…" he muttered, a short, thickset man with gray hair and a genial look. "What can I do for you girls?" His eyes alighted on Lily, then refocused, as though it had taken him a second to place her in his mental Rolodex. "Mrs.

Ellis. Not been having any more trouble with the Jeep, have you?"

"All good." Lily smiled. "We're actually here about something a bit more... unusual."

Jessica slid the folder across the desk and explained, as succinctly as possible. She decided to leave out the part about ghosts and stuck to the facts. "We just wanted to know if you recognized the tires. Deputy Troy seemed to think it was a sedan?"

Shooting them both a curious look, Mr. Russell opened the envelope and slid out the photos. Troy had printed two; one a distance shot of the tire tracks, the other a close-up of the imprint they'd left.

"Potenza," Mr. Russell said at once, nodding. "Those are the brand I use on all the cars I rent out. They're good in the snow, which is specially important if you're not used to handling the weather we get out here." He paused, tilting the photo this way and that. "Looks like an all-wheel drive vehicle... recently rotated. Hmm." He scratched his chin. "You know, I did rent a sedan out a week ago, with a tread like this. Course, hard to say from the tracks alone, but..."

Jessica and Lily exchanged looks. This was more than Jessica had dared to hope for — she'd just been looking for a make or maybe a model number for a car. "Really? Do you remember who you rented it to?"

"I can soon find out." Mr. Russell grinned. "I'm not that disorganized yet." He tapped his temple then reached out to pick up a three-ring binder. He flipped it open to the front page and ran his fingertip past some names. "There we go. Gray Ford Taurus, rented to a Mr. Jack Montgomery. He's staying over at Miss Daisy's for the holidays."

Their eyes lit up.

"And we're going there for the charity dinner tonight," Jessica said, her eyes gleaming.

"Yes, but not to chase some ghost…" Lily frowned.

"Thank you so much, Mr. Russell," Jessica beamed.

"Hold on now." Mr. Russell fretted. "That's a common make and model. I can't be absolutely sure — "

"We understand!" Jessica called over her shoulder, already grabbing Lily's arm to tug her from the shop. The bell tinkled merrily as they exited with one last thank you, leaving Mr. Russell to frown at his rental binder in their wake, shaking his head.

That was a real result, and Jessica was even more determined to get to the bottom of it all.

CHAPTER 11

Cheerful Christmas music emanated from Miss Daisy's Bed and Breakfast as Jessica and Lily walked up the entranceway. Twinkling lights welcomed them on the porch. A big homemade wreath of woven spruce adorned with red berries and glitter sprayed fir-cones was fixed to the oak front door. They entered the lobby into the spacious reception room, which also served as a guest sitting area. The handful of guests relaxing in chintz covered chairs around the blazing log fire didn't look up as they paused to gaze around.

The scent of mulled wine hit Jessica first, followed by wood smoke and fresh pine from the prettily decorated Christmas tree next to the check-in desk. A model train set ran in a circle around its base — Jessica realized it was Montrose in miniature, complete with a tiny version of the B&B.

"We're early," Lily said as she pinged the brass bell on the counter top. She'd put on a baby blue wool dress for the evening, it matched her eyes exactly.

"Yes, because we decided we should be," Jessica reminded her. She felt cold despite her velvet navy dress decorated with red cherries over dark tights and elegant leather boots. It wasn't nerves, she told herself, because they weren't going to make a big deal of anything, and Luke being at the dinner was just a great chance to connect with him again…as friends, she added firmly.

She gazed about, and felt a smile spread across her face. She'd stayed here for Lily's wedding, when her and her parents' houses were both filled with out-of-town guests. Every morning over breakfast Miss Daisy had filled Jessica in on goings on in town, making her feel just like a local. She'd had a wonderful time.

Miss Daisy swept out of the back room behind the check-in desk. Wearing a floral dress, long socks over rose pink tights and her standard embroidered converse hightops, she peered through steamed up glasses. "What have I forgotten now — oh!" She pulled up short at the sight of them, beaming. "Hello, dear hearts. There's another half an hour to go! Luke hasn't arrived yet, and we can't start the charity dinner without him now can we?"

"Do you need our tickets?" Lily dug out the red, green and gold printed cards from the pocket of her pink coat and held them up.

"Not just yet, Lily," Miss Daisy said. "Now, is Grant coming, because I've allocated everyone seats?"

"He'll be over soon as he can," Lily replied with a smile.

"Actually," Jessica took a breath. "There's someone staying here we'd like to talk to."

"Would you?" Miss Daisy's brows rose behind the glasses. "Now who would that be?"

"Jack Montgomery," Jessica said in a rush.

"Ah, you'd like to speak to Jack?" Miss Daisy said with a smile that could almost be described as mysterious. "Well, he is one of my guests."

"Has he been here long?" Jessica asked, thinking he wouldn't be the intruder if he'd only recently arrived.

"Almost a week already. Why do you ask?"

Jessica's stomach knotted. She couldn't quite bring herself to say that she thought he might be a trespasser. Or worse. What if she was wrong? What if he'd simply rented a similar car to whoever was coming around High Meadows House and scaring poor Mrs. Ryan? "We… I was just wondering what he's like. We might have a — a mutual acquaintance."

"Well, he keeps to himself, mostly. He's here on business, you see. A quiet man, but very polite. English, and he speaks very nicely." Miss Daisy flashed a sweet smile. "Handsome, too, if I do say so myself. And around your age."

Lily looked worried and Jessica quashed a sense of guilt. "Business? Really?" She sounded skeptical. "What kind of business brings someone here?"

"Oh, come now. We're not so remote as all that." Miss Daisy clicked her tongue. "Though I know we might seem like small fries to you big city folk."

"No, I —" Color rose in Jessica's cheeks. "Sorry. I didn't mean it like that. I just… didn't know there was a lot of industry around here."

"Jack's an antiques collector. Plenty of treasure troves in these parts for a man like him, he said so himself." Miss Daisy's smile was faltering.

Jessica barely noticed. Treasure troves! She thought of High Meadows House. All the beautiful old furniture, ornaments and clocks that even she knew must be worth a lot of money — surely it would qualify as a 'treasure trove' for an antiques collector…or was he a dealer? A feeling that it was beginning to make sense crept over her. "Do you know if Mr. Montgomery has visited High Meadows House at all?" she asked, careful to keep her voice even.

Miss Daisy paused, tilting her head to one side. "I wouldn't know, my dear, but I wouldn't be surprised. Clara Ryan has some extraordinary pieces over there, and they're probably quite valuable. If she ever wanted to sell, that is — which I'd say was highly unlikely."

"I'd agree," Jessica replied, thinking of how precious anything that had belonged to Joe was to her.

"But if you're so curious about Mr. Montgomery, you might ask him yourself. He promised he'd come by tonight," Miss Daisy said. "And I really must hurry, the guests will be arriving very soon now." She bustled back toward the kitchen, leaving them standing at the counter.

Jessica turned to Lily and dropped her voice to a near-whisper. "I think he might be casing the joint."

"Casing the joint?" Lily arched her brows wryly.

"Well, perhaps that was overstated, but it still adds up."

"It does seem a little suspicious…' Lily agreed. "But let's not jump to conclusions. You heard Mr. Russell — it might not even have been his car's tracks. It's a common model, and those tires are used a lot in winter around here."

"I still think we should talk to him." Jessica persisted. "Miss Daisy said he'd be coming tonight, we — "

Luke strolled in, casual in a cream sweater and chinos. "Hey, my favorite cousin and her favorite friend."

"Oh, you didn't bring the puppy," Lily said, then grinned and went over to hug him.

"You didn't actually think I was going to — " Luke laughed as he casually lifted her off her feet to hug her close.

"No of course I didn't, just teasing." She stood back to let him greet Jessica.

He didn't say anything, he just swept her into his arms and held her tight. She stiffened in surprise then relaxed, letting his arms envelope her, the warm smell of him wash over her. She felt like she could have stayed there forever, then he let her go.

"Glad you could make it," he said softly, his blue eyes gazing into hers.

"I…I…" she flushed, she could hardly tell him why they were already there.

Miss Daisy came back from the kitchen. "Luke! I thought I heard your voice. Now, I was just about to put out the place settings, and I have the box for the draw. Lily, will you take these name cards from me, they're all going to tumble off?" She laughed. She was clutching a cardboard box covered in red and gold paper with the poster of

Luke and the puppy stuck to the front. There was a stack of neatly folded cards on top of the box.

Lily gathered them carefully, then paused to take a quick look at the handwritten names on each. "Whoa, I can put anyone anywhere I like!"

"I'm afraid you cannot," Miss Daisy said firmly. "I have a seating plan. Let's go through shall we?"

She led the way, Lily followed, Jessica hesitated and Luke casually took her hand as though it were the most natural thing in the world.

In preparation for the event, Miss Daisy had opened up the pocket doors that normally separated the common room from the big dining area. This, too, had been decked in holiday cheer, with fairy lights and paper garlands festooning the ceiling and each chair adorned with its own small wreath on the back.

The table was already laid, tall creamy candles in gleaming candelabra were lit in a line along the center with sprigs of holly and berries filling in the gaps. Each place was set with mismatched crockery, sparkling glasses and polished silverware.

Miss Daisy put the box on the pine dresser, set against one white painted wall. "Now, Lily, we will put the cards out. Luke is at the head of the table," she put a hand out and Lily shuffled the cards to find his name.

"Here you are." She gave it to her.

Luke went to the top of the table, Jessica's hand still in his. "And Jess is next to me," he said and held a chair out for her.

She looked at Miss Daisy.

"Exactly where I'd planned for her to be," Miss Daisy said gaily and let Lily put her name card down with a big grin on her face.

"Sit," Luke insisted, and she did so graciously, a smile curving her lips.

Luke sat down as Miss Daisy took all the cards and placed them on each setting. Lily was opposite her, Hugh Fellows, the book shop owner was next to Lily, with Grant to sit beside Jessica, when he arrived. Lily's parents would be down the other end of the table, as would Mrs O'Dowd from the flower shop, and Ed Stanton, owner and editor of The Montrose Post. She didn't recognize any other names, but Jack Montgomery wasn't amongst them and nor was Caitlin, which she was relieved to hear.

People started arriving and Miss Daisy went to take coats and show them through. It wasn't long before champagne corks were popping and the room filled with happy chatter.

"Here's to your Montrose Christmas, Jessica," Luke raised his glass to her.

She touched it lightly with hers. "And to yours," she replied, then took a sip.

He did the same, then relaxed back in his chair, watching her, almost as though puzzled.

"What?"

"How did I forget?"

"I…don't know how to answer that," she replied.

He put his glass down and leaned towards her, his eyes locked on hers. "How did I forget how beautiful you are, inside and out, and why didn't I remember… until now?"

"If everyone is seated…?" Miss Daisy called out, looking around above the tops of her spectacles. "May we have a word of welcome from this evening's sponsor, Mr Luke Jensen."

Jessica was glad of the interruption because her heart felt as though it had stopped and then started again in a tumble of skipping beats.

Luke made a nice speech, thanking everyone for the generosity, telling them about the animals and the shelter. Everyone clapped, and Grant arrived, apologetic and slightly breathless, having rushed back from the hospital. Then the first course was served, Ellie-May had come to help Miss Daisy, along with her mother, who gave close directions to her ditzy daughter. Hugh Fellows began a dissertation about the meaning of Dickens' 'A Christmas Carol' and they all joined in with ideas which turned to light chatter which turned to laughter and the evening passed in relaxed and convivial ease. The dessert of Bombe Alaska had been cleared away and eggnog served when Miss Daisy stood up again.

"Now, please pay attention, everyone, it is time for the raffle." She went to the dresser and picked up the box she'd carried in earlier. "I need all your tickets, please." She went around the room, allowing everyone to drop their printed tickets into the box. Once she'd collected them all, she took it to Luke. "You have to close your eyes and pick out just one," she ordered.

"Yes, ma'am." He gave her a grin then rooted around and pulled out a ticket. He held it in his hands to hide the name. "And the winner is…Miss Jessica Brooks!" He called out then tossed the ticket back into the box.

Jessica laughed in delight, her brown eyes sparkling. "But I never win anything!"

"What's the prize?" Estelle called out from the end of the table.

"Yeah, tell us the prize," Jakob demanded, his cheeks rosy from the wine.

"A bottle of pink Taittinger champagne!" Miss Daisy announced to applause then went to the dresser and took it from the lower shelf.

"Isn't that the same bottle we had last year?" Ed Stanton asked dubiously.

"And the year before," Jakob added.

"And the year before that," Mrs O'Dowd said to more laughter.

"Oh, it sounds like a Montrose heirloom," Jessica said as Miss Daisy came to present the bottle to her. "Perhaps I should donate it to next year's draw?"

"Only if you're sure, dear heart." Miss Daisy was already holding the bottle back.

"If you do, I can offer you a consolation prize," Luke said, leaning towards Jessica.

"What would that be?" She asked, her eyes dancing.

"Dinner with me," he replied.

She heard Lily gasp.

"Then I'll definitely donate the bottle back," Jessica laughed.

That caused a few happy whoops and everyone applauded again even more loudly.

"Drinks will be served by the fire," Miss Daisy told them all as they finished their eggnog and Ellie-May and her mother began clearing the table.

They began wandering out of the dining room, making for the large reception area and the chintz armchairs and sofas gathered about the blazing fire. Luke took her hand and led her through, then stopped as they neared the Christmas tree.

"Listen, I've got to go and check up on a couple of patients I'm holding overnight at the clinic, but I meant it about taking you out to dinner."

"I'd love to go," she said, the words almost tumbling out. She was aware everyone was watching, while pretending not to.

"I'll call you in the morning," he said, then moved to kiss her.

She turned to offer her cheek, but he took her chin, and softly turned her face, to kiss her lightly on the lips. "Goodnight, Jessica."

"Goodnight, Luke," she said quietly, as he turned and walked out.

She sighed, then turned to find everyone's eyes on her. Her cheeks blushed pink and she put her hands up to cover them.

"Love is in the air," Jakob started singing.

"Pop, you just stop that," Lily called to him.

Grant came over to give them both fresh glasses of eggnog.

"I've got to go too, Lil," he put his arm around her, "just a quick drop by at the hospital then I can head home for the night. Estelle's going to give you a lift back."

"Ok, sweetie pie," she gazed up at him, love in her big blue eyes.

He kissed her, waved to Jessica and was gone a moment later.

Lily grabbed Jessica by the arm and they moved to a window alcove with a built-in bench seat covered by a thick fluffy sheepskin.

Jessica was beaming, amazement and confusion battling with unbridled joy.

"You and Luke! It's all our dreams come true," Lily said, eyes wide and sparkling.

"I can't believe it," Jessica laughed, "He asked me out to dinner." She held her glass to her chest. The image of the house, and picket fence rose in her mind again, this time Luke had his arm around her and she was clutching the puppy in the photo, its little paw bandaged.

Miss Daisy came over and put her hand on her shoulder.

"Jessica, the guest you wanted to talk to," she told her. "He's over there." She pointed to an open doorway, where a figure stood leaning on the door jamb.

He was tall, with thick dark hair, chiseled cheekbones and eyes the color of a turbulent sea. They were fixed on her, a look in them she couldn't decipher, and suddenly the image of Luke and the picket fence dissolved in a haze of confusion.

It was the man who'd stopped the runaway horse. The hero of the hour. It was Jack Montgomery.

CHAPTER 12

Jessica suddenly felt rather breathless. What on earth was she going to say? *He looked so...amazing. No, not amazing, intimidating. So don't let him intimidate you,* she told herself. *He might be guilty...even if he didn't look guilty, even if he looked like... never mind what he looked like.*

She stood up and resolutely lifted her chin, then the front door opened and Caitlin walked in.

As usual, she'd dressed to kill — stiletto heels, a ridiculous black leather mini-skirt and electric blue silk blouse. She paused to check herself in the mirror, pushed a blonde wave back in place, then, pouting with her fire engine red lipstick, she spun round and made a beeline for Jack Montgomery.

"Hey there, I heard there was a handsome stranger in town." She flashed a wide smile at him.

He took a sip from the glass in his hand, his eyes glinting under dark brows.

There wasn't much that could intimidate Caitlin's rhinoceros hide but she faltered as he remained silent.

"I was just being friendly," she tried again.

"Fine," he replied finally.

"And it's Christmas, so maybe you could find a girl a drink?" she simpered.

Jessica and Lily remained in the alcove, watching as though mesmerized. Jack suddenly threw a glance their way and they both instantly took a step backwards.

"What would you suggest?" Jack turned his gaze back to Caitlin.

"They do a fabulous Mistletoe Margarita here," her smile grew wider, then she turned and strolled over to the bar to perch on a stool, long legs crossed, one heel hooked in the footrest, toes pointing downwards for a better display of her assets.

Jack took his time following, his face coldly neutral. He wore a black polo neck sweater under a charcoal gray suit, perfectly tailored to fit across his broad shoulders.

They were now too far away for them to hear, or to be heard.

"I didn't take her long to get her hooks into him," Lily said quietly, although no-one was close enough to overhear them.

"Maybe they're well suited," Jessica said, standing where she couldn't be seen from the bar.

"What are we going to say to him, Jess?"

"Nothing until she's gone."

A loud peel of laughter cut through the air as Caitlin threw back her head in apparent raptures.

He didn't join her laughter. She laid a hand on his arm;

he swiveled very slightly on the bar stool and she let her hand drop.

"He's kind of intimidating," Lily whispered.

"Or just plain rude," Jessica replied. "And don't forget that he's been frightening Clara for no good reason, and we're not going to let that lie."

Miss Daisy sailed across to the bar and stopped at Jack's elbow. He immediately stood, his features softening slightly. She was speaking to him, her head tilted to one side, a bright smile on her face, she barely reached his shoulder and had to look up at him. She turned and pointed towards the alcove, still chattering. Jessica slid back to make sure she couldn't be seen, then peered around again.

He was coming their way.

Lily's eyes widened. "Jess…" she sounded rattled.

"We're just going to question him, Lily," Jessica said with determination, then brushed her dress down, straightened up and put her face into neutral.

He seemed to fill the doorway.

"Jack Montgomery," he announced, his voice deep and resonant. "I believe you would like to speak to me?" He thrust out a hand to shake hers.

Determined not to blush, she looked him in the eye. Miss Daisy had been right about the accent — definitely British, and upper-crust sounding, at least to Jessica's ear. Her knowledge of British accents started and ended with 'Upstairs Downstairs' which her mother had loved to watch with her when she was little.

For a split second, she debated shaking his hand, then she remembered why she'd come looking for him and pointedly folded her arms over her chest. "Jessica Brooks. I'm a friend of Mrs. Ryan's."

An expression of surprise twitched a brow, or possibly suspicion, he dropped his outstretched hand back to his side.

She focused on those amazing sea-green eyes, *eyes the color of the ocean, eyes she could drown in...*

She realized he was talking and gave herself another mental shake.

"... I'm in town for the holidays, and for business."

Lily hadn't said anything, but had moved closer to her side. Tension seemed to emanate from her, she was almost vibrating with energy; Lily may be small, but she could be fierce, and the expression in her narrowed blue eyes fired Jessica up.

"So you weren't at High Meadows House last night?" Jessica replied, lowering her voice a fraction.

A muscle in Jack's jaw tensed, his gaze flicked towards the staircase, which led upstairs to the guest rooms — no doubt wishing for an easy getaway. "Not last night, no."

Lily was astounded. "Not...? You mean you have been outside her house?"

"You scared poor Mrs. Ryan half to death!" Jessica suddenly filled with fury at the admission. "What the hell did you think you were doing?"

Jack's eyes darkened. He stepped closer to Jessica who caught the scent of his cologne, a musky, warm, masculine scent that instantly reminded her of richly ornate, old-fashioned settings, like the exclusive private clubs in Manhattan where women were definitely not welcome.

She hated how much she liked that scent.

"It's a private matter, and has nothing to do with you," he almost growled.

Lily gasped and clutched Jessica's arm.

Jessica forced herself to remain strong. Not to cave at his nearness, or the intensity of his gaze. He was one of those men who, when he looked at you, made you completely unable to focus on anything else. "We are close friends of Clara," Jessica almost hissed the words. "We called the police out and we'll do it again if you don't have a good explanation."

He regarded her, sea-green eyes darkening, his sculpted mouth flattened in irritation bordering on anger. "Very well." He flicked a glance at the group of dinner guests now chattering animatedly by the fire, including Estelle, who had been casting a few sharp looks at them. Caitlyn seemed to have vanished too, probably off hunting more prey.

"Would you like to join me in the library, it's quieter there."

Lily gazed up and nodded at her, and together, they followed their mystery prowler out of the room.

It was a very small library, but with the same high ceilings as the reception hall, crown molding and colorful rugs on the hardwood floor. Bookshelves lined the walls, and soft lamps gave the room a warm glow. A floral sofa with velvet cushions and a worn leather chair stood across from each other, separated by a low coffee table. The fire in the white painted surround had almost burned to ashes. He picked a couple of logs from the big wicker basket, placed them on the glowing pile of embers then blew it back to life.

Jessica had the impression he spent quite a lot of time in here. A green bound book lay closed under the leather chair, its title was *A History of Vermont*. He gathered it up and placed it on the mantel shelf, next to a line of felted reindeer decorations. He remained standing until they were seated on the sofa, then sat on the chair, leaning back and crossing his legs.

"Well?" she said, without preamble.

"This is something I do not want to broadcast," he said.

"What is *this* exactly?" Jessica replied. "Because so far, I'm struggling to understand what possible reason you could have for scaring an elderly lady out of her wits."

Jack leaned his head back to regard her, as though he were weighing something in his mind, the burgeoning fire lighting one side of his face, casting the other side in shadow. "It's a personal matter and I'd appreciate you respecting that…" He dug in his pocket and removed something from his wallet, sliding it across the low coffee table between them.

Jessica picked it up. It was a photograph, blurry and cracked with age, but even in the relatively low light she recognized it at once — because she'd seen this exact photograph before. Her eyes widened and her head snapped up to look at Jack.

"Is that…?"

Lily leaned across, strawberry blonde hair brushing Jessica's arm. "That's Joe, isn't it? Clara's Joe. Where did you get this?"

A different light gleamed in Jack's eyes, a softer one. "Is it Joe Ryan? Are you sure?"

Jessica looked at the image, then Jack, and raised the photograph up to compare their features side by side. Now that she could see them together, the resemblance seemed obvious. Jack had the same sharp cheekbones, the same firm jaw. Even the same shaped eyes, almond and a little wider-set than most people's, in a way that made the blue-green color of his all the more arresting. Of course, the photograph was in black and white, but the similarities couldn't be ignored.

"Are you… related?" Jessica placed the photograph carefully back onto the table..

"You've got to be," Lily stared at the image. "It's obvious now you look."

"I don't know. Not for certain." A haunted look she thought she'd glimpsed earlier returned. Jack exhaled deeply and leaned back into the chair, looking momentarily lost. "But I'm pretty sure that Joe was my grandfather."

The words sucked all the air from the room. Jessica and Lily traded startled looks. In all of Clara's stories about Joe — of which they'd heard many by this point — there had never been any mention of a child, let alone a grandchild. Especially not a grandchild from the British Isles.

Clara had said she and Joe used to have friends over in England, ones he'd made during the war, but…

"My grandmother's name was Annabelle Curtis. She married my grandfather Henry just as the war ended, my mother was born a few months later. It wasn't so unusual at the time — the war had disrupted everyone's lives. Their romance had been rather tempestuous..." His focus drifted to the fire. "Grandma didn't tell my mother the truth until she was dying. She said she hadn't wanted to hurt her, and had even kept the secret from Henry, my grandfather. He'd already passed away and never knew the truth. She explained Henry wasn't my mother's birth father. She and Henry had become engaged, then they called it off after some sort of ridiculous argument. She then had a romance with an American airman, a man called Joe Ryan. He was shot down shortly after they'd met and reported missing, presumed dead…" he paused, thoughts apparently playing on his mind. Discussing private family matters to complete strangers was probably an absolute anathema to him. "Henry never knew about the affair, but in the meantime he'd come to his senses. He apologized to Annabelle and they wed…Neither had reached their twentieth birthday." He shrugged. "It was just the madness of war. They made a go of it though, and had a good marriage."

Whatever Jessica had expected, it wasn't this.

"Clara said Joe was posted missing, presumed dead," Lily murmured, almost to herself. "His plane had been shot down, and he'd been held captive…"

"It wasn't until years later that Annabelle heard Joe had survived," Jack went on. "He'd written to her after his liberation apparently, but the letter never reached her. She learned through old friends from the war." Jack shook his head. "Annabelle decided not to tell Henry the truth about Joe; it would break his heart, and she wasn't entirely certain which of them truly was the father. Not for a long time anyway, not until she realized why no more children came their way." He took a breath and let it out slowly.

Jessica was barely moving, she was utterly astounded and hanging on his every word. So was Lily.

He continued. "I think Grandma was right in what she did, and she was right about my mother's reaction. Mama took the news terribly badly, my father had passed away a few years before, she was fragile… She refused to contact Joe; she had no interest in learning anything about him, or about their story. She'd always believed Henry was her true father and didn't want to accept any other possibility. She'd have felt betrayed if she thought I'd ever come here. But…she died last year," he paused, his expression troubled, conflict clouding his eyes. "I was curious. The only thing we had of his was his flying jacket; he'd given it to Annabelle to keep her warm the night before his plane was shot down. She'd hidden it away, I found it, and the photograph, while clearing out the house. I just wanted to know more about him, that's all."

Finally, Jessica found her voice again. "So you decided the best way was to sneak around Joe's home at night?" She sounded harsher than she'd intended, her throat was dry and constricted.

Jack winced. "I didn't even know he was dead until I got here. I went to see where the house was, thinking perhaps to knock on the door. I wore Joe's flying jacket, I'd thought it would help authenticate who I was. I got as far as the drive and heard the cry of fear, so I left. I tried again, but… I had second thoughts. I'm not sure if she knew about Joe's relationship with my grandmother. I don't want to cause an elderly lady anguish, but I had rather hoped to meet her and explain…and I'd liked to have learned more of my grandfather."

Looking into his eyes, studying his expression, Jessica wanted to believe him. There was something strangely compelling about this man — the mysterious past, the details he knew about Joe, the worry in his eyes when he talked about his mother refusing to accept the reality of her father. And then there was the way he'd fearlessly thrown himself in harm's way at the Christmas market.

But he'd also lied about why he'd come here…and Jessica's city instincts were beginning to pulse.

"You told Miss Daisy you're an antiques collector," Jessica challenged him. "You said you were here on business."

"I do collect antiques. That's true, I just — "

"It's not really why you're here though, is it?" Lily quietly interjected, her lips pursed, and both Jack and Jessica turned to look at her. Lifting her eyes to look directly at Jack, she asked "Why not just tell everyone the truth?"

"You make it sound so simple," Jack replied slowly. "The truth broke my mother's heart. The last thing I want to do is hurt anybody else in the same way."

"Well, you've a strange way of showing it," Jessica retorted, then wished she'd held her tongue when she saw the hurt in his eyes.

He stood up and walked out without a word, leaving Jessica and Lily to gaze at one another, unsure how to process what they'd just heard.

"Do you believe him?" Lily whispered.

Jessica heaved a sigh. "I don't know. He sure looks like Joe, but why not just write to Clara? Why sneak about in the dark?"

"It wasn't dark, it was dusk," Lily replied. "He said he only found out Joe had married when he came here, and that he'd died."

"It would hardly be a surprise to find he'd married, most people do…" Jessica said, then stopped when she suddenly recalled Luke, and the image of the house, and picket fence. Suddenly Jack seemed like an interloper, like someone who could sweep the dream away for reasons she couldn't fathom. She cleared her throat. "Anyway, why now? Is it because it's Christmas?"

"Why should that matter?" Lily was confused.

"Clara's lonely and apparently wealthy…" Jessica was trying to put her thoughts in order, and trying not to be irrational. "She'd be more vulnerable at this time of year than maybe any other."

"Well, maybe he's lonely too?" Lily said.

Jessica turned to her. "You're always too forgiving, Lily, we don't know anything about him other than what he's told us."

"I think Clara deserves to know the truth. It's another link to Joe, and it's for her to decide, not us." Lily's eyes shone with emotion as she stared at the fire. "I think we should help Jack and Clara connect."

CHAPTER 13

Estelle and Jakob dropped them at home, with no word spoken about Luke or Jack, for which Jessica was very grateful, but once inside Lily had instantly gone into raptures about Luke and that kiss, then speculation about Jack and what should they do; all of which kept Jessica from sleeping despite being exhausted from the previous night's disruptions.

Next morning, Lily was up early, determined to call High Meadows House and talk to Clara, but Bethany told her Clara would be out all day at the house of an old friend who lived along the valley.

"Right in that case, we're going to investigate!" Jessica put her empty coffee cup onto the kitchen counter and stood up.

Lily groaned. "How?"

"I'm going to take a look in his room, see if his passport is there, and you're going to act as look out."

"I am so not!" Lily was adamant.

"All you have to do is hang around the reception area and hold him up if he comes in, until I come back downstairs."

"Jess, we can't go rooting around people's rooms. Anyway, he will have locked his door."

"Oh…yes." Why hadn't she thought of that? All the excitement of last evening probably. "Then his name will be in the reception book. Miss Daisy always asks guests to sign in."

"What if he just lied?" Lily was unconvinced. "Seeing as you think he's a total rogue anyway."

"Miss Daisy asks to see people's passports if they're foreigners. I think it's in case they leave without paying. Most hotels do the same."

Lily thought about that. "If Miss Daisy saw his passport then she has verified who he is, and she was the one who pointed him out to us." She ended in triumph. "So we don't have to check up on anything."

That left Jessica frowning for a moment. "But we should be cautious, Lily. I know you think his story is touching, but we're about to introduce a complete stranger to a vulnerable old lady and we have some responsibility to make sure he is what he seems and not — "

"Not some insane murderer who's going to do her in and run off with her grandfather clock?"

"I was going to say check he wasn't a snake and would charm his way into a large inheritance."

"How do we do that?" Lily crossed her arms and looked up.

Jessica suddenly smiled. "You're a ghost hunter!"

"What?"

"Track down his family! That's your new business, so why not use your skills to find out his background."

A frown formed between her brows. "Genealogical research you mean?"

"Yes. It'll be good practice...unless him being from England is too difficult."

Lily suddenly grinned. "No, that's part of the challenge!"

"Ok...So shall we start digging?" Jessica asked.

"It couldn't hurt." Lily straightened up. "I mean, we're probably overreacting, but we could see what we can find out at the library in the meantime."

* * *

"Oh, how are you two both doing?" Matilda was delighted to welcome Jessica and Lily back to the library, and listened carefully to their request to find out more about an English family by the name of Montgomery.

"Obviously I won't have anything here unless the family had lived in the valley, so we need to check that first." She dug out the whole card catalog and they all leaned over the desk and pored over it together twice before accepting there was nothing there.

"What now?" Jessica turned to Lily, who turned to Matilda.

"I could send a fax enquiry to one of the big English record libraries." Matilda tucked her hair behind her ear thoughtfully. "First of all, that would determine if the family name and place of residence are connected. From there, we can ask if they have any information that would help trace find his ancestry. I also still have a few friends back in the Boston library system, and I know one of them keeps back copies on microfiche of the English Times newspaper. If Montgomery were a well-known name, they might appear in the Society pages."

"Really?" Lily's eyes lit up at the suggestion. "That would be incredible. And also, good to know that we can request that sort of information for the future…"

"Will you be investigating a lot of mysterious British visitors' families in the future?" Matilda asked, amused.

"Possibly," Lily replied airily. "Or the British origins of families in town; I know at least a few local families who can trace their roots back to the UK, if any of them are interested in hiring me."

"How long would a request like that take?" Jessica interjected. In the back of her mind, she calculated her days left in Montrose, and winced. Two weeks had seemed like forever when she'd first arrived, but she was already nearly halfway through her vacation.

"Normally a few days," Matilda replied. "Maybe a week at the most. But this being the holiday season and all, it could take longer…Where's he from?" She lifted her pen to make a note on a jotter open on the desktop.

"I…we don't know," Lily said, looking at Jessica.

"Is it important?" Jessica asked.

"It will be very difficult without some place to start," Matilda replied.

"Jessica's leaving in just over a week," Lily said.

"Then it would help if I had as much information as possible." Matilda shook her head. "I'll try to do what

I can, but bear in mind there's already a rush before the holidays and then they won't re-open until Tuesday next week due to Christmas and Boxing Day. "

Lily and Jessica traded disappointed glances.

"That's alright," Lily said. "Thank you again for checking on it for us. Maybe someone in Boston can find something sooner."

Feeling somewhat less hopeful than they had when they arrived at the library, Lily led the way back outside and toward home. "Look, Clara is the most important person here. We have no right to keep this information from her, and she might be told about it anyway. And I think meeting Jack will be an absolute joy for her," Lily said. "If he starts suggesting anything wild, and she starts talking about changing her will to leave all her worldly possessions to him, then we can have a sit down with her. Until then, I think we should just… let the wheels turn, stay alert, but let them live their lives. You know?"

"I suppose." Jessica ran a hand through her hair, exhaling a misted breath. The snow had a crystalline quality, since the top layer melted during the day, then re-froze at night. It also meant black ice coated chunks of salt and ice gathered at the edges of a lot of the plowed sidewalks, so Jessica had to pick her way more slowly than back in the city. "You don't think 'Tell Agatha' would have any advice, do you?" Jessica asked, after a few minutes of carefully walking.

Lily laughed. 'Tell Agatha' was the Montrose Valley Post's agony aunt, known for her wisdom on problems that ranged from dating advice to guest etiquette to what sort of holiday gifts were appropriate to buy for in-laws who had recently offended you. "We can't ask 'Tell Agatha' for advice on a suspicious British man visiting his long-lost step-grandmother; everyone would know who we were talking about in an instant."

"True." Jessica's shoulders dropped, she felt dejected. She was out of ideas already, and they were no closer to verifying whether Jack Montgomery was someone they could trust.

Lily must have noticed her turn in mood, because she clapped a hand on Jessica's shoulder, squeezing lightly. "Hey, there's no sense in worrying about it now. Matilda's going to look into things. In the meantime, we should get back to the holiday fun, and lunch! Come on, best foot forward."

There was a phone call waiting on the answer machine when they got back. Luke wanted to take Jessica to dinner at seven, he'd come pick her up, unless she called to cancel, and even if she did, he wasn't going to listen.

"What are you going to wear!" Lily was beside herself. "Oh you're going to be my cousin-in-law! You'll be true family, Jess. What color shall we choose for my bridesmaid dress?"

"Lily, you've got to let me think." Jessica could hardly register that she was going on a date with Luke, but she gathered her wits enough to think about a dress. "Black, plum or russet?"

"Russet. It will go beautifully with your hair, and I can lend you my gold silk scarf."

"Gold?"

"It's rose gold, come on, let's try it!" Lily was halfway up the stairs before Jessica had taken her snow boots off.

The dress was wool and the color of dark autumn and Lily was absolutely right, the rose gold silk wrapped carefully around her long slim neck was the perfect foil.

"Right, enough of the dress rehearsal," Jessica declared. "I'm going to wrap in a dressing gown and we can have lunch. Then I'm taking a long hot bath, read a book and have some quiet time before I get ready. And," she held a finger up. "Not one more word about weddings."

Lily laughed, and she only mentioned bridesmaids dresses a half dozen times throughout the whole afternoon.

Come six, she brushed her chestnut hair to gleaming, applied only enough makeup to enhance her dark eyes and finely formed lips and pulled the dress back on over thick dark tights. She let Lily wind the scarf artfully about her neck, and, along with leather boots, was as ready as she was going to be.

"You look fabulous," Lily sighed, sounding just like Estelle.

The wool dress flowed perfectly over Jessica's willowy figure, her face aglow as though lit from within, she truly did look beautiful.

She barely had time to be teased by Grant, who'd just arrived home, when Luke knocked on the front door and came into the living room. His eyes lit up when he saw her and he broke into a broad grin.

"Hey, Jess, you really have grown up haven't you?" He

came straight across and hugged her close to his chest, then a light kiss on the lips. He held her for a moment longer, blue eyes gazing into hers. Enveloped by his coat, the softness of his pale blue sweater, and the scent of his cologne, a wonderful warmth washed over her, as though she were finally returning home to where she belonged.

Lily was squeezing her hands together, standing on tiptoe and smiling hugely, Grant was grinning and Thor was wagging his tail madly, wanting to be included.

"Hello, Luke," she managed, suddenly ridiculously shy for no good reason.

"I've brought the car, or would you prefer to walk? It's a beautiful night," he said, her hand still caught in his. "There are carol singers in the streets, it's busy but not too crowded, what do you think?"

She smiled, delight alight in her eyes. "Yes, that sounds wonderful, I'd love to."

He helped her into her red coat, Lily fetched her hat, which had been left in the kitchen for some reason, and they set off under a starlit sky with snow crunching beneath their feet.

CHAPTER 14

They talked as they walked, he took her hand in his. He made her laugh, regaling a story about a hamster that had escaped from its cage that morning and he and his assistant had searched the clinic on hands and knees only to find it curled up asleep in a box of paper tissues.

They turned into main street, where the sound of singing caught their attention. Lilting voices resonated in the crisp air, echoing between snow capped houses and stores; they paused for a moment to drink it in, then strode on to find a group of carol singers making their way slowly toward the center of town.

Everyone wore Santa hats, clutching lyric sheets in one mittened hand and candle-lit lanterns in the other. A few played Christmas bells or flutes, adding melody to the songs. Jessica recognized Mrs. O'Dowd and Mr. Gunter, the farmer whose draft horse caused such a panic at the market a few days ago, singing his heart out beside her. Miss Daisy was there, sharing a song sheet with Ed Stanton. Jessica wondered if there was anything between them, then dismissed the idea. Miss Daisy spotted her and Luke leaning together under a lamp and gave them a merry smile. A couple of the vendors from the market carried baskets and were handing out candy canes and chocolate-covered pretzels to passersby and receiving donations to the local church in return.

Charmed, they stopped to enjoy the renditions of "Jingle Bells," "Deck the Halls," and "Joy to the World", then followed them to the corner of Maple and Crestview streets. The choir gathered outside the Sugar Maple Lounge, the oldest bar and restaurant in town, its tall, elegant street lamps illuminating the singers beautifully.

The owner opened the restaurant door just as the carolers started to sing "We Wish You a Merry Christmas." Diners inside crowded the windows to get a better look, and more people came over to join the small audience clustered outside.

As the carolers moved on, Luke held Jessica in place.

"This is us," Luke said and escorted her to the open door.

"Mr Jensen! Great to see you," the landlord beamed and stood aside to let him through. "My Suki's doing just dandy after you fixed her leg. I've saved you a real nice table near the fire." He led them through crowded tables of early diners, motioned to a waiter to clear a place just vacated, then hurried off to fetch a fresh gingham cloth and silverware.

Luke helped slip her coat off and hung it on the nearby stand, then pulled out a chair for her to be seated. She settled into the soft cushioned seat of the traditional wooden armchair and surveyed the cozy restaurant. Dark polished wood floor, pine-paneled walls, low lights over tables, garlands and swags and a Christmas tree. The whole place was buzzing with lively conversations on the last Saturday before Christmas, she sighed, it was just perfect.

"Perfect timing," Luke said, the blazing fire throwing a warm glow over them both. "Have you been here before?"

"No, I mostly either ate at Lily's or Miss Daisy's B & B when I was here for the wedding."

"Yeah," he nodded slowly. "That slipped by too fast. I was pretty caught up in things back then…"

He picked up the menus, handed one to her and started to peruse the specials. Meanwhile, Jessica was spiraling back ten years, to the handsome troublemaker she'd fallen for at camp. Not that Luke had been much of a handful — he never put anyone in danger, and his charming ways meant he never got in any serious trouble. But he did like to push the boundaries anywhere he could. When they went to Mr. Gunter's farm to ride the sturdy Welsh ponies, he'd spur his on to a gallop; when they went canoeing on the lake, he'd start races and place bets on who'd cross the finish line first. Wherever there was a hubbub or commotion, you could be sure Luke was somewhere in the middle of it.

As someone who'd been terrified of even accidentally bending the rules, let alone breaking them, she'd been drawn to Luke's casual defiance. He wasn't a bad boy — but he didn't let the rules define his whole life, somehow he always knew how to tread the line just enough to stay out of trouble. Jessica wondered what that must feel like, the carefree freedom to do what you choose. She wondered, too, whether he'd calmed down in recent years, or was he still hiding that wild streak somewhere beneath the professional veterinarian exterior.

"Any drinks for you folks?" The young waiter arrived with pen and notepad in hand. "We have hot toddies," he suggested with a smile. A tall, lanky lad, dark hair falling over his eyes, his shirt too short at the cuffs and collar too large about his neck.

"Jess?" Luke raised his brows.

"Toddies are usually a little too strong for me, thanks. Red wine?"

"We have some great Californian wines, or mulled if you'd like?" the waiter asked.

"Oh, definitely mulled," she said, and Luke flashed her another of those smiles.

"I'll have the same," Luke told the waiter, who nodded and hurried off. "They've got the best mulled wine in town." He turned his gaze back to her. He'd always had a way of really looking at you, as though he could already see your answer, knew what you were going to say. "So what's stopping you?" he asked.

"Hmm? Stopping me what?" Jessica blinked, trying to drag her attention back to the conversation.

"From staying here."

"Oh." She shook her head ruefully. "A job, real life, practicality…all the usual complications."

"You know, it's funny," Luke mused as he leaned back

in his chair, pushing up the sleeves of his pale blue jersey. "For some people, your life is the dream. Living in the big city, with a high-powered job, making real money–"

"Let's not get too carried away," she cut in, smiling.

"But you get what I mean."

"Sure. Of course. That was my dream, too, for the longest time. It's like Frank Sinatra says—if you can make it in New York, you can make it anywhere. And I've worked so hard to get to where I am." She really had. Years of school, followed by an unforgiving unpaid internship, before she finally got a position at a company where she could work her way up and her own place to live.

"But?" Luke prompted, lifting a brow.

"I don't know." Jessica looked down at the red and white tablecloth, unable to hold his gaze any longer. What did she really have to complain about? Her life might be predictable, but it was comfortable — her bills always paid, her schedule manageable, leisure time spent in the city's countless attractions. If she had to work some unexpected overtime here and there, well, that was par for the course in the tech industry, particularly in such a highly sought after position. She'd known what she was getting into when she chose her major — long hours, a lot of repetitive work, but at the end of the day, an exciting career with endless possibilities.

The waiter returned with their drinks, and there was a pause while Jessica took a sip, then beamed at Luke. "You're right, it's delicious."

"You were saying?" Luke prompted.

"So if it didn't mean you had to stick it out in the city, you'd enjoy your work?" he said.

"Yes, I guess so, although there are plenty of other things I'd love to do."

"Like what?"

"Oh simple stuff, you know. Designing, decorating, updating old houses," she laughed. "All the usual."

"It's not that usual, not everyone wants a creative life," he replied, his tone more subdued.

"I guess my career just isn't quite how I pictured it," Jess said after a moment. "That's all. But then, what in life is? Maybe this is real life after all." The mulled wine worked its magic and she began to relax, and regard him as the close friend he once was — as well as the handsome, interesting man he had become.

"I get that. Working at the clinic isn't exactly how I'd pictured it would be either."

"Really? How so?" She propped her chin in her hand, glad to focus on his life rather than hers. Since when had she gotten so melancholy about her achievements? Back in school, Jessica had been proud of all her accolades — the many extracurricular activities she participated in, the perfect grades she maintained, the summa cum laude distinction on her degree. Every new milestone used to fill her with excitement, the thrill of reaching her goal, always searching for the next one. Now…

"Well, for instance, I didn't expect being a vet would involve dealing with so many people." He grinned ruefully and threw his hands up in defense, "Not that I'm against people on principle, but I always assumed I'd get to spend more time with patients than their owners."

"Are people really that bad?"

"Not all of us." He laughed.

The waiter returned to take their order. Luke chose the cider-braised beef with a side of greens, while Jessica settled on the venison stew, which sounded like it would pair well with her mulled wine. As they waited for their food to arrive, Luke opened up with stories from the clinic.

"It's not even Christmas Eve yet, and I've already treated three cats for ingesting tinsel."

Jessica laughed. "Is that common?"

"You have no idea." He grinned and rolled his eyes. "They've had the prescribed meds, they're all fine."

"Any other Christmas season dangers to look out for?" Jessica asked lightly.

"Oh, the usual. Stealing food from the table and becoming sick, Christmas tree needles in paws, turkey bones stuck in jaws… we even had a parrot one year who'd stolen a bowlful of unpopped corn. The owner thought he'd eaten them all and was worried, but when I examined him, it was obvious it hadn't. Later, they found out the bird had been dropping them behind the radiator when the heating was ramped up and the corn started popping. The noise sounded like fireworks going off and gave them a hell of a fright."

That made her laugh, he reached out and touched her hand. She felt the same sparks fly and leaned closer to him. Luke had always been a touchy person, even when they were kids.

"But you still like your job, right?" she asked, in a softer voice this time. "Even though it's not exactly how you pictured it?"

For a moment, Luke fell silent, thinking. Then he nodded. "It can be hard when it gets emotional. I often deal with animals in distress or trauma, and sometimes…" He broke off for a moment, his attention turning inward. "You can't save them all. And it doesn't matter how many times you go through it, those situations can still break your heart."

Now Jessica was the one reaching out and resting her hand on his. He rotated his palm up, giving her fingers a tight squeeze before letting go.

"At the end of the day, though," he continued, exhaling deeply, "I feel that I'm contributing something important to the world, you know? For every animal I can't save, there are many more I can help. That's important to me. Makes me feel like I'm making a difference, like I can give something valuable back, make things better."

Nodding, Jessica pressed her lips together, letting his words sink in.

"Maybe that could help you?" Luke said after a pause. "If you're struggling to find your purpose, maybe you just need to reframe the way you think about your job. You're doing something valuable. Something important."

"I guess so." Jessica ran a finger across the base of her mulled wine glass. "I mean, yes, computers are the future. It's not just what tasks the programs can run, it's about opening up information and knowledge to everyone. For example, right now you have to go to a library and track down details, and it can take hours, sometimes even days," she was thinking of her and Lily's session in the microfiche room. "I know that's kind of fun, but it takes time, it's hard to cross check things, and often it's just something you need to know for a quick reference. There's something called the world wide web now. Computers are going to bring all this knowledge to our fingertips — one gigantic library — right at the end of our keyboard. That's pretty huge. Imagine the information we'll all have access to. Think of how many things in life could be improved by that — for everyone."

At that, Luke smiled. "Wow, that's really something. Is that why you went into it?"

Jessica paused, thinking for a moment, "Well, I wasn't sure that's how it would work at the time, but now the possibilities seem endless. And it's something my parents were proud of me for working in."

The waiter brought their orders, and as they tucked in eagerly, the conversation drifted away from jobs and onto their families. Despite Lily's mom being sisters with Luke's mom, Jessica had only met Luke's parents a couple of times, once at camp and once at Lily's wedding. Both times they'd seemed nice. Supportive.

"My mom's my biggest cheerleader, she's so like Estelle, positive and constantly bubbly," Luke told her. "But Dad, well…" "He's alright, really. Just old-school. Bit of a tough cookie."

"Sounds like he would have gotten along well with my father," Jessica offered, and they traded knowing looks.

It surprised Jessica, how easy it was to talk to Luke. He was a good listener — unlike most of the guys in New York she'd gone on dates with. Her conversations had often felt like an exercise in futility. They barely paid attention to anything she said, obviously waiting for their turn to talk — or in many cases, not waiting at all, just interrupting with their opinions.

But Luke paid attention to every word. He processed what she said, asking follow-up questions that made her think about the situation in a new light.

By the time the waiter subtly slipped a dish with the check and a couple of chocolates onto the table, Jessica realized two hours had passed. She'd barely noticed the time flying by, conversation had been free flowing and easy.

"My treat." Luke took the check before she even got a look at the numbers. He fired another one of those disarming smiles, and swiftly counted out notes, leaving a healthy tip.

"Thank you. It's been wonderful."

As Luke took Jessica's coat from the stand and held it out for her, Jessica's heart beat just a little faster. It was all she could do not to fumble her arms into the sleeves.

Waving a cheery goodbye to the owner, they drew collars up as they left the warm confines of the restaurant, pulling on hats and gloves to ward against the frosty, still night air. He took her hand as they crunched along the snowy sidewalks through town, both strangely quiet now they had left the busy, noisy restaurant. Their breath steamed in the night air, a cloud of fog that trailed them under the streetlights.

Montrose was beautiful at night. Frost glittered on window panes, and light flurries cast halos around the street lamps. The stillness of the air made everything feel like a painting, all the bustle of the day's activities packed away for the night, everyone cozy inside, very few people were out and about now. They entered the tree lined road leading to Lily and Grant's farmhouse on the outskirts. Overhead, a few patchy clouds had gathered to hang in the sky, stars visible in the dark spaces between. Jessica knew from experience that if she were to drive just ten minutes outside of the town limits, beyond the streetlights' glow, hundreds more would appear.

Luke followed her gaze, his smile soft. "Do you remember Bonfire Fridays?"

"How could I forget?" Every Friday at camp, the staff had lit a big bonfire in the main activity field. The younger kids all gathered around it, sitting on tree stump stools to roast marshmallows and sing camp songs, while the older kids tended to gather toward the edge of the field. Lying on their backs, they watched for shooting stars and told ghost stories. Just silly, local legend type stories, though some of them had been genuinely spooky. "You used to tell the worst stories."

Luke raised his brows in mock offense. "I'll have you know, I have always been considered a consummate storyteller."

"Exactly! That was the problem." Jessica nudged his side. "Too creepy. I couldn't sleep some nights!"

Luke wrapped an arm around her shoulders and squeezed gently. "My apologies. I'll remember now: no science fiction or ghost stories for you."

She leaned into him, laughing. Then stayed there, his arm folded around her shoulders, as they walked up the drive, and the last yards to the front door. Lily had left the porch lamp lit, but downstairs was now in darkness, with the upstairs windows softly glowing behind pulled curtains. As they paused by the bottom step, Luke's arm slid away.

The night air suddenly felt colder where the reassuring pressure of his arm had been. Jessica suppressed a shiver, tipping her face up to catch his eye.

Luke remained close — close enough for the fog of their breaths to mingle in midair.

For a moment, neither of them moved. She could hear her own breathing, feel her heart beating. The only thing she could focus on was his lips. And how close they were to hers.

Luke's eyes tracked her every motion, he gently placed a hand beneath her chin, lifting her face, then gathered her in his arms and kissed her deeply and passionately.

Slowly, they released their embrace, and as she opened her eyes again, Luke was looking at her with a wistful expression, his eyes dark in the shadows. "I'll call you."

"I'd like that," Jessica said, smiling contentedly.

"I have to see you go in," he insisted.

"Do you?" she said

"Yes, it's a rule."

She opened the door and slipped through as he waited, hands in pockets, then she closed the door and leaned against it, her heart still thudding loudly. Her lips tingled from his kiss, she raised her hand to touch them lightly with her fingertips. Then suddenly thought of the other woman, the one who'd broken his heart, and wondered if it had been like this between them at the start. She shook it from her mind, this was theirs, it didn't matter what had gone before.

CHAPTER 15

Lily had stayed up, wanting to hear all about the date, and had pretty much decided on dusky pink for her bridesmaid dress. Jessica was still glowing and didn't have to say anything, the smile of her face said it all. She fell into bed after a mug of cocoa with Lily in front of the dying fire, and slept in happy contentment until the first rays of sunlight woke her.

Breakfast done, Thor accompanied around the paddock behind the farmhouse, Jessica and Lily headed to High Meadows House in sparkling sunshine under a cloudless blue sky. The whole drive over, Lily chewed on her thumbnail, a bad habit Jessica hadn't seen since their camp days. Nerves were showing for both of them, and conversation was somewhat stilted in the car.

"Don't worry," Lily murmured once they reached the porch. As they waited for Bethany to answer the door, Lily lowered her hand and managed a bright smile. "It'll be fine."

Jessica sighed. Her friend knew her too well — well

enough to read the worry that had been gnawing at her all morning.

"What if she's upset?" Jessica replied. "I would be, if I found out my husband had a secret child I didn't know about."

"I don't know." Lily tapped her chin, thinking hard. "If Grant had a baby from a relationship that ended before we even met, a child he didn't know about … Maybe I'd be surprised. Freaked out, even. But I'd still want to meet them." The door opened and Lily snapped her mouth shut.

"Lovely to see you again," Bethany greeted them. "Clara's in the sitting room. You can go right on in, I'll be in the kitchen if you need me."

In what was quickly becoming a routine, they shrugged off their coats and hurried up the hallway. The house felt warmer than it had on their previous visits — or maybe Jessica was adjusting to the cooler temperatures. Back in New York, like most apartments in the city, Jessica's steam heating was controlled by the landlord. He seemed to believe the thermostat only had two settings: off or boiling. In the depths of winter, she'd often had to open all her windows just for a breath of cool air.

In the sitting room, Clara Ryan sat with a crocheted blanket over her lap, nursing a cup of coffee in front of a roaring fire, a magazine open on her lap. A smile spread across her face when they entered, and she scooted over to make room beside her on the couch for Lily. Jessica took the settee opposite, and Lily shot her another reassuring look.

"Tell me, girls. What have you found?" Clara leaned forward eagerly, eyes shining with anticipation.

"Well..." Lily took a deep breath, still fidgeting with her fingers. Then she sat up straight and took a deep breath. "How much did Joe tell you about his... um, his time in England? During the war."

Clara frowned thoughtfully. "As I said before, he never liked to talk about the past much, especially that era. I can't imagine what he went through in the prison camp. He had nightmares for years..."

Lily winced. "What about before his plane was shot down? Did he ever talk about those days?"

"Sometimes. I met a few of his friends from the base over the years; Joe tended to open up a bit more whenever they were visiting. They liked to tease him about his carryings-on. I never knew how much to believe — you know how boys are." She chuckled. "It all feels so long ago now, why do you ask?"

Jessica cleared her throat, "Clara, this might come as something of a shock..."

"We met a man who's visiting Montrose," Lily picked up the thread. "From England. He claims — well, to be fair, he said he isn't sure, but..."

"He believes Joe might be his grandfather," Jessica softly finished for her.

A beat passed, while Clara looked from one to the other, and back again, her mouth slightly open..

Gently, Lily reached over to touch the back of Clara's wrist, where she gripped her coffee mug. "I'm sure it's a lot to take in. And it might not even be true. But he says that his grandmother had a wartime romance with an American pilot, one whose plane was shot down. She believed he'd been killed, and she married someone else. The man only just learned about this recently…"

"What's his name?" Clara asked softly. Her hand had started to shake a little and she reached over to place the coffee cup onto the coffee table. Suddenly she looked more fragile than when they had entered the room.

"Jack Montgomery," Jessica replied. "His grandmother was Annabelle… something? I don't remember her last name."

"Curtis," Lily supplied. "If that means anything to you?"

Clara shook her head. Her eyes were shining a little too brightly to blame on the reflection of the fire across from her. "So the figure I saw…?"

"He said he has Joe's old flying jacket, passed down from his grandmother," Jessica said. "He was afraid he startled you, the first time he showed up, so he left to avoid causing any problems. Why he decided to come poking around if he wanted to not cause problems, I couldn't tell you, but —"

"He does look a lot like Joe, and he has the same photograph of him, the one wearing the jacket…" Lily interrupted, brow furrowed as she studied Clara's expression. The older woman looked deep in thought, her face clouded as though her mind were a thousand miles or 50 odd years away. "At least, so far as we can tell. You'd know better." She fidgeted with her hands, looking like she was battling the urge to take another bite of her thumbnail. "He's asked if it might be possible to meet you. But we didn't tell him one way or another. We don't even know if his story is true."

"This all must be very upsetting," Jessica added gently. "We're happy to tell him no, if you prefer."

"Upsetting?" With a shiver, Clara blinked out of her stupor. "Oh, no." A smile broke across her face, slow at first, but getting broader by the second. "This is incredible! Joe and I always talked about having children. We tried, but…" Giving a rueful smile, she shook her head. "It just wasn't in the cards for us, I suppose. Joe would've been thrilled to learn about this. Oh, I must meet him! Could you arrange it? Where is he staying?"

Far from reassuring Jessica, Clara's excitement only deepened her worry. What if Jack wasn't who he claimed to be? Or worse, what if he had ulterior motives for this sudden appearance?

Some details of his story matched up, yes, but there was the business with the antiques. Jessica's gaze wandered from Clara's shining face, around the room instead. She was no expert, but even she could tell how valuable some of the contents of High Meadows House must be.

"He's staying over at Miss Daisy's," Lily was saying. "We've told him we'll help connect you two, if you're open to it."

"Of course I'm open to it!" Clara beamed. "I don't have plans until Christmas Day, but — gosh, that's coming up soon isn't it?"

With a pointed look at Lily, Jessica said, "Why don't we see if Jack is free to stop by with us tomorrow?"

In response, Lily tilted her head, apparently confused about why they'd need to tag along. Clearly, she didn't recognize Mrs. Ryan's need for backup in a situation this emotionally charged.

Jessica forced a broad smile that she didn't feel. "How about we bring Jack over mid morning for tea, introduce you both, then Lily and I will let you two catch up? How does that sound?"

"That would be lovely, But I have an even better idea! Why don't you all come for lunch instead? We could find out about this Jack, and how he is related to my Joe. I'll speak to Bethany about what we can put together by tomorrow, she's bound to have some things in for the holidays," Clara said, still smiling.

At this, Jessica relaxed a fraction. She couldn't quite bring herself to pop Mrs. Ryan's happy bubble — besides, who was she to say that this couldn't turn out to be a heartwarming family reunion after all? But she felt better knowing that she and Lily would be around, just in case.

* * *

Luke hadn't called whilst they were at Clara's, or he hadn't left a message on the answer machine, anyway.

"He'll be busy at the clinic," Lily said when she noticed Jessica's gaze drifting towards the telephone and biting her lip. "Don't worry, Luke's solid, he doesn't play games."

"Oh I know that," Jessica forced herself to be upbeat. "Just thought it would be nice to hear his voice, that's all."

Lily laughed then headed for the kitchen singing 'love is in the air', making Jessica smile. Lunch was creamy chicken soup and fresh bread.

"Ok, another volunteer shift at the Christmas market for me this afternoon — I didn't want to push you into doing it twice," she told Jessica. "So maybe you could ring Miss Daisy's B&B and tell Jack the news?"

"Sure, then I'll go catch up on some Christmas shopping," she agreed.

But when Jessica tried calling to leave a message for Jack, the line was busy. After a couple more attempts, she was forced to accept that a quick call was not going to work. She would have to deliver the message in person.

Lily dropped Jessica off at the B&B on her way to join the volunteers at the market, and she headed inside to find Jack and tell him the news.

Part of her hoped that Jack would be out, so she could leave the message with Miss Daisy instead. Somewhere deep down though, she hoped he'd be in — only to assess how suspicious he seemed, of course, nothing more. There was something magnetic about his personality. She felt drawn to him, his dark brooding good looks, the deep voice and English accent, his obvious intelligence, even his flashes of irritation were attractive. No, she would have to be very clear, this was a supervised meeting with Clara, to find out the truth about Jack, and she would not let any irrational feelings get in the way of protecting the elderly lady and her precious memories. Reaching the B&B, Jessica pulled back her shoulders, raised her chin up, and climbed the front steps. A bell tinkled as she entered, followed by an irritable meow.

Jessica looked down to see William, Miss Daisy's enormous ginger tomcat, lolling on a chair next to the check-in desk. "There you are, you little devil! I haven't seen you since Lily's wedding." Jessica crouched to scratch William's ear, and he rolled onto his back, evidently forgiving her for disturbing his nap.

"He's still upset with me for hosting that dinner the other night," Miss Daisy said, stepping into the reception area from the kitchen doorway, wiping her hands on her Mrs Claus apron. "He doesn't mind our guests, but big parties are a bit much for the old grump. Isn't that right, William?" She looked down fondly at him. "He's been acting up ever since, knocking things off shelves, messing with the books... For some reason he seems to like knocking the phone off of its cradle best of all."

William meowed in response and rotated again, Jessica leaned to rub his ears, then realized her jeans were covered in pale fur. Laughing, she brushed them off. "That explains it. I tried to call you earlier, but I kept getting the dial tone."

"Oh, William, you are the naughtiest cat," Miss Daisy groaned and hurried over to the desk. "At it again," she muttered as she picked up the dangling phone and replaced it where it belonged. "Anyway, how are you, dear heart? What can I help you with?"

"I was actually calling with a message for Jack Montgomery."

"I see." Miss Daisy's eyebrows rose, making it quite clear she didn't really 'see' at all. "Is anything amiss?"

"Oh, no, it's fine." Jessica wondered how much Miss Daisy knew about her lodger and his suspected provenance, but she decided it wasn't her business to share. If Jack was telling the truth, he deserved the right to decide who he told about it and when. "Just extending an invitation. Could I leave a note for him?"

For some reason, this brought a sparkle to Miss Daisy's eyes and a smile warmed her lips. "You know, dear heart, I believe he's in his room right now. Why don't you pop up and give him the message in person?"

Jessica was taken aback, she wasn't in the habit of knocking on a strange man's hotel room. Especially a man like Jack Montgomery. "Oh, I, um… wouldn't that be imposing?"

"Nonsense." Miss Daisy scoffed and waved a hand. "Lovely girl like you? Which man wouldn't mind an interruption, especially for an invitation out! He doesn't know anyone in the town after all." She gestured to the staircase. "Room twelve. You remember your way around?"

Having stayed in room eleven the previous summer, Jessica knew the route well. "I do. Thanks, Miss Daisy." Jessica hesitated, frowned, then headed for the staircase. William decided to tag along and bounced up the stair carpet in short hops.

They reached the top step and he flopped directly in her path.

"Not helpful," Jessica whispered, but she'd always been a sucker for animals, so she knelt to give him one last tummy-rub before continuing along the hall.

Number twelve was the last room on the second floor, a big suite with a sitting area and balcony that overlooked the B&B's backyard. In summer, Miss Daisy hosted cookouts there every Sunday, grilling up some of the best burgers Jessica had tasted.

She tapped lightly on the door. Maybe if she didn't knock very hard, Jack wouldn't hear her, and she could go back downstairs and leave a written note after all…

"Come in!" called a deep voice from the other side of the door. "It's open."

Shoot. He was home. Oh well, too late to back out now. Taking a deep breath, Jessica turned the knob and eased open the door.

The sight that greeted her made her hesitate in surprise. The room was almost as neat and tidy as Jessica's apartment back in the city. Clearly, Jack wasn't a person who lived out of a suitcase, even the desk in the corner was neatly organized.

As for Jack himself, he was perched on the window seat with a sketchbook propped in his lap. He didn't turn when she opened the door, but kept his eyes fixed on the view outside, which he was busy sketching. Even from here, Jessica could tell it was good. Somehow, with just a single charcoal pencil, he managed to capture all the shades of winter visible through the window: the undulating drifts of snow on the ground, the laden evergreens that lined Miss Daisy's property, wispy smoke curling from the chimney of the next house over, just visible through a thicket of snowy pines.

"I'm still working on the last pot of tea you brought, but thank you, Daisy," Jack said without turning.

"That's lucky, because I'm fresh out of tea," Jessica replied.

Jack's head snapped round in surprise, his pencil skidding over the drawing to smudge the trees. She felt a brief, guilty flutter, then suppressed it as Jack's surprise turned to suspicion.

"Jessica? I hadn't expected to see you," he said. Like the other night, his tone was tight, every word precise.

Jessica remembered the curt way she'd spoken to him, the hurt in his eyes and the abrupt manner he had then left the room. The guilty flutter grew another size. "You're very good," she said, nodding at the sketchbook. Hopefully he'd take that as an invitation to start again on a better foot.

Instead, Jack flipped the sketchbook shut and set it aside, ignoring her attempt at civility. "Do you need something, or have you come to give another lecture? This is my private room, who let you up here?"

Jessica bristled. "Are you always this charming?"

"Are you always this nosy?"

"When it comes to making sure people aren't being taken advantage of, yes." She crossed her arms and squared her shoulders.

Jack gave an irritated sigh. "Jessica." A wary expression

crossed his face, clouding his eyes. "I'm not sure what it is that you think I'm trying to accomplish here. I've already explained the situation to you, and you've had a more thorough explanation than my own family. If that wasn't enough to convince you I'm genuine, then I doubt anything will. Why don't you tell me why you are so distrustful? What is your intention in coming here today?"

For all her intentions of defending Clara, the hurt she could see behind his anger made her pause. She tore her gaze from his to stare at the carpet instead. It seemed William had visited Jack at some time recently too because there was cat hair stuck to the pile. "I'm sorry, I don't mean to be…" she took a breath, and raised her head to look directly at Jack. "We spoke to Clara Ryan this morning. She'd like to meet you. You're invited for lunch at High Meadows House. Noon tomorrow. Lily and I will be there too."

The room fell quiet, then Jack stood, and crossed the room towards her, his expression softer, all the bristling anger fading away. Somehow he looked more open, more vulnerable, his walls of defense momentarily lowered.

"Thank you," he said quietly. "I'll be there. You can trust me."

All the earlier guilt mingled with her pent-up worries and a rush of sympathy.

She gazed up into his eyes, locked on hers with a look of intensity she couldn't decipher. She still had absolutely no idea what to think of this man.

The safest option seemed to be keeping her distance,

putting her New York armor back on. Even if part of her longed to learn more about who was underneath Jack Montgomery's cool exterior. She relented a little, her voice softening. "Please understand, this is a huge shock for everyone. We don't want to see Clara upset or hurt, we need to be able to believe you are telling us the truth. The memory of Joe is all she has left, we don't want that to be ruined."

Jessica could see on his face that Jack understood. After all, hadn't he gone through the same emotions with his own mother? He said he was only here to find out about his heritage.

"It wasn't my intention to cause trouble, I hope you can see that, and I appreciate your help. It's been a lot for me to accept too, and I've been wary of sharing my story. I don't have any immediate family left…" He stopped suddenly, as though the glimpse he'd offered of himself was too much. "I look forward to meeting Mrs Ryan tomorrow, I'll see you there. Thank you again, Jessica."

With that Jessica nodded and turned to leave the room, her thoughts in a whirlwind. She'd seen a side to him that she hadn't before, a softer, more gentle side, which had only confused her feelings towards him even more.

As she descended the stairs and let herself out the front door, Jessica made a promise to herself not to make any more judgments until they had more in the way of facts. She could manage that, at least.

CHAPTER 16

Luke still hadn't called. Sleep eluded her that night. Every time she was just about to drift off, something startled her awake again — the hoot of an owl outside or the distant cry of a fox. Closer to hand, there was a drip somewhere in the bathroom. She stood up, jiggled the sink handles, and returned to bed, only for the wind to pick up, setting tree branches tapping at her window.

In the end, Jessica pulled her pillow clean over her head, blocking both ears. Exhausted now, she finally dozed off, falling deep into dreams of High Meadows House. She was walking its halls at night again, only this time alone, the furniture casting eerie shadows on the walls while she followed the trail of a distant whisper. Turning the corner into Clara's sitting room, a huge shadow leapt toward her and she bolted upright in bed, heart hammering.

Outside, dawn was already painting the curtains pale amber.

She slumped back on the pillows, watched the sunlight grow brighter and gave up on sleep. By the time Lily and

Grant came down to the kitchen, she'd made a head start on breakfast, cooking a big batch of oatmeal with apple slices, cinnamon and honey.

The morning ran by. She and Lily walked Thor, then whilst Grant and Lily ran some pre-holiday errands, Jessica called her mother to check in. Talk of long-lost children and Clara's delight had made her realize she hadn't spoken to her in over a week. Predictably, the call was full of Simon, and how she'd decorated his apartment for Christmas, and how wonderful he was at looking after her. There was also mention of a girlfriend who sometimes came over. Simon tended to skim through girlfriends, most of them the glittering type attracted to his world of high finance. This one didn't sound much different. Beneath the bright chatter, Jessica could hear the tremble of uncertainty in her mother's voice, the fear every widow must harbor about a lonely future. Only at the very end was Jessica able to tell her what a lovely time she was having, how nice it was to see Lily and Grant and some talk about the Montrose holiday spirit. It was rather banal, but Jessica had no idea how to begin explaining Clara, or Jack, or any of the things that had happened that week. It was far easier not to get into the details, or not yet anyway.

Once she had rung off, Jessica realized she hadn't thought about Jack all morning, but the closer it got to noon, the more butterflies gathered to knot her stomach. Not for Jack, but for Clara. Yesterday, she'd been excited by the prospect of meeting Joe's descendant. But what if Jack didn't live up to her expectations? Or what if, after she slept on it, she'd changed her mind? What if Jack's sudden appearance brought up all kinds of fresh fears about what Joe suffered during the war? Or jealousies she hadn't considered. What if Jack was curt or brusque with her, how would that make everyone feel?

Jessica couldn't help putting herself in Clara's shoes. She hated surprises. And as surprises go, this one was off the charts. It was all a lot to take in, and if she was struggling with it, she could hardly imagine how Clara was feeling.

They drove over to High Meadows House a little before noon, wanting to be there before Jack arrived. Nobody greeted them at the front door this time — they only heard a muffled "Girls, is that you? Come on in!" called from inside.

It soon became obvious why. Bethany bustled back and forth from the kitchen to the formal dining room, ferrying plates and napkins. A fire blazing in the grate, the chandelier sparkled, and all memories of dust sheets, and sleepy, unused rooms had been banished, replaced by this beautiful, welcoming tableau.

Clara was there too, fussing with the arrangements. She kept circling the table to refold the napkins, and adjust the silverware beside settings until everything was just so.

"It looks so beautiful," Lily gasped and Jessica agreed.

Glossy green holly ringed polished candelabra lined along the center of the linen-covered table, crystal glasses sparkled under the huge chandelier, its lights reflected in maplewood paneling, gilded picture frames and large mirror hanging over the fireplace.

Every now and again, Clara paused and fidgeted with a silver locket around her neck, seemingly deep in thought, her critical eye surveying and assessing every detail. Dressed handsomely in a dark blue silk jacket over a black dress and delicate sapphire earrings to match.

"The turkey's just keeping warm in the oven," Bethany said. "But the pies still need another few minutes. The scalloped potatoes, too."

"How many people are we expecting?" Lily joked. "You must have been cooking all night!"

"I don't know what kind of food Jack likes," Clara said. "I thought I'd better prepare a few options. We made some of Joe's favorites; maybe he inherited similar tastes." Clara chuckled at this, a soft smile on her face.

"How can we help?" Jessica asked.

"Perhaps put more wood on the fire," Clara said, although it was already crackling away with yellow and amber flames leaping around a heap of burning logs.

The doorbell rang before she could move, and they all froze in place for a moment.

Jessica spun around, so did Lily as they heard Bethany call out that she was on her way to answer it. Clara's hands were fidgeting with the locket again, but she stood tall and erect, moving closer to the doorway to greet her guest. Jessica joined her, as did Lily, providing moral support. They could hear Bethany greeting the guest in the hallway, accompanied by the low tone of a man's voice. A moment later the door to the dining room swung inward, and Jack stood at the threshold.

Jack looked even more handsome than he had at the B&B yesterday, or at any time they'd seen him before. He'd dressed for the occasion; his tailored suit fit perfectly over white shirt and dark red tie, thick wavy hair brushed and gleaming, as were his leather brogue shoes. No sign of winter boots – he must have driven over.

His eyes flicked straight to Jessica's, then away, focusing on Clara instead.

Clara had gasped and stood rooted to the spot, her hand at her throat, eyes fixed on Jack's face. "My goodness. You are almost my husband's image…" Clara took a step toward Jack as though in a trance, then stopped herself. She flashed him an apologetic smile. "I'm sorry. Where are my manners? I'm Clara Ryan, Joe's wife. Welcome to High Meadows House."

Jack stepped forward and extended a hand. "Jonathan Montgomery. Jack, to my friends."

Clara tutted and pushed his hand aside, stepping forward for a hug instead. "We don't shake hands with family here." She wrapped thin arms around him, her head didn't even reach his shoulder. He hesitated a moment, then returned the hug lightly, as though she were made of porcelain.

"It's my greatest pleasure to finally meet you," he spoke quietly.

"Let me get a better look at you," Clara said with a tremor in her voice, releasing Jack from the hug, but taking both his hands in hers. She stood back, appraising him, drinking in the details of his face, tears forming in her eyes and threatening to overflow.

He gazed down, his expression almost frozen, although there was a troubled look in the depths of his eyes. "I'm sorry Joe isn't here, too."

"He would have been deeply moved," Clara's voice shook. "To think he had a grandson…a boy he could share his stories with, and…and…his life. Just to have even known of your existence would have brought him such joy." Tears finally overcame her, falling down lined cheeks, she dabbed at them with a handkerchief.

Jack placed a protective arm around her quivering shoulders. "Would you like to sit down? I really didn't want to upset you."

Jessica surreptitiously tapped Lily, who, like her, was mesmerized by the whole situation. Jessica nodded toward the door. "We'll leave you to it," Jessica said. "Bethany will need a hand in the kitchen."

They hurried out of the room, though not before she cast a look over her shoulder. Jack was pulling out a chair for Clara at the head of the table, helping her be seated. Clara had finally found her voice again, and was chattering excitedly about how much he resembled Joe, her features alight with happiness and excitement Lily shut the dining room doors behind them with a click, Jessica walked on with a lump in her throat. She felt a sense of remorse. What had she been so worried about? Jack seemed genuinely pleased to meet Clara, and she was clearly thrilled to meet him.

Bethany had the kitchen organized in almost military style, everything was very well in hand.

"How's it going?" she whispered, although they wouldn't be able to hear a word from the dining room.

"It's so touching," Lily held her hand over her heart. "I'm going to cry, I just know it."

Jessica felt the same way, but busied herself arranging serving dishes and plates while Bethany finished stirring the gravy. Lily sniffed and pulled out her handkerchief.

All three of them strained their ears, trying to listen.

Clara suddenly let out a bright peel of laughter, then Jack's baritone note of amusement, followed by more laughter.

"What on earth are they talking about that's so funny?" Jessica murmured.

Lily raised her brows with a grin, then snuck a quick spoonful of cranberry sauce when Bethany wasn't looking. Bethany turned around and Lily quickly pulled it from her mouth and crossed to the sink to wash it.

Bethany frowned at the cranberry sauce, picked it up and moved it over to the platter where the turkey was about to go. The oven started beeping, distracting Bethany again.

Lily leaned in close to Jessica. "Sometimes you need to just enjoy the moment. Live spontaneously. You know?"

"No." Jessica shot her friend a faux-disapproving look. "I most certainly do not know. My life is planned, structured, I have to look out for myself, you know."

Releasing a long-suffering sigh, Lily looped an arm around Jess's waist and squeezed once, before releasing her to go help Bethany with the turkey. "I'll get you to do something wild someday, Jessica Brooks."

"Good luck with that," Jessica called after her, although

Lily's words hit home. Maybe she had allowed her city instincts to sour her attitude. She loved Montrose, and the people in it, she needed to learn from them, open up more, be more trusting.

They placed the food on large serving dishes. Clara and Bethany really had prepared enough for a small army — a whole turkey, complete with stuffing and cranberry sauce, scalloped potatoes, a chicken pot pie, and a heap of roasted vegetables.

"Everything smells incredible," Lily said as they lined up, each with their own tray to carry to the dining room.

Clara and Jack's conversation broke off when Bethany opened the doors to the room. Clara's eyes were red-rimmed, her cheeks flushed with high color, but she looked utterly happy.

For his part, Jack looked more relaxed than Jessica had ever seen him. He leaned back in his seat, his smile wide and easy. Upon catching a glimpse of her in the doorway, however, he straightened and cleared his throat.

"You've prepared a feast," Jack said, his gaze on the browned and basted turkey.

"Forgive me. I don't have guests often. I got a little carried away." Clara beckoned the girls to join them at the table. "Bethany is such an incredible cook, we just thought we might bring Christmas forward a day or two."

Bethany retreated to the doorway, embarrassed by the praise, but clearly very proud of the laden table. "I just need to keep an eye on the dessert, I'll pop back in a bit when you've had chance to enjoy this."

"Thank you so much Bethany," Clara replied, "you really are a wonder. Where would I be without you?"

As the door closed again, Clara turned back to address the table. "Now, where were we? Oh yes, Jack has just begun telling me about his childhood in England."

"Why don't we all enjoy some of this fabulous food?" Jack said.

"Of course," Clara instantly replied. "Would you like to carve the turkey? Lily, perhaps you could pour the wine?"

After the business of serving and passing food around the table had settled, they began to eat.

Clara told them how she and Joe ended up in the house, which Joe had inherited from his father. "Neither of his brothers wanted to stay in Vermont," Clara explained. "They both fled south for warmer climes as soon as they were old enough. But Joe, he was a homebody through and through. It was somewhere he pined for in the prison camp, dreamed of getting back here. He always said he'd been born in this house, and he planned to die in it, too." She paused, tears suddenly overflowing, and reached again for her handkerchief.

"Don't mind me. Grief's a funny thing. You think you're over it, and then it sneaks up on you out of the blue…" She forced a shaky smile, and Jessica's chest ached with sympathy. "Anyway, he had his wish in the end. So at least there's that. One promise fulfilled."

Once again, her fingers were gently stroking the locket that hung around her neck. Jessica felt sure there must be a photograph of Joe inside.

Silence fell for a moment. Then Clara clicked her tongue. "But don't let me sadden the day. This is a time for celebration! You were asking about the house, Jack…" Clara launched into an explanation of the history — how long it had been in Joe's family, that they'd bought out his brothers to own it outright and how much work and time it had taken to restore it.

Jack seemed keenly interested, Jessica noticed. He asked about the restoration, and the difficulties, then about the furniture, pointing out several antiques in the dining room and complimenting them. He spoke of the makes and styles, which made Jessica realize he hadn't been lying about the antiques business, he was very knowledgeable.

But the fact that he was so interested in the house and its contents continued to concern her. After all, Joe Ryan didn't have any direct descendants. Jessica had no idea if Clara had an extended family, but she couldn't help thinking about the fact that Clara was sitting on an old, historic, valuable property, filled with antiques that must be worth a fortune.

As lunch progressed, Jessica kept her own council, determined not to let her city habits overshadow the moment, and working desperately hard to keep an open mind. Jack and Clara were already forming a close bond, and there was no real reason to doubt his motives for coming to Montrose. Besides, she reminded herself, this wasn't about her, it was all about Clara, and Jack too of course, and who was she to deny an older lady such happiness?

CHAPTER 17

Jessica had thought about Jack almost non-stop since lunch the previous day. They'd had a fabulous time, and lingered well into the afternoon. Jack had been so kind and gentle with Clara, a perfect gentleman, prompting questions here and there, but mostly listening attentively. It was clear that he was trying to absorb every detail, and Clara was in such high spirits she was more than happy to share memories of Joe and their life together.

Finally, coffee had been served, with Clara insisting Bethany join them, which she did, blushing with pride as everyone showered her with compliments over the delicious food. In surprise, Jessica had exclaimed it was almost 4 o'clock. They felt like they had outstayed their welcome, and amid protests from Clara, hugs and thank you's all round they were soon outside in the fresh afternoon air and heading their separate ways home.

It wasn't until much later, sipping tea by the fire at Lily's house, that Jessica realized Jack had hardly said a word about his own family, his background, or history. In fact, he had been content to just sit and listen.

There was now no question in her mind that Jack was Joe's grandson, but...

"We've got to find out," Jessica announced over breakfast.

"Find out what?" Lily was still nursing her coffee.

"Where he lives in England. He didn't say…didn't you notice?"

"Um, no. Look Jess, I really think we should just step back and leave them to it."

"But we've asked Matilda to enquire about him, and she needs to know where he's from. He never mentioned it — I was waiting for him to tell us…it's suspicious."

"It is *not* suspicious." Lily was adamant.

"Fine, but we told Matilda we'd try and find out, and we should," Jessica decided.

"How?"

"I'll just ask him."

Lily sighed and started tidying the dishes. "Did Luke call yet?"

"I…I'll just go and check the answer machine," Jessica said, then dashed off to see if there were any blinking red lights on the telephone. There weren't. Her heart sank. Why? She trailed back to the kitchen to help Lily.

"He'll call," Lily said. "And if he doesn't I'll call him and ask him exactly what he thinks he's doing?"

"No, absolutely not, he's just busy…"

"I'm gonna do it, Jess."

The argument rumbled as they washed up, then Lily

announced she had to drop by at her parents. "There's just a few presents I'm leaving there that I don't want Grant to find."

"Why would Grant find them?"

"He goes hunting, always the same every year. He wants to know what he's got so as to figure what to give me," Lily explained.

"Seriously..." Jessica thought about it. "Is it a married thing, because I don't think my parents did that?"

"No, it's a Grant thing," Lily laughed. "Are you coming or are you still on Jack's trail?"

"I'm going to get his address and give it to Matilda," Jessica insisted.

Which was how, half an hour later, Jessica found herself sitting across from Jack Montgomery in the café attached to Daisy's B&B. Ellie-May busied about preparing their orders in the background — in the fifteen minutes since they'd sat down, Jessica had already seen the poor girl drop a carton of milk and a whole tray of cookies, so she figured the drink orders would take a while.

When she'd arrived at the B&B, Jessica had knocked on Jack's door to ask if he'd like to have a coffee with her. She'd been ridiculously nervous, but she'd acted cool, well, pretty cool anyway.

"Thank you for stopping by," Jack said, patently puzzled. He looked as handsome as ever in a crisp white button-down and navy chinos, with a sweater slung over the back of the chair in the warm café. His shirt sleeves were pushed back just far enough for Jessica to catch a glimpse of his broad forearms, his elegant understated gold-and-leather watch, the only jewelry he wore. "I was hoping to get a chance to speak to you again. I wanted to thank you for the introduction to Clara."

"It was no problem." Jessica turned her gaze to meet his. At this distance, she realized his green eyes weren't one solid color, but a whorl of blues and dark greens mingling to create an overall effect similar to the ocean on a tropical island. The kind of eyes a girl could easily lose herself in.

"Maybe not, but you don't know how grateful I am to make this connection," Jack said quietly. He bent a little closer over the table, and Jessica felt herself mirroring him unconsciously, her body leaning toward him.

"Here we are, one latte and one black coffee," Ellie-May announced, startling Jessica.

She sat back in her seat, grateful for the interruption. "The latte is for me." Jessica took the cup, flashing Ellie-May a reassuring smile.

"I'm so sorry for the delay," Ellie said, blonde strands escaping a loose ponytail and adding to her flustered appearance, and straggling over the collar of her dark blue uniform. "I'm still getting used to the new coffee machine and, well…" She shot a rueful look over her shoulder at the mess she'd made in the kitchen.

"Please, don't worry about it," Jessica said lightly with a reassuring smile. "We're in no rush."

Ellie-May hurried back to the counter to take a new customer's order.

Jack shot Jessica a grin. "That's something I love about

Montrose. Nobody seems to be in a hurry around here. It's refreshing."

"Are things too hectic back at home?" Jessica asked nonchalantly. She lifted the latte to take a careful sip, savoring the creamy texture and smooth coffee. Ellie-May might take a while to do it, but she made a fantastic cup of coffee — given enough time and cleaning supplies to mop up the mess she left behind.

"You could say that." Jack raised his black coffee for a taste, nodding.

"Where's home?" she asked.

"Deepest Dorset, in the south of England. A tiny little village called Chilcot."

"Sounds kind of cute." She took another sip of coffee. "You have a house there?"

"Yes." A shadow passed over his face. "I'm not there as much as I should be, there are a lot of demands on my time."

That was probably as close as she was going to get for an address, so replied lightly. "I can relate."

"Oh?" Jack lifted an eyebrow, those arresting eyes fixed on hers once more, with a gleam of amusement in them. "Is your slice of Montrose busier than other people's, then?"

It took Jessica a moment to figure out what he meant. Then her cheeks flushed. He thought she lived here. Well, it made sense. She knew people in town, and she'd gotten herself involved in his affairs. Clara's, too. "Oh, no, I actually don't live in Montrose," Jessica said, a statement that raised Jack's dark brows. "I've been visiting the valley since

I was a girl, Lily is my best friend, but I live down in New York."

"City?" he asked, looking taken aback.

"The very same."

"Apologies if I seem surprised," he said. "It's just… you don't strike me as a city girl."

Jessica suppressed a smile. "No? How do city girls strike you?"

"Well, for starters, I'd imagine they'd have more of an accent…"

She laughed. "Get me mad or let me have one too many glasses of wine, and believe me, the accent will slip out."

His mouth twitched into a wry smile. There was something disarming about him — until now, she'd only ever seen Jack Montrose acting formally polite, angry or sullen. Although yesterday they had seen a very gentle, empathetic side that he generally seemed to keep hidden. His expression took on a hint of bemusement now, a slight edge that she found she liked. "I believe I've seen you mad already, and I didn't notice a shift in your speech."

"Mad? No." Jessica shook her head, dislodging a curl of chestnut hair, she pushed it back. She noticed Jack's eyes tracking the movement, before refocusing on her face. "You saw me mildly irritated."

Jack's smile stretched into a grin. "Ha! If that was mild irritation, then I must retract my earlier statement — I do see the city girl in you now."

"Don't tell anyone," Jessica replied lightly. "I'm trying to reform."

"Is that why you're all the way up here in winter?" he asked, tilting his head. "I thought most northeastern yanks fled to warmer climes this time of year, assuming they can escape the grind."

"I happen to like the cold!" she replied. "Well, maybe not the cold by itself." She thought of Manhattan's long, gray, interminable winters. "I like snow, and being close to nature, and…" She reached for her latte, lifting it in a toast. "Warm drinks around a cozy fireplace with friends, eating too many sweet things, and cozying up to listen to holiday music in the evenings."

"A woman after my own heart," Jack replied, and the smile was gone now, replaced by an open, interested expression. The way he watched her made Jessica feel somehow exposed. She shivered, not sure whether she liked the feeling or not. It felt risky.

"I'm a winter person too," Jack went on. "Give me a warm fire on a cold night over sweltering on the beach any day."

"Now you really sound British. Let me guess, you like rain, too?" Jessica eyed him over the rim of her coffee cup.

He let out a loud, genuine laugh and leaned back in his chair. "Guilty as charged. It can be relaxing! Especially at night. As long as you're indoors and not out in the thick of it."

"I suppose I can see that. I like the sound of rain at night. And thunderstorms…"

"We've got nothing on you lot in that department." Attention drifting to the windows of the café and the snow outside,

Jack took on a nostalgic look. "I spent a summer in Savannah, Georgia one year. My God, the storms they had…"

"Why were you in Savannah?"

Whatever the reason, the question seemed to throw Jack off. The easy smile vanished, and the cool, polite façade that Jessica was accustomed to returned. "Antiques sourcing, officially," he said.

"And unofficially?" Jessica couldn't help asking, even though he appeared discomfited by the topic. Jack paused a beat before replying.

"Unofficially… I'd been dealing with some personal matters at home. I wanted a break somewhere where nobody would recognize me."

"Recognize you?" That confused her. "Are you well-known in your hometown, or notorious somehow?"

A shutter fell over Jack's features, and he drained the rest of his coffee in one long sip. "No matter, that's all in the past now. Thank you again for stopping by. I should get back to work."

"I thought you weren't actually working on this trip," Jessica said, startled by the sudden shift in temperature. What happened to the lighthearted, friendly guy she'd been talking to a minute ago? Why the hot and cold?

It would be easier if he simply acted too good for the world all the time. Then she could safely write him off as insufferable. But Jessica kept glimpsing other facets of Jack — the same warm, inviting man who she'd watched make Clara Ryan laugh, and inadvertently cry, then listen to her stories for hours.

"No rest for the wicked, and all that," Jack was saying, rising out of his seat.

"And here I was, just starting to think you might not be wicked."

"I wouldn't go that far," he said, but the jovial tone sounded forced now. Pushing his chair into the table he made to leave, and Jessica experienced an unexpected swell of disappointment.

What had she thought would happen? From day one, she'd noticed his arrogance and curt manners. He'd been acting nice today because she'd got him what he wanted, an audience with Clara Ryan. Now, she'd asked one too many pertinent questions and he was shutting off again.

But then he paused, and turned back to her, his eyes shadowed under dark brows. "Would you like to have dinner tonight?"

Jessica blinked, and couldn't think of a reply for a moment, then the image came to mind, Luke and the house with the picket fence. "Dinner?" She shook herself, coming to her senses. "I'm sorry, I already have a date."

A stupid lie — she cursed to herself, willing her cheeks not to blush and give her away.

"Right. Of course." If Jack was disappointed by the statement, he didn't let it show. He simply nodded, as though he were ending a business meeting. "Well, I'll see you about town sometime." With that, he walked out of the café, heading back to the B&B, leaving Jessica to stare after him and wonder what on earth that was about.

CHAPTER 18

As promised, straight after coffee, Jessica set off to meet Lily at her parents' house. A Santa was holding court near the cafe, letting out jolly laughs at intervals as a line of kids waited for a turn to tell him their wishes.

Jessica wondered idly if it was the same Santa she'd seen in the sleigh, who had nearly lost his seat when the horse bolted. Thinking about that reminded her of Jack's intervention — another of his actions that she struggled to parse. Normally, Jessica was good at reading people. She'd sensed what a pain her boss was going to be on day one at her job, and she'd known from her first day of summer camp that she and Lily were going to get on like a house on fire.

When it came to Jack Montgomery, though...why had she stupidly said she had a date tonight?...And why hadn't Luke called? She walked on, head down, and arrived at Estelle and Jakob's house a few minutes later.

"One of Mr Gunter's horses has had a difficult foaling and Luke's had to go backwards and forwards to it,"

Estelle immediately told her. Which meant they'd been talking about her and Luke.

Lily deftly turned the conversation to Clara Ryan and they spent the rest of the morning, and lunch, discussing the remarkable turn of events and what it meant. As soon as they got back to Lily's farmhouse, Jessica headed straight to the telephone intending to call Matilda and give her Jack's address in England.

The answering machine light was blinking red.

"Hey Jess, how's my favorite girl? Sorry I've been caught up in work, but I can't wait to see you again. Pick you at seven tonight? See you then!"

Luke! Thank heavens he'd called, and now they were onto the second date...which was meaningful...She put the phone down, then picked it back up and dialed Matilda's telephone number at the library. Matilda took Jack's address down carefully and told her it should really help. She hadn't heard anything from anyone yet, but it would surely be only a matter of time.

She went to tell Lily the news that she really was going out on a date that night! The rest of the day passed in a haze, she only had two dresses left to choose from — she couldn't wear the same she'd worn to their last date.

"Plum with that teal scarf Grant bought me — " Lily said.

"The teal scarf you've never worn?"

"Because teal just drains me, but it looks fab on you," Lily insisted.

She wasn't sure, but by the time she was dressed, she figured that Lily was right, as usual!

***

Luke arrived with that crooked grin and same warmth in his eyes. He gave her a light kiss on the lips on arrival, then took her hand and led her to his car, calling good night to Lily and Grant on the way out.

"The Hidden Kitchen, you been there?" Shadows in the car interior sharpened his high cheekbones, firm jawline and the curve of his lips. The image of the house and picket fence fixed itself back in her mind, with the mountains of Montrose in the background. "Jess?"

"Oh," she laughed low. "Sorry, um, no, no, I haven't."

He took her hand as they strolled to the restaurant tucked away in a discrete courtyard off main street; a canopy over its front door, the path lined with small, snow-etched, pine trees in terracotta pots.

A low murmur of intimate conversations filled the room, rendering the soft background music irrelevant. The overall effect was so charming that Jessica's breath caught. Candles in hanging lanterns, evergreen garlands strung along the windows, across the fireplace, and more above the windows. The dining area was furnished with round tables and chairs, and a brass and mahogany bar took up one wall, where people on high stools sipped cocktails.

A hostess in a smart black cocktail dress greeted them and took their coats, then showed them to their table, it had a view out over main street. Luke drew out Jessica's chair, allowing her to settle before sitting across the table.

She smiled appreciatively, yet again reminded of what a gentleman he had always been.

"They've got a seasonal menu, usually based on local food from the valley farms," Luke was explaining. "But they really ramp it up around Christmas. I'm looking forward to this — I haven't been here this winter yet."

Jessica scanned the menu then cast her eyes around to see what her fellow diners were enjoying to help her choose. At the table next to theirs, a couple had just been served butternut squash soup with toasted pumpkin seeds and maple cream, another table were enjoying the lightest, fluffiest cheese soufflé she had ever seen.

"I want everything," Jessica admitted, laughing.

"One of everything, then. Done." Luke grinned, and she shook her head.

"I can't actually eat that much. Besides, the desserts here look incredible" They settled on a cheese board to start, and a tender steak for mains.

Once their wine was poured, and the aproned waiters faded away, conversation flowed easily. As they ate, Luke shared more stories from the vet clinic. He'd visited Mr. Gunter's farm to check on the horse that panicked during the Christmas parade, along with performing a cesarean on a mare that had foaled. "Mother and son doing well," he said with a grin.

"What happened?" she asked, then wished she hadn't when he started to explain.

"Sorry," he broke off when he noticed her expression. "Too much detail."

"I do miss that place though. I loved grooming the horses," Jessica sighed. "And it was so much fun going on rides back in the day."

"Guessing you haven't kept up your horsemanship since camp?" Luke replied, one eyebrow arched.

"There aren't a lot of riding rings in New York City."

"But you'd remember the basics. Enough for a gentle hack at least. Why not call over to the Gunters', see if he'd be willing to let you take a horse out sometime?"

Jessica's cheeks flushed. "I couldn't." She shook her head. "It's been so long. Honestly, I wouldn't even remember where to begin."

"It's like riding a bike," Luke replied. "It'd come right back to you. Anyway, Lily rides sometimes; I'm sure she'd be glad to take you along."

There it was again — that strange distance Jessica felt cropping up between them. Just when she'd begun to relax, he'd say something like that. *Couldn't you take me riding?* she thought, not able to bring herself to say it. Then told herself to stop being an idiot, his work called him out at all times, making daytime dates would always be difficult.

"Will we see you at Lily's on Christmas Day?" she asked, keen to change the topic.

Luke nodded. "Sure, I'm planning to stop by. Lily would never let me hear the end of it otherwise."

"Is she the only reason?" Jessica suppressed another rush of confusion.

"Estelle, Grant, Jakob…you," he grinned and she smiled, the tension lifting from her shoulders.

She'd had the prickly sensation of being watched, but ignored it until she caught a flash of movement reflected in the restaurant window beside them. She glanced over towards the bar, only to freeze in her seat.

Jack Montgomery was sitting on a bar stool, drinking alone. His cut glass tumbler caught the light as he swirled his drink, creating tiny facets of flashing light. The moment she looked in his direction, he lowered his eyes, but Jessica felt certain he'd been looking her way.

Shaking her head, she refocused on Luke, who was telling a story about last Christmas and a disaster involving Lily's mother Estelle's turkey. "I told her she shouldn't risk deep frying it, but she had a friend who moved up here from Louisiana that swore by it. Of course, the whole thing erupted in the kitchen, first thing Christmas morning, and — "

A loud, nasal voice cut through the subdued restaurant chatter. "Hey gorgeous, you beat me to it." A voice Jessica would've recognized anywhere.

She looked over to see Caitlin Johnson sliding onto the bar stool next to Jack's. As usual, she'd overdressed for the occasion in a form-fitting red dress with a dangerously low neckline. That, combined with her hemline, left little to the imagination. She'd paired the dress with a faux diamond necklace and matching earrings that glittered too brightly. Her blonder than blonde hair pinned into an elaborate updo, with tendrils cascading down her back in an attempt to look effortless.

Caitlin lowered her voice and Jessica couldn't hear what

she was saying, but she couldn't help noticing the way she rested a hand on Jack's forearm, or catching the artificial trill of her laughter. She'd crossed her long legs, her red skirt slit up one side. Jack had almost certainly noticed, as had just about everyone else.

Luke turned to follow her line-of-sight to the bar with a wry smile. "Well, well, if it isn't Montrose's very own femme fatale, and with a new victim in her sights. Maybe this means she's going to give up trying to steal Grant back."

Caitlin glanced over at them, then pretended not to.

Jessica spoke quietly. "Let's hope so. She's already put Lily through enough."

"The whole ghost-hunting nonsense was a typical debacle," Luke said. "At least Ed Stanton removed the ad once Lily called him."

"Oh, it didn't end there." Jessica filled him in on the basics of their investigation at High Meadows House, and how it led to inadvertently reuniting a long-lost grandson with his step-grandmother. She left out her suspicions, and putting Matilda on Jack's trail. She also tried to keep out her confusion over his attitude, this was surely not the time to explore that tangled mess.

But even without her commentary, by the end of the story, Luke was frowning. "Don't get me wrong, it's always a wonderful thing when family reunites… but doesn't it strike you as a bit coincidental? Why did this man come looking for Joe Ryan now, of all times? Joe's only been dead for just over a year. It seems kind of convenient."

"Shh." Jessica darted a quick look at the bar. "That's him. He's called Jack Montgomery."

Caitlin was sitting closer to Jack now, head thrown back as she laughed at something he said. Jack didn't look particularly enthralled — but she noticed Caitlin's hand brush his arm again. He didn't pull away, instead he turned to signal the barman to refresh Caitlin's champagne glass.

She suppressed a twist of irritation. How dare Caitlin claim him for herself!

Luke spotted her gaze. "Maybe Caitlin will suss him out," he said dryly. "She's certainly making a play for him."

"I know. I almost feel sorry for him." Jessica leaned closer to Luke conspiratorially. "I said the same as you, though. It's pretty sure he is who he says. The family link is clear, but why did he wait so long and why did he stay here after he found out Joe died? He already knows how upsetting the revelation of a lost family can be, so why risk that with Clara?"

"I suppose all we can do is trust him for now, but keep an eye out." Luke looked thoughtful. "And Clara Ryan's sharp for her age. She used to bring her cat into the clinic, until he passed a couple years ago. I swear, she remembered his medications better than me."

Jessica suppressed a smile. "That's reassuring, at least." Her gaze drifted back to Jack. To Caitlin's hand on his forearm. "Lily said the same thing. That we should trust him as long as Clara does." Her brow furrowed. "There's something about him that worries me, something that he's holding back on. It worries me, and we're responsible, you see. We introduced them."

When she turned back towards Luke again, he was regarding her with a look she couldn't fathom.

"What?" Jessica asked, taken aback.

Luke shook his head. "Nothing. We'll all agree to keep an eye on Jack, will that make you feel better?"

"I think so, yes," she replied. As long as she wasn't the only wary one in town, it would be more difficult for Jack to take advantage of anyone. "Thank you for that, Luke."

"Of course." He smiled, his head slightly to one side.

Jessica continued to steal glances at Jack, he didn't seem to be responding to Caitlin's obvious overtures, but he wasn't exactly fighting her off either.

Dessert was too much and they opted out. Luke again insisted on paying, and he helped her on with her coat. Jack glanced her way a couple of times and she merely nodded to him on the way out of the restaurant into the wintery night air.

Through the restaurant windows, she could see Jack paying his tab, Caitlin still stuck to his side like glue. The last thing she wanted was to be standing out here when those two exited.

"We should get going," Jessica said quickly.

"Sure." Luke extended an arm to walk her to the car. As gallant as ever, he helped her keep her balance on the icy sidewalk. The drive back to Lily's was mostly in silence. Luke seemed relaxed, navigating the snow salted roads with ease, while Jessica stared through the windscreen, the lamplight throwing alternate strips of light and shadow across their faces.

He opened the car door for her outside the farmhouse, walked her to the front porch and took her in his arms once more. His kiss was passionate, hungry almost. She melted under his caresses, responding to his touch. "We could go back to my place…" he whispered.

"I…I…" She wanted to say yes. More than anything she wanted to say yes and allow herself to be consumed by the desire and the dream…but did she? Was it truly Luke, or everything he represented? Where were her true feelings in all this? Was it him, or was it the dream? And what if it were the dream? He'd been burned already, what would happen if she did that to him again…how would his family react, and Lily? "I need to be sure, Luke. I'd rather wait." She spoke huskily, her lips on his, the warmth of his body against hers, both of them aroused and wanting each other.

He broke away. "Yeah, you're right. I'm sorry." He stepped back. "I think we know each other, but we don't really. We're not kids any more, we've grown."

"And grown more complicated," she spoke quietly, then sighed.

"Is there someone else?" He gazed down into her eyes, the light too dim to read anything in them.

"No, no, of course not." The denial was too quick.

He kissed her again, long and hard, taking her breath away. Then he let her go.

"I'll call you, Jess," he said and turned and left.

She gazed after him, standing on the step as the red rear lights of his car turned out of the drive and disappeared along the lane.

CHAPTER 19

Christmas Eve dawned bright and sunny.

"You said no!" Lily asked again.

"We don't really know each other, Lily, it just feels like we do." Jessica sipped coffee from a mug, rings under her eyes from another night not sleeping. Had she done the right thing? Why didn't she just go for it? She took everything too seriously, it was just a night together not a marriage proposal.

"I've always hoped you two might make a go of it, especially after that kiss at camp…" Lily sighed, her eyes on the pancakes sizzling in the pan.

"You knew about the kiss!" Jessica was stunned. "All this time, and you never said a word."

"Well, you know…" she spread her hands. "I was just waiting to see if anything came of it."

"Well… I just… I have to be sure… and I don't want him to be hurt again." She suddenly felt disconsolate.

"No, you're right. He probably doesn't know his own mind either. It's only been a couple of dates." Lily said kindly, then made a grab for the pan and flipped the pancakes. "Don't burn, please don't burn."

"Who was it who broke his heart?" Jessica asked the question that had been playing on her mind.

Lily slid the pancakes onto plates then sprinkled her special cinnamon and powdered sugar over the top. "Astrid Linden — you wouldn't know her, but I mentioned her on our calls a few times. She's a vet, they worked as partners. They were together two years, she moved in with him. We all thought it was settled, like they were made for each other. She was stunning. Swedish ancestry, very matter of fact, and really nice, you know." She paused to pass Jessica a knife and fork. "But I wouldn't say she was warm, not like you." Lily smiled, kindness shining in her eyes.

"So what happened?" Jessica paused over the pancake, fork in one hand, syrup bottle in the other.

"Like I said, she wanted a career in the race horse world and a lot more than Montrose could offer. She was genuinely keen on Luke, but it didn't run as deeply as he felt. When she was offered a job in Florida, she asked him to come with her, he refused, and that was the end of it."

"Poor guy," was all she could think to say.

"Yeah," Lily's face fell and they ate in silence for a while. "And Jack and Caitlin, wow!"

"Maybe they deserve each other," Jessica sliced her pancake up.

"Oh come on, he was really kind to Clara."

"So, maybe he deserves an Oscar."

"You're turning 'city cynic' again, Jess," Lily admonished.

Jessica put her fork down and sighed. "You're right. It's…I don't know, I just can't think straight."

Lily gazed at her, a frown between her eyes. "Well, let's not worry about it now, I have a surprise for you today."

"What?"

"Clara Ryan called last evening. She's invited us all to High Meadows House today for her Christmas Eve luncheon. She hosts it every year, usually it's for the senior set, you know, those who own the big houses — but this year it's going to be us too!" Lily told her, rising excitement in her voice.

"Wow," Jessica said, not sure what to make of it. "And I suppose he'll be there."

"You mean Jack?" Lily cocked her head.

"Who else?" Jessica gave her a wry look.

"I suspect he'll be center stage," Lily said then grinned. "You'd better figure out what you're wearing."

She couldn't wear the same as last night, he'd already seen her in that, and the velvet dress with red cherries. So, the russet dress, which happened to be an English design — not that, that meant anything. Although she'd worn that to dinner with Luke, not that he'd be there. She didn't realize it but she was bouncing between thoughts of one then the other. Why had Astrid Linden been so cruel to Luke? He was the nicest guy ever, and the best looking, plus he lived here in Montrose. And Jack had a date with Caitlin last night…

* * *

"I wonder what she's going to serve?" Lily broke into her thoughts. "Since she already cooked a whole feast just for us and Jack the other day." They'd driven over with Grant and were walking down the long driveway to High Meadows House. The early morning sun had given way to noonday clouds and a light flutter of snow had started falling. A dozen cars already lined the road and they were at the back of them all. As they got closer to the house, they caught the conversation of a couple walking ahead of them. "I can't wait to meet Clara's grandson!" exclaimed the woman. "It's so extraordinary."

"Where did she say he was from again?" the man asked. "England?"

Jessica traded a sidelong glance with Lily, who shook her head. Apparently, Clara had decided to go public with the news about Jack. No wonder people were curious — Clara had lived in Montrose Valley her whole married life. Anyone who knew her knew she didn't have any children of her own. It was a story that would soon be on everybody's lips.

The front door was wide open. Bethany was in the doorway, greeting everyone with smiles, taking coats and directing people.

Jessica, Grant, and Lily followed the couple up the hallway to the sitting room which had been cleared of books and magazines, and was now restored to an elegant reception room, filled with guests chatting and sipping pre-lunch drinks. Clara was wearing an elegant high-neck dress frock in old-fashioned black lace over purple silk and a row of large, gleaming pearls. She looked every inch the Lady of the Manor.

"No, we had no idea," Clara was saying to the people to her right. "Isn't it just so exciting?"

Jessica recognized Ed Stanton, the editor of the local newspaper.

"It's an incredible story," Ed said, nodding enthusiastically. "Maybe we could interview your grandson for a piece in the Post."

"Oh, I'm not sure he'd like that. He seems rather reserved…Oh, Lily! Jessica!" Clara looked up, noticing them where they hovered in the doorway. "Come sit over here, you must say hello to Ed." She turned to them. "These are the ladies of the hour; without their help, I might never have met Jack."

"We were all at the charity dinner together, at Miss Daisy's." He smiled. Tall and lean, he had the air of an academic.

They looked around, as if expecting to see her.

"She has sent apologies, she's helping out at the church children's party," he added in explanation. "Lily, I do hope we are still friends again after that confusion over your article?"

"Actually, I owe you a thank you." Lily laughed. "Without that article, we would never have spoken with Clara, and this whole grandson business might never have come to light! Jessica's been amazing, helping to bring Jack and Clara back together."

Jessica stepped forward to shake Ed's hand. "Hello, again."

"I remember you two tearing about the town!" Ed smiled. "You were inseparable, and we always knew just where you were. Your father had every police officer call in to the station if they saw you — you know, just keeping an eye on things!"

"No!" Lily's mouth fell slightly open. "I had no idea."

Ed laughed at that.

Despite the people already in the room, and the sound of more arriving outside, there was still no sign of Jack. Jessica asked Clara, "Does Jack know how many people you've invited today?"

"I told him it would be an intimate gathering of my closest friends!" Clara smiled.

Jessica decided they had very different definitions of 'intimate'. A commotion by the door caught her attention. Heads swiveled, and the gossip in the room swelled to a peak, then cut off. A moment later, Jack Montgomery entered.

He wore the same suit again with a blue-green silk tie that brought out his sea-colored eyes. His gaze found Jessica's, then he turned to Clara.

"Jack, it was so good of you to come on such short notice," Clara called as she beckoned him towards her. The room fell totally silent as Jack crossed the carpet and lightly hugged Clara, kissing her on both cheeks in greeting, before standing back slightly.

"Let's do this the easy way," Clara said, then, raising her voice slightly, and holding Jack's hand tightly, "Everybody! This is Jack Montgomery, my long-lost grandson from England. It's such a treat to have you all here today, there will be lots of time for you to meet him, but for now, let's move through to the dining room or I'll be in trouble with Bethany!"

Everyone smiled, murmuring their hello's as Jack politely responded, then they all set down their glasses and slowly processed across the hall to the dining room.

Clara had set place markers, Jack was next to her and directly across from Jessica.

Jessica couldn't help thinking of Jack cozied up at the bar last night with Caitlin Johnson, of all people. Had he been interested in her? She'd clearly been flirting — and they didn't meet by chance; 'Hey, gorgeous' had been Caitlin's greeting, he hadn't acted surprised at all.

It doesn't matter, I was there with Luke. Then she told herself off, it was beyond inappropriate to be wondering about another man's love life while she was on a date with someone else.

Once everyone had settled in their places, Clara lightly tapped her wine glass with a knife, then formally introduced everyone for Jack's benefit. The local folk all knew each other, and many were regular attendees apparently. When she reached Lily and Jessica, she broke off with a grin at Jack. "And of course, you know these two already."

"How could I forget?" Jack replied, eyes fixed on Jessica, a hint of a teasing glint in them.

"Likewise, Mr. Montgomery is quite memorable," she replied.

A frown flicked between his dark brows at the return

to surnames, though he was too well-bred to let it show. "Thank you again for the invitation, Clara. Do you host this luncheon every year?"

"Yes, it's become quite the tradition. Though, I must say, it's not usually this popular." She chuckled, and everyone else in the room echoed her. "What sort of traditions does your family observe back in England around the holidays? Anything special?"

From across the table, Jessica heard Jack's slight indrawn breath. She shot him a sympathetic look, worried that Clara had inadvertently struck a nerve. For all of Jack's interest in his birth grandfather, Jessica hadn't heard him mention many family members by name.

"The usual, I suppose. Roast Turkey and Christmas Pudding on the day itself, then there's the hunt on Boxing Day."

"That's the day after Christmas," Clara informed the table, as a couple of people looked inquisitive.

Jack stifled a grin, though only Jessica seemed to notice.

"What do you hunt?" someone else asked.

"Foxes," Jack replied.

"On horseback, with hounds," another voice said. "I've read about it."

Jessica held his gaze. She was about to ask if that was why he'd stopped the runaway horse, because he was familiar with handling them, but—

"I hope I'm not prying," Marcella Cullins cut in with the air of someone who very much wanted to pry. "But, is there a Mrs. Montgomery in the picture?"

"No, there isn't," Jack replied, his smile becoming somewhat forced.

"That will be a relief to the eligible Montrose Valley bachelorettes," someone else further down the table remarked, to another round of chuckles.

"Oh look, the food's here!" Jessica called, hoping to give Jack a reprieve from what was quickly devolving into a public grilling about his life and background. Much as she herself wanted more details about him, she hated to see someone put on the spot like this.

What did the Boxing Day hunt comprise of, for example? She'd heard of such things, or rather seen it on those old shows her Mom was so fond of. He must have his own horse. Who looked after it?

She must have been staring again, because Jack's eyes snagged hers.

Her comment, along with Bethany's arrival, had distracted everyone. Two ladies Jessica didn't recognize followed Bethany, dressed in black and white — Clara must have hired a couple of servers for the occasion. All three women bore enormous serving platters over to the long sideboard. This was the first of a planned five courses: a starter salad of winter greens, cranberries, and goat cheese would be followed by stuffed acorn squash and roast beef with horseradish sauce, then a champagne sorbet palate cleanser before the yule log cake and tea with petit fours.

"What'd I tell you?" Lily whispered as Bethany explained the menu they could expect. "A whole feast."

"I'm going to leave this town a whole size up!" Jessica

murmured in response, but was enjoying watching Bethany in her element, directing the waitresses to start serving the guests, her eagle eyes watching all the details.

"Why haven't we come to this before?" Grant murmured, leaning over to catch Lily's attention.

"Because we weren't invited before, silly." She whispered, before spearing a mouthful of salad.

"You're going to have to carry on ghost-hunting so we can keep getting invited to these luncheons," Grant replied loudly enough for people to hear.

There was a light thunk followed by Grant grimacing. No doubt Lily had kicked him under the table. Jessica stifled a laugh with her napkin.

Next to her, Clara was deep in conversation with Jack, who seemed relieved to be the center of only one person's attention now, rather than a dozen.

" — about your grandmother," Clara was saying. "Annabelle, was it?"

Jack nodded. "She was a very proud woman. Very independent."

"I'd imagine that might've been difficult in those days," Clara replied.

"I suppose so." Jack's expression shuttered, the way he always seemed to when someone mentioned his family.

Chancing a glance around the rest of the room, Jessica realized everyone within earshot besides her and Clara was involved in other conversations. Seizing the opportunity, Jessica leaned forward slightly, until she gained Jack's attention. "You don't talk about your family very much."

"No," he agreed. From anyone else, such a curt reply would've made her leave the topic alone. But he held her gaze.

"Why not?" Jessica asked softly.

He released a sigh. "Because even when it's well meant, family often involves a lot of... pressure. There are certain expectations one cannot escape."

Jessica's throat tightened. She thought about her family's well intentioned pressure too. "Yeah," she murmured. "I know what you mean."

"That's actually what I've liked so much about visiting Montrose Valley," Jack said, turning to include Clara in the conversation, who smiled at him. "Life feels simpler here," Jack went on. "As if I can just... be myself."

"I've always enjoyed that too," Clara replied. "Joe and I did a lot of traveling when we were younger, and right after we first retired. But no matter how beautiful the places we visited were, within a few days, I found myself homesick for Montrose."

What must that be like? Jessica wondered. She'd certainly never experienced homesickness. Even when she was a kid and her parents dropped her off at camp — the other girls would be crying and hugging their mothers goodbye. But Jessica was too excited to miss home. She cried more at the end of the summer, when she had to hug Lily goodbye and return to her regular life.

Even now, as a grown adult, she didn't miss her New York apartment. She felt more at home crashing in her best friend's attic, than she did in her own place. *What does that say about me, or my life?*

"It's wonderful that you've found somewhere to feel that way about," Jack was saying. "Too often these days, I'm more eager to leave home than return to it." He spoke openly. "Hence this long stay, I suppose."

"And over the holidays, no less." Clara shook her head, though she was still smiling. "What must your poor family be doing without you?"

"They're not close family, they'll manage," Jack was dismissive. There it was again — that flicker of emotion, gone too quick for Jessica to parse. *Why doesn't he want us to know anything about his family? Is he hiding something bad?*

But watching him, Jessica didn't think so. His reluctance seemed genuine. If he were lying, why not simply make up a sob story to get everybody on his side? No, this seemed more like actual avoidance. Whatever or whoever Jack had left behind in England, he didn't want to think about them right now.

"What are you doing for Christmas tomorrow?" Jessica asked impulsively.

Jack shrugged. "Miss Daisy is cooking dinner, and I'll spend the day reading. There's an excellent window nook in my room — well, you've seen it," he added to Jessica.

Clara's eyebrows climbed her forehead, though she stuck to the topic. "I'd invite you here for Christmas, but I'm afraid I won't be hosting tomorrow. Bethany has insisted I come to her house for the holiday, despite my protests that she needs a day off…"

"No, no." Jack waved a hand. "Don't worry about me.

I'm actually looking forward to a quiet holiday season for once." He smiled, but there was something self-deprecating about it that tugged at Jessica's heartstrings.

"Come and join us for lunch," Jessica said before she could stop herself.

He nodded. "I'd like that."

She smiled. Then Luke came to mind, and she caught herself. What had she just done?

CHAPTER 20

Something warm, fuzzy, and damp woke Jessica next morning, panting directly in her face. She groaned and cracked one eyelid to find Thor sprawled next to her, licking her chin. "Ack!" Jessica wriggled out from under him, laughing as she wiped her face on her sleeve.

Nearby, she heard a gasp and then Lily's voice as she shouted, "Thor, get down here! Jess, I'm so sorry, I didn't realize he'd gotten the door open…"

Thor gave Jessica one last look and then jumped down and raced off.

"Merry Christmas!" Jessica called after him, to a chorus of laughs from Lily and Grant.

"Merry Christmas!" they chorused back.

Half an hour later, dressed in the matching Christmas pajamas that Lily gifted both her and Grant the night before, Jessica descended to a changed house.

Lily and Grant were old school about their Christmas decorations, which meant the tree itself didn't go up until the night before, after the rest of the house went to sleep.

Traditionally, Jessica supposed, they'd be decorating it for the kids to wake up to in the morning.

"How'd we do?" Lily cried as soon as Jessica entered the living room. The tree was beautiful, thick and pine-scented and draped in several different strands of twinkling lights, some silver and some gold. In addition, dozens of ornaments of all shapes and sizes covered the tree from about the mid-section down. "Grant wouldn't add more to his part." Lily pouted, nodding to the top half of the tree.

It had considerably less over-ornamentation than the bottom, but there was an elegance to it, each ornament hung equidistant apart, right beneath the perfectly positioned gold star on top. "Because it looks better when there's enough space to see each ornament!" Grant protested from the kitchen. He joined them a moment later with a tray of hot cocoas — well, two hot cocoas, and a coffee for himself, though he'd added marshmallows to it. "That's your pile, Jess." He nodded to the closest of three large present piles stacked under the tree.

Jessica flushed. "You didn't have to get me all this! I thought we set a ten dollar limit."

"Per gift, but we never agreed on how many gifts," Lily interjected, batting her eyes. When Jessica continued to look worried, Lily nudged her. "Don't worry. Most of them are from my parents."

Jessica groaned. "Your parents got me gifts too?" She'd brought boxes of Aigner chocolates, a New York classic, for Lily's mother and father. There were treats for Lily and Grant too, as well as a cute rose-patterned sweater that looked exactly Lily's style, and a pair of house slippers for Grant, who was always jokingly telling Lily how jealous he was of her warm, cozy collection of them.

But were those gifts enough? She bit her lip.

Lily must have noticed, because she heaved a sigh. "You're in an overthinking spiral. I know we might have overdone it, but it makes us happy to give them, okay? You don't need to give a mountain in return, I promise. Just let us spoil you. It's fun!"

Jessica suddenly beamed. "Alright, if you insist." She dropped cross-legged to the carpet beside the tree, immediately joined by Thor. Laughing, Jessica dodged his tongue this time, reaching around him for the first gift on her stack.

They settled into an easy rhythm, taking turns opening and exclaiming over their gifts. Grant got Lily a new CD player for her car, to replace the old cassette player, along with a few of her favorite bands' albums. Lily got Grant the most elaborate coffee maker Jessica had ever seen, complete with more knobs and levers than she would know what to do with. Grant immediately dashed off to the kitchen to test it out, which led to them all having more coffee than usual.

The caffeine jitters had just set in when the doorbell rang, followed without pause by a flood of people tromping into the living room without waiting for an answer.

"Merry Christmas!" called Estelle, heading up the pack. Lily's father, Jakob, was right behind her, along with Luke's parents and siblings and their children.

"Luke will be along later," his mother told Lily, who Jessica caught shooting her a surreptitious look. "He had an emergency at the clinic."

As the pleasant bustle of the holiday got underway — Lily and Grant taking turns to ferry out plates of cookies, Estelle insisted everyone else unwrapped their gifts before she'd touch her own — Jessica's mind kept drifting back to yesterday. To Jack and wondering if he would come, and the consequences, and why did she even ask him?

Luke arrived just before lunch, swooping through the house to hug everyone and pass out gifts. He'd gotten everyone the same thing, including Thor — matching socks depicting a cat dressed up in a Grinch outfit. In Thor's case, the socks had been sewn shut and stuffed to make little chew toys, which he promptly proceeded to destroy in a couple of bites.

"Oh well," Luke commented, watching this. "At least he had fun while it lasted." He held out a pair of socks to Jessica last, giving her a rueful smile. "I'm not sure whether they're exactly your style, but…"

"I love them. Thank you." Beaming, she accepted the socks, then held out the gift she'd brought. "I managed to save you one, though it wasn't easy to fend off Lily." She hadn't bought the gift with Luke specifically in mind — it was just the last of the stocking stuffer boxes, but then again, Luke clearly hadn't bought the socks just for her either.

The party had migrated to the living room, for the most part, leaving them alone in here for a rare moment. He took her hand then pulled her towards him and kissed her on the lips. "Happy Christmas, Jess."

She smiled up at him contentedly. With the distant sound of Christmas music playing in another room, and flurries drifting past the window, the scent of Lily's baked honey ham filling the air, Jessica couldn't imagine a more perfect holiday.

Luke turned to open his gift. "Dark chocolate bonbons? And hazelnut butter truffles? I'm impressed you managed to keep Lily from stealing these."

As if sensing a discussion about her, Lily appeared in the doorway, eyes darting straight to her cousin's gift. "Luke, did you get any of the hazelnut ones? Can I swap you?"

He and Jessica traded bemused smiles. "Here, take them. I shouldn't eat too much chocolate before work anyway; don't want to have a sugar crash mid-surgery." He passed Lily the box.

Jessica frowned. "You have to do a surgery?"

Luke grimaced. "Afraid so. One of my patients has a bone lodged in his stomach. The aides are prepping him, so I was able to slip out for a bit, but I need to be getting back."

"Now?"

"Yes, now. Sorry, I've already told the folks." He took her hand. "Come wave me goodbye."

She went to the front door with him, and waited while he pulled on his coat and boots. *Jack was coming over sometime… was she relieved Luke was going? How deep was she getting in with Luke… how deep was he getting in with her?*

"I'll try to come back later." He put his arms out for her and she moved into his embrace.

"I'll be here," she whispered as he bent to kiss her, a long, lingering kiss.

The doorbell rang.

"Oh." Jessica stepped back. "Um. That's probably Jack. I invited him over since he's been all alone up at the B&B..." She trailed off.

"Very neighborly of you," he spoke dryly.

"Was I wrong...?" Jess started, but Luke waved his hands.

"No. I'm just trying to figure you out, that's all."

The doorbell rang again. Jessica opened the door as Lily called from inside the house.

Jack stood there, eyes moving from Luke to Jess and back.

"Hey, man, good to see you." Luke slapped Jack's shoulder on his way out.

As Luke departed, Jack's gaze tracked him, before he returned his attention to Jessica with a slight frown. "Thank you again for the invitation. I hope I'm not intruding."

"How can you intrude if you're invited?" Jessica replied, tilting her head to one side.

"Fair point." Jack flashed a brief smile, then lifted a grocery bag in offering. "I come bearing a gift of cranberry jelly. Miss Daisy seemed to think it would be needed."

Jessica laughed and took the jar. "Come on in."

He shrugged off his coat as she closed the door, her

mind whirling. *This was just her way of apologizing for being so suspicious of him, she told herself. Pax, a nice Christmas gesture to a stranger far from home…* her other voice told her that it was nothing of the sort. That she was intrigued by this man, and if she were honest with herself, she was attracted to him. She had to know her own mind.

She led the way through. "Can I get you anything? Water, coffee, tea… I'm pretty sure Estelle's putting some wine on to mull in a minute or two."

"Tea's fine for me, thanks." Jack lingered in the doorway, glancing over his shoulder up the hallway, in the direction Luke went.

"They're in the living room, but if you come through to the kitchen I can make tea the way you like it…whatever way that might be!"

"Earl Grey, if you have it."

They didn't, they had black tea, which he took with milk, no sugar. Things were a little stilted between them. Once she finished making his tea, they joined the rest of Lily's family in the living room for introductions. Estelle congratulated him on his new found relationship with the Ryan family, and welcomed him to Montrose. Jakob was quieter, weighing the man up. Lily and Grant chatted amiably, then headed for the kitchen to work on lunch. Estelle and Jakob weren't far behind and this gave the younger kids a chance to gather around Jack. They loved his accent, constantly asking him to repeat certain phrases and words.

"Say squirrel again!" That one seemed to be a favorite.

Jessica laughed as Jack repeated the word over and over, all the while shooting her good-natured glances. He seemed good with kids. Laughing at their bad jokes, telling jokes of his own. During a lull in the conversation, Jessica slid onto the sofa beside him. "Do you have a lot of children in your family?" she asked, forgetting, momentarily, how questions about his family made him jittery.

For once, Jack didn't tense up. But his expression took on a wistful note. "No. But I wish there were. I don't even have any siblings. I always thought it would be fun to have one."

"Depends on everyone's temperaments," Jessica replied wryly, and Jack lifted an eyebrow at her.

"Don't you get along?" he turned his gaze away from the blazing fire and onto her.

"My brother's a bit of a workaholic. Not that having a work ethic is a bad thing," she added quickly. "But he can be pretty single-track minded about it." She leaned her head back against the sofa, warm and comfortable, finding herself surprisingly at ease in his company. "For example, since my brother and I are both perpetually single, my mom's always reminding us that her chance at having grandchildren anytime soon is currently nonexistent."

"Do you want to have children?" Jack asked, his eyes steady, expression neutral. He might be one of the first people to ask her that the way one asked an actual question.

His open-mindedness surprised her. And it made it easier to be honest. "I'm not sure. I think so? I love spending time with them." Jessica paused to glance across to the far end of the room, where Lily's young cousins were currently engaged in tug-of-war with Thor. "But only with the right partner," she added more softly. "I know how much work it took for my parents to raise me and Simon; I'm not sure I could handle it on my own."

"I bet you're more capable than you give yourself credit for," Jack said quietly. His eyes hadn't left her face, his expression somber. "But I understand what you mean. The basis of any strong family is the parents. I'd want a partner I love and trust more than anyone in the world before I embark on something that momentous."

"Here, here." The corner of Jessica's mouth ticked up in a smile. "Is that so much to ask?"

"Sometimes." Jack's face fell, and Jessica mentally kicked herself.

Suddenly, all his dodges and deflections when it came to questions about his family started to make sense. Something must have gone wrong — wrong enough to bring him all the way to the United States chasing a grandfather he'd never met. Whatever it was, Jessica felt guilty for dredging up past hurt. She thought about her father's death, and how sometimes, it was nice to talk about him, but other times, she just wanted to forget for a while, if she could.

"Family can be... a lot," she heard herself saying softly. "Don't get me wrong, I love mine, but sometimes..." She thought of her and her brother's most recent argument, a week before she left New York for Montrose Valley. At the time, all she'd been able to focus on was the unfairness of it, the way he blamed her for not making as much as he did, when the fact was, he'd had a four year head start in the world, and she was still earning her way up the ladder.

Now, though, looking back, she could picture the anxiety underneath his anger. Fear of the future driving his constant badgering.

"There's a lot of pressure to do things the right way," Jessica said quietly. "Even if it's not the right way for you." When she looked up again, Jack's eyes had taken on a sadness.

"Yes. Other people's expectations can weigh so heavily on you. People expect you to be someone you're not, just because of your name or where you come from." Jack shook his head, mouth a hard line. "Why can't we just exist? Why do we always need to be performing for each other?"

"You can say that again." Jessica cocked her head, a slow smile beginning. "Let's make a deal. I won't judge you if you don't judge me?"

Jack laughed under his breath. "No matter what I do? I find that difficult to believe."

"What, you don't believe a yank can refrain from being judgmental?" Jessica's grin widened.

"I find it difficult to believe any human can resist the urge. We're programmed to mark the odd one out of the herd; it's instinctive."

"Well, if you're already the odd one out of your own herd, then why would you go around judging other herds' outcasts?"

At that, Jack laughed outright. She liked his laugh —, and it looked as though it surprised him as much as it did her. "I suppose we social pariahs might as well stick together."

"Don't go sounding too enthusiastic," she joked.

"Fine." He held out a hand. "From now on, Montrose Valley is a judgment-free zone for the two of us. Free from all societal expectations and external forces."

"Not sure how long that can last," she said, "But you've got a deal." She reached up to take his hand. He shook, just once, formally. But her palm tingled where it made contact with his, his hand so large it swallowed hers for an instant. Then he let go, just as quickly, leaving her in a confusing rush of emotions.

"I'd better go and see if I can help in the kitchen." Jessica stood, eager for some space, or some air, or just to clear her head away from Jack.

Lily must have been waiting for her. "So. Jack seems like he's having a good time."

"I hope so, since I dragged him out into the cold."

"Oh, yes, I'm sure he's very put out about the cold. Not at all enjoying the fact that a lovely young woman invited him to a party…"

"Lily." Jessica groaned.

"What? I'm only stating the facts!" Lily waved her hands in a gesture of surrender, then turned serious. "What about Luke?"

Her face fell, and she realized Estelle was watching from over by the stove.

"I just don't know…" Jessica lowered her voice. "Besides, it's a moot point. I'm going back to New York in a few days."

"Unless you and Luke really do make something of it," Lily spoke quietly.

The dream slid into her mind; she shook it away. "It has to be for the right reasons, Lily."

"Yeah, I get that," she sounded subdued.

Jessica sighed. She felt like she'd signed up for your standard, run-of-the-mill bad idea.

The slight damper on their mood didn't last long, lunch was served, toasts were made and mulled wine was enjoyed. It was a jolly happy affair, and enjoyed by every one of them. Everyone agreed on a walk in the snow after the meal, apart from Jack, who said he really must be going back to Miss Daisy's.

They shook hands with him and trooped out, trying to pretend it was pure chance that Jessica remained behind to wave Jack off. Jessica had figured what they were doing, Lily's family were as kind and as astute as she was. Whatever happened had to happen for the right reason, no pressure, no judgment, just step back and let people find the depths of their own emotions. Jessica loved them all the more for it.

"It's been a really nice Christmas." Jack had pulled on his great coat and was standing in the hall, almost in the exact spot Luke had stood earlier.

"And for me," Jessica replied.

He held his hand out. She took it; he didn't let go. His

eyes locked onto hers, a smoldering light in their depths. He gently pulled her to him, lowered his face as she raised hers. He kissed her, passion building, sending frissons of desire through her body. She lost herself in his embrace, a world of just the two of them, a world she realized she never wanted to leave.

CHAPTER 21

She didn't tell Lily, or at least not until Grant had left for the hospital next morning.

"So what are you going to do?" Lily asked.

"I can't…" Jessica had her head in her hands, leaning elbows on the kitchen counter, wearing the Christmas pajamas under a dressing gown. "I don't know. I don't think Luke is actually in love with me."

"Maybe you'd better cool it with him…until you know your mind," Lily said gently.

"I…yes, of course. That's what I intended," she signed. "Horrible timing."

"Crazy more like," Lily tried a lighter note.

"Ha!" Jessica exclaimed. "Totally off the wall, especially as I'd been warning everyone about Jack."

"The irony hadn't escaped me." Lily pushed another mug of coffee towards Jessica. "Luke called while you were in the shower. He's coming over."

"What? Why didn't you tell me?"

"I'm telling you now, after you've had enough coffee and told me what happened with Jack."

"What time is he coming?" Jessica looked over at the kitchen wall clock.

"Not for another hour, so you've got plenty of time to figure out what to do."

Jessica groaned and put her head back in her hands.

* * *

She was staring out of the kitchen window when he arrived an hour later. Gazing at the snow-covered mountains in the distance, clouds forming on their peaks, a winter blue sky beyond. Meadows, farms, trees, all etched in white — the scene could be a picture out of a book. A book she was about to close the cover on.

"Hey, Jess." Luke walked in.

She raised her eyes to his, but couldn't say anything.

"I was going to ask if you'd like a day out driving round the valley, stop for lunch somewhere…but maybe we'd better talk first?"

"Oh, Luke, I'm just…I'm so confused." She shook her head, chestnut curls catching on the roll neck of her dark red sweater. "I'm sorry…I…" tears gathered in her eyes.

He came with his arms held out. "Hey, come on. We're friends, we go way back."

"I know and I'm being such an idiot." She was crying now, his arms around her, her head in the crook of his shoulder.

"I assume it's Jack?" he spoke softly.

"No, it's me," she said through tears. "I can't…I don't think I'd be interested in him if I truly loved you, Luke. And I've probably just said that all wrong, but…but I think it's true." Sobs were breaking her words, and he stroked her hair soothingly.

"Jess, look at me." He gently cupped her chin.

She leaned back a little to gaze into his eyes.

"I don't know either. I'm attracted to you. I always was, but I don't think it was ever…" he sighed. "It's not the soul binding kind of love. I thought we might want it to work between us because we've been looking for something missing in our lives. But that's not a foundation that's going to last a lifetime."

"I know, and I recognize that," Jessica controlled her tears, and pulled out a tissue from the box on the counter to wipe them away. "I just wish it could have been though."

He smiled at that. "So do I, Jess, because you're the best."

"No, you are…and the most understanding, wonderful friend I ever had." She threw herself back into his arms and let his warm embrace comfort her until her tears dried.

* * *

"So that's it?" Lily had heard Luke leave and came into the kitchen. Jessica was once again perched on a stool, elbows on the counter with the box of tissues half empty in front of her and the waste bin full of crumpled ones.

"Yeah, that's it," Jessica said quietly. "He felt the same way, or said he did. We weren't soul mates, and he's right, we're friends, and he's the best of my friends, along with you." She sniffed and dragged another tissue out of the box.

Lily put her hand over hers and squeezed it. Her face said all that she wasn't putting into words. Jessica would have been family, helping out at the vet's clinic, seeing each other whenever, watching their families grow. Living the Montrose life along with her. The whole dream just disintegrated. "I'm sorry, Jess."

"Shall we take Thor for a walk?" Jessica sniffed.

"Yeah, he'd love that."

* * *

The day dragged until Lily turned on the TV and found an old movie to watch. They curled up by the fire, blankets on knees, hands wrapped around mugs of hot chocolate, watching but not watching the flickering images. They all had an early night, Jessica slept better than she'd expected, maybe it was part of letting go of her childhood dreams and accepting the reality of the world. She thought of Jack, what was the reality of his world?

He called mid morning, just after they'd come in from walking Thor. "Can I pick you up?"

She hesitated, she'd only just finished with Luke yesterday, did it seem too soon? "I…I, where to?"

"I'll see you at noon."

Noon came and there he was, casually dressed, a charcoal turtleneck sweater under the great coat, dark trousers, polished shoes, a smile and a light in those sea-green eyes.

"High Meadow House," he replied in answer to her question, there's something I'd like to show you.

"Ok, great," she said, amazed to be going anywhere with him.

Bethany answered the door with her usual smile as though Jessica and Jack were a normal couple just making a casual call. She took their coats and led them up the hall, then gestured to enter the sitting room, the cozy, warm room where Jessica first met Clara days ago.

Clara sat in her usual chair, close to the fire, with a pile of knitting in her lap. She'd abandoned it for the moment, focusing on Jessica as she entered, offering a bright smile. "How lovely to see you, my dears," Clara said. Was Jessica imagining it, or was there a hint of a twinkle in her eye? She set her knitting aside and rose from her seat — Jack went to help her up, but she waved him off.

"Now you two go up and I'll be back with tea in a few minutes." Then, still with that twinkle in her eye, Clara exited from the room.

"Come with me," Jack said.

He led the way out of the sitting room and headed for the stairs. Clara and Bethany were nowhere to be seen. She had the feeling they were playing at matchmaking, which made her smile.

Jessica followed him through to the hall and staircase. He walked so quickly that she struggled to keep up, but he turned around to be sure she was still with him. He looked distracted, like his mind was a million miles away from this house.

Finally, they climbed up to the top floor and paused on the steps up to the attic.

"Where are we going?" Jessica asked, unable to keep a slight tremble from her voice. The last time she'd come up here was with Lily and had found it rather creepy.

"I want to show you something," was all Jack would say. He'd picked up a flashlight that had been left on a low bookcase nearby — suggesting he'd been up here recently — then he surged up the steps into the dark.

Jessica followed. Once she reached the top, she could see someone had cleared a space around Joe Ryan's old trunk and dragged over a tea chest, so there was a spot to sit down. A lantern had been left hanging off a nail driven into a rafter. Jack reached up to turn it on. It brightened the dusty old attic considerably — enough for Jessica to be able to tell that someone had cleaned a bit, too. The layer of dust wasn't as thick as the last time she ventured up here.

Jack gestured her to sit on the tea chest while he knelt next to the trunk. He lifted the lid, several of the contents were spread in neatly ordered piles.

"You've been looking through Joe's things?" Jessica asked softly.

Jack nodded. "With Clara's permission, of course. I wanted to see what I could learn about his time in the war, back when he knew my grandmother. And look." Jack reached into the trunk and withdrew a battered paperback book — a copy of Graham Greene's *The End of the Affair*. Jessica had never read it, but she'd seen the old movie based on it, and knew that the author had written it shortly after the war had ended. From inside the back cover, Jack slid a folded piece of paper, the cursive on it faded with time.

"I found this when I was flipping through some of the books in here," Jack murmured, passing Jessica the slip of paper.

She unfolded it, bending closer to the light to read. Their heads almost touching.

My dearest Annabelle,

I've not heard from you since my last letter. I understand if you don't want to talk. I should honor that. But I just want to say thank you, and that I hope you have found happiness.

It's strange — I feel as though I'm writing to you from a completely different lifetime from the one we shared. Perhaps I shouldn't mail this; perhaps the past is better left undisturbed. Maybe that is what you meant to imply, when you didn't respond. But you were a bright light in my life at a time when I was in desperate need of one. I'll always treasure the memories we made together.

I've found a new light now. I've married. That's what I wanted to tell you. Clara is everything I could ask for. I wish you could meet her, I think you'd get on. I love her more than I could've imagined possible. I hope that you've found the same contentment I have. Know that I will always think of you fondly, as I hope you think of me.

With fondest love.

Joe didn't sign the letter. Probably because he never sent it, Jessica realized. Otherwise it wouldn't be here, in this trunk.

"Look at the date." Jack leaned over to tap on the date at the top right hand corner of the letter. 1947. "My mother was still a small child then…" Jack shook his head slowly, staring at the letter in Jessica's hand. "If Joe had sent this second letter; Annabelle might've told him about my mother, and we all might have known one another while people were still alive. We could have been a family —" He broke off.

Jessica reached over to rest her hand on his, he rotated his palm, opened his hand to let her weave their fingers together.

"Jack." She waited until his eyes met hers. "I'm so sorry, but do you think it could have worked the way you imagined? Your grandmother wasn't even sure who the father was then. You said it was only later she realized your mother must be Joe's child."

"Maybe, I suppose I'm clinging onto something that I wanted, rather than they wanted."

"A family?" She guessed.

"Yes, which doesn't make sense because I have one, but we weren't close. Duty, position, all those things, but somehow love got lost among it."

He searched her gaze, like he was seeking something.

Throat tight, Jessica whispered, "I lost my father just over a year ago. My mother… Well, the loss broke her.

And my brother and I are trying to hold together the pieces, but we don't exactly get along at the best of times, let alone…" She fell silent.

Jack squeezed her hand tightly. "So many losses, and so many missed opportunities to grow together, rather than apart." His gaze slowly drifted from Jessica's to the letter in her hand, and the book he still held. He looked at Jessica again, a searing, determined expression that caused her pulse to skitter in her chest. He suddenly pulled her to her feet. His hand firmly gripping hers. "I don't want to make the same mistake my family did. I don't want to let opportunities slip away when they're within reach."

Jessica's mouth went dry, unable to peel her gaze from Jack's. She'd never seen him like this, intense and focused, but also with open vulnerability in his eyes. *I could look at this man forever,* she realized.

Jack bent his head until their foreheads brushed, their eyes still locked. "Jessica. Since the day we met, you have challenged and confounded me."

She laughed, breathless, Jack was so close now she could feel the ghost of his breath on her lips, the heat radiating from his skin. "Is that a compliment?" she joked.

"Actually, yes." His eyes sparked with amusement, one corner of his mouth twisting up. "I've never met anyone quite like you. Except, perhaps…" Here, his gaze flickered, just for a split second, to her lips.

She felt her lips part in answer, drawing in a shuddering breath.

"Well, except for myself, I suppose," Jack murmured.

"Even when you're frustrating me, I can't help but understand where you're coming from. Confronting me the way you did. If it had been me in your shoes, and Clara was my friend, I would've done the same thing," he admitted quietly. "Perhaps that's why it rankled. Because I understood your motives too well."

Jessica pressed her lips together, not trusting her voice to stay steady if she spoke.

For his part, Jack seemed to be steeling himself. At the same time, his free hand rose to hover in the air just beside her cheek, close enough for Jessica to feel the heat coming off him. "Jessica, I… I have feelings for you. I don't know if you feel this too, or where you're at, but —"

In response, she closed the distance between them. There was barely any to cross, really. Just a hair's breadth of space. She lifted her head up and forward, her lips feathering across his.

Jack's hand slid around the back of her head, his fingers winding through her hair. He drew her closer, pressed his lips to hers, a long, slow melding of a kiss. He tasted of cinnamon and smoke from the fire downstairs, mingled with a headier flavor that was all him, the same taste as the scent that wrapped around her now.

Of all the kisses Jessica had experienced in her life, she'd never shared one like this. One that felt so instinctively right. She inhaled sharply, lips parting. At the same time, Jack pulled away too, like maybe he'd come to his senses at the same instant she did. Air rushed between them, cooling the space. Jessica felt her heart going wild.

Does he think that was a mistake? Just as she opened her mouth to ask, Jack's hand slid down the back of her neck, his forehead tilting forward to rest against hers. "Wow," he breathed.

Jessica exhaled a soft, incredulous sound. "Yeah." Of all the directions she'd imagined her and Jack would go, this one didn't make the list.

This kiss, even more than the last, felt so right. In spite of her logical, risk-averse brain screaming at her that this was impossible, could never work, Jessica stayed right where she was, sharing the same air as Jack, every molecule in her body on fire with his nearness.

A gentle, reassuring smile lifted the corner of his mouth, accentuating the sharp angle of his jaw. "I don't want to rush you. We hardly know each other. I want to give you all the time you need for this."

Time. That was the one thing Jessica didn't have enough of.

CHAPTER 22

They had tea with Clara; they kept talk light and friendly, but Jack sat next to her on the sofa and once they'd said their goodbyes, he took her hand and walked her to his car. They didn't speak on the drive back, both were lost in thought. He dropped her at Lily's and told her he'd call, then drove away.

"Did you kiss?" Lily had heard all about the letter and their discussion, but she wanted the facts!

"Lily, I…" she blushed, laughing. "We're grown ups, it's allowed!"

"Is he taking you out again?" Lily slid another piece of toast onto Jessica's plate. They were just finishing a late lunch because it hadn't seemed to be on Jack's agenda today.

"Maybe. He said he'd call."

"Wow, an Englishman, who'd have thought it." Lily shook her head. "Anyway I'm glad you're home early because we're going to Mom's to eat leftovers tonight. It's a tradition!"

"Ok…but" she hesitated, tears unexpectedly springing in her eyes. "Will Luke be there?"

"No, his new partner hasn't started work yet, so he's run off his feet with work." Lily tilted her head. "It's fine, we all understand, and it was his choice too, don't forget."

"Maybe…oh Lily, I feel like I'm on a merry-go-round. First Luke, now Jack. I don't know what to make of it. It's too fast, I'm hardly registering what's happening, and I'm going back to New York in three days."

"All the more reason why you need to spend a nice quiet stress free evening in my parents' crazy household." Lily laughed.

The evening was full of chat and laughter, and warmth and understanding. A few of the cousins had dropped by and Grant came with them. They ate too much and played board games. It was the perfect antidote and Jessica slept until dawn had long since broken the next morning. She had three days left, would the day bring another call from Jack. Maybe she should have made herself clearer about her timeline? But wouldn't that just look pushy?

Breakfast was french toast, which she insisted on making because Lily had done way more than her fair share of cooking.

He telephoned in the afternoon.

"May I take you out for dinner?"

"Yes, yes, I'd love to."

"Pick you up at seven."

She figured he didn't go in for long telephone conversations.

At seven on the dot, headlights lit up the driveway. Jessica gave the outfit she'd put on one last critical look in the mirror — thick, glittery tights paired with a simple black dress, the neckline just low enough to suggest a date night, rather than an office party. She'd paired it with a plain gold necklace and matching bracelet — gifts from her mother last Christmas.

Lily was behind her, peering through the curtains. "He's coming up the walkway!" she stage-whispered. "Wow, Jack really cleans up nice."

"Stop," Jessica groaned. Lily and Grant had been lightheartedly teasing her all afternoon.

"I'm just saying!" Lily batted wide, innocent eyes, then hurried down to answer the doorbell.

Jessica came behind a little more slowly, high heels held in her hand. Lily flung the front door wide open with a huge smile, arms wide. Jack had a split second to shoot Jessica a startled look, before Lily pulled him into a hug.

"I'd demand to know your intentions with my best friend, but given you're an English gentleman, I assume they're honorable," Lily said as they broke apart, her face still split in a cheeky grin. "So I'll just say, have her home by bedtime."

Jessica flushed, but when she glanced at Jack, he was grinning, too. "Naturally," he said in his deep, somber baritone, "I would never dream of any improper behavior. Jessica?"

Their kiss flitted through her mind, and she smiled. "Of course not. See you later tonight, *Mom*," Jessica said, teasing, as she leaned in to give Lily a quick hug.

"Don't forget your coat and scarf!" Lily scolded, darting

to the closet to fetch Jessica's long red coat and the rose gold silk scarf.

A few layers later, they left, Jack taking Jessica's hand on the slippery front walkway. His rental car, with the fateful tire tracks they'd once used to follow him to Miss Daisy's, sat idling, the heat blasting to keep it warm.

"Sorry about the ninth degree," Jessica murmured as she buckled herself into the passenger seat. "Lily's a bit protective, that's all."

"I'd be more worried if she wasn't looking out for you," Jack replied.

"So where are we going?" Jessica peered out the windshield.

He didn't answer, though he looked relaxed, one hand on the wheel and the other resting on the gearshift.

"Dinner."

She turned to give him a look. He laughed, then turned his hand over and held it out. Jessica slid her palm into his. His fingers wove between hers, folding around her hand perfectly, as though they were made to fit together.

"Have you ever been to the La Monte?"

"No, but I heard the place is impossible to get into." She'd driven by it once or twice on visits to the valley — and listened to Estelle waxing rapturous about their seafood, which she'd tried when she and Lily's father celebrated their 30th anniversary there. But Jessica had never dined anywhere that fancy. She'd heard rumors that the menu didn't even have prices on it.

Jack just grinned, as though this were an everyday occurrence. "Fortunately, I know a man."

"You've only been in Montrose Valley a couple of weeks and you already know a man?" Jessica laughed.

Jack turned onto a narrow road that led up the mountain. La Monte, true to its name, sat near the peak of one of the mountains surrounding Montrose Valley. The view was half of the draw — the food being the other. "I bought a beautiful antique clock from the owner a couple of weeks ago. He was overcharging, which we were both aware of, but I hadn't seen a piece that well-kept in years and couldn't resist. Anyway, he offered to toss in a meal with the bargain. I was saving it for my last night here, but I'd rather share it with you."

He squeezed her hand gently, and Jessica squeezed back, smiling. Outside the windows, a beautiful, clear night had fallen. Stars stretched above the valley, dark shadows cloaked trees and vales, broken by lights from houses and farms. From here, the central plaza of Montrose, still decked in its Christmas finery for a couple more days, was visible as a shining beacon, the brightest thing for miles around.

"I can see why my grandfather loved this place," Jack said quietly, as the car climbed higher. "When I was younger, all I wanted to do was run away to London the first chance I got. I thought a big city would teach me who I was, how I wanted to live. And I suppose, in a way, it did. I realized that the bigger the city is, the more cramped it can feel."

Watching the horizon, Jessica nodded thoughtfully. "New York's the same for me. I feel claustrophobic there.

But here, there's so much space. Like you can do anything you set your mind to." When she looked back over at Jack, she caught him watching her, before his gaze moved back to the road.

"I was going to say, it seems easy to make a home here."

"I wish." Jessica sighed wistfully.

"Do you?" Jack glanced at her again, one eyebrow lifted, his expression inscrutable. "If you could snap your fingers and make it happen tomorrow —"

"What, quit my job and move here with no house or prospects?" Jessica laughed.

But Jack shook his head. He took another curve, this one around the far side of the mountain, so Montrose temporarily slid out of view. Other towns replaced it on the opposite side of the valley, more constellations, galaxies that Jessica would love to get to know. She imagined going on drives every weekend, exploring all the little valleys and towns around the one that had stolen her heart.

"If money were no object," he said. "Where would you go?"

"Montrose," Jessica replied. She didn't need to think twice. "In a heartbeat."

The restaurant appeared ahead of them, up a final stretch of road. The front of the restaurant was marked by a stone archway, beyond which lanterns led the way up a stone path toward the building itself. They parked near the front, a valet opening their doors for them. Jack circled around to offer Jessica his arm, and together they stepped under the arch.

In the dim light of the flickering lanterns, the restaurant looked like something out of a movie. Rustic stone walls and wood-beamed ceilings with modern floor-to-ceiling windows that overlooked the valley and the surrounding mountains. Ivy adorned the exterior, adding to the charm and someone had added twinkling lights, giving the whole place an otherworldly appearance.

"I'm so underdressed," Jessica fretted, tugging at the hem of her dress.

But Jack shook his head, tightening his arm around hers. "Nonsense. You're perfect."

A concierge opened the door to usher them inside and take their coats. Jessica paused to gaze a moment, La Monte was every bit as breathtaking as Estelle had told her.

Soft, ambient lighting lit the dining room, a big stone fireplace on the far wall, elegant bouquets of fresh flowers on each table. In the far corner, a live quartet played soft, classical music, just loud enough to add to the atmosphere, rather than drown out conversation.

A handful of diners dotted the room, which was filling up fast, to judge by the headlights appearing one after another on the windows behind them. Jessica trailed after the waiter as he led them to a table at the farthest point of the restaurant, where two corners of the windows met. Sitting here felt almost like sitting on a cloud; as far as the eye could see in both directions, there was just endless, beautiful night sky and twinkling valley towns.

"It's beautiful," Jessica murmured.

"It certainly is," Jack replied softly. But when she tore

her gaze from the view to look over at him, Jack was staring straight at her, ignoring the view entirely.

"What?" Jessica asked after a pause, when he still hadn't torn his gaze from her.

Jack cracked a smile. "Sorry. I'm just… It's the little things, you know?"

"Like the fanciest restaurant for miles around?" Jessica raised an eyebrow, and he laughed.

"No, I mean being able to come here." At her blank stare, he added, "You've no idea how refreshing it is to simply be allowed to exist."

"In what way?" She wasn't sure what that meant.

"The polite lack of intrusion. Everyone getting on with their lives, and allowing everyone else to do the same. While just being there, if needed… I've been met with nothing but kindness. Another reason I love Montrose." His fingers twined around hers, his thumb brushing along the outside of her wrist, raising the fine hairs along her skin in his wake. "And I intend to make the most of every day I have left here."

CHAPTER 23

Lily spent the next breakfast teasing Jessica with light-hearted speculation and more searching questions about Jack's life, although Jessica still couldn't really shed much light on that.

"He's pretty consistent though," Lily said, laughing. "I mean, he says he'll call and *voilà*, he calls!"

"Yes, and he's just the perfect gentleman," Jessica said, her eyes sparkling. "I can hardly believe it." She shook her head, dazed with the unexpectedness of it all. They were laughing gaily as they came back indoors from walking Thor around the track behind the farmhouse.

Matilda Collins had left a message on the answer machine — the library had received a response to its request for information on Jonathan Montgomery. They both frowned as they listened to it.

"No, no, no," Jessica said.

"She's gone to a lot of trouble." Lily replied although she was troubled too.

"But we've just accepted him for who he is, we don't need to dig into his life."

"No, but the file's going to sit there until we do something," Lily said.

"Tell her to destroy it."

They discussed it through the morning and lunch and all the way to the library.

"We've started it, Jess," Lily said. "We should follow through, and we both agreed we do this so we can be sure of who he is." She was staring out the windscreen, gloved hands on the wheel as they turned into the parking lot.

And Jessica hadn't really found a good enough reason to put this off, because whatever she'd learned about Jack, there was still a lot missing.

The deal she'd made with Jack kept running through her mind: '*a judgment-free zone*' they'd said. And she was breaking it already. Last night, the wonderful meal, the kiss goodnight. The passion between them had sparked a fire in them both, a deep desire she'd never felt before. Was that all it was, desire? Or could it be more? One thing she'd really learned about him was that he guarded his privacy. She still didn't really understand why, but it was important to him, and here she was, breaking it.

She followed Lily up the steps into the library. The atmosphere seemed subdued post-Christmas — the jar of candy was half-empty, and as they entered, Matilda was in the middle of taking down a few of the Christmas decorations. She caught sight of them and hopped off her ladder with an apologetic smile. "Got to prep for the New Year's festivities now," she said, by way of explanation. She gestured to the counter, where Jessica noticed a fresh pile of decorations — these were all hand-made illustrations by local kids of their New Year's resolutions: *Read more books, Eat all my vegetables,* or, Jessica's personal favorite; *Be a superhero.*

"Looks like fun," Jessica said.

"It should be! We're doing a mini-countdown here for the kids at New Year's in Greenwich Mean Time—since that's only 7pm here." Matilda winked. "Perfect for the parents who want to get them in bed at a reasonable hour. You two should stop by!"

Jessica's face fell. "I wish," she managed to say. "I'll be back in New York, working." She forced a weak, unconvincing smile. "But, hey, launching a new software program at midnight should feel pretty cool."

"That's the spirit," Matilda said, though to judge by the sympathetic look she shot Jessica, she didn't seem to buy it. "Anyway, your request from England came back. Let me just find it…"

They waited while Matilda shuffled through a few more papers until she found the one she wanted.

"Here we go." She handed over a fax with a return address in London. The cover letter gave a brief disclaimer about how many Jonathan Montgomeries were in England (over 200), so the disambiguation was a bit tricky. But the library explained that it assumed the petitioner was referring to Jonathan (Jack) Montgomery, of Montgomery Hall, Devon, since his name had been in the newspapers frequently of late.

Jessica handed the faxes to Lily. "That's impossible. It's

got to be one of these few hundred other Jonathans. He said he lived in Chilcot."

But Lily turned the page to the actual contents, and her eyes widened.

"What is it?" Jessica demanded. Panic shot through her. Why would newspapers write about someone? Was he a criminal?

Rather than responding, Lily simply rotated the papers so Jessica could read.

The second page of the file was a full-page black-and-white copy of a newspaper called *The Express*. To judge by the big font sizes and the amount of exclamation points on the subtitles, Jessica guessed it must be a tabloid.

And right there, front and center, unmistakable despite the grainy quality of the photocopy, was Jack. He wore sunglasses, and had one hand extended, like he was about to block his face. But the photographer caught him an instant before that, revealing his telltale sharp jawline, the angle of his nose. He was halfway up the steps of a historic-looking building, wearing a suit that looked like it must have cost more than Jessica's entire wardrobe. Behind him, an absolutely gorgeous woman.

The caption beneath the photo declared: *Britain's Most Eligible Bachelor Back in Town!* And underneath that. *Sir Jack Montgomery seen leaving London bachelor pad with latest girlfriend, model Felicity Moore —*

It cut off, with a note to read more within.

"Sir Jack? He's…" Jessica stared at it, hardly able to take it in.

Lily reached over to turn the page, but the next item in the stack wasn't a continuation. Instead, it was the front cover of an entirely different newspaper, this one called *The Daily Mail*. Jack's photo wasn't front and center here, so it took a moment to locate him — in the lower right hand corner, standing solemnly beside a couple of other men all in black. *Montgomery Family Mourns Loss of Matriarch, Lady Annabelle (nee Curtis)*. That one was dated two years earlier. But the very next page in the stack the British library sent was another Daily Mail article from last year: *Tragedy Strikes Montgomeries Again: Less than a year after the death of her mother, Lady Meredith Montgomery takes her own life…*

"Oh no," Lily breathed.

A knot formed in the center of Jessica's chest. Suddenly, all his avoidance of talk about family made terrible sense. And so did the need to protect his privacy.

There were more pages — shots of Jack in pools and at beaches around Europe. One image of him with another stunning woman, the caption called her "his current girlfriend," although it was several years old.

"I can't believe this," Jessica murmured, her voice pitched low so that Matilda wouldn't overhear.

"I can't believe he's famous. Or that he's… what did it call him?" Lily snatched the earlier pages, flipping back to the very first one. "Ah, yes. Britain's Most Eligible Bachelor."

"Give me that." Jessica reached for the page. "Oh Lily, this is so awful." Her face had blanched. "He probably came here hoping to get away from all of that." His words ran through her mind. *People expect you to be someone you're not, just because of your name… Why can't we just exist? Why do we always need to be performing?*

Lily had become very somber and nodded. "I agree. Unless Jack tells people himself, nobody needs to know about this." Then, moving purposefully, she snatched all the papers from Jessica, squared her shoulders, and strode over to Matilda. "Matilda? Do you have a paper shredder we could use?"

Matilda's eyebrows rose. "You don't want the file?"

"We've learned enough," Lily replied firmly. "Thank you. We won't be needing it anymore."

"Alright." Matilda held out a hand, still with that curious expression. "I'll shred it. Anything else I can help you with?"

"That's all, thanks." Lily took Jessica's arm and marched her out of the library. "We are just going to have to forget about this whole awful mess."

CHAPTER 24

The day passed without any more phone calls or visits, and Jessica spent most of it in shock. She'd betrayed Jack's trust.

Not a word was to be spoken about it ever again, they kept repeating all day, but only finally stopped talking about it when Grant came home for dinner.

Next morning he was sitting at the kitchen table with the post-holiday edition of the Montrose Valley Post, staring at the front page. "Did you know about this?" he demanded the moment she entered, shaking the paper.

"Know about what?" Lily asked, yawning, as she stepped through the door, squinting through the window at Thor racing happily around the yard.

But Jessica had frozen where she stood, her gaze fixed on the newspaper Grant was waving around. Right there, front and center, was a grainy reproduction of The Sun's tabloid photo. *Montrose Valley Christmas Celebration Attracts British Nobility,* declared the headline. And the byline…*Sir Jack Montgomery, 7th Baronet of Montgomery Hall…* Jessica's hands rose to her cheeks. "Oh, no…"

An exclusive, by Caitlin Johnson.

"That little..." Lily cut herself off, eyes wide, fists clenched.

"As a rule, I don't believe anything Caitlin says, but is there any truth to that story?" Grant asked. "Jack's minor royalty?"

"He's not *royalty*," Jessica replied, reaching for the article.

"You're quoted in there, by the way," he added, with a grim expression.

Sure enough, Jessica quickly realized why. *Thanks to the investigative work of a couple of local sleuths, we now know the real identity of the polite, handsome stranger who has charmed his way into our town's hearts. "There's something about him that worries me," one of our intrepid sleuths, Jessica Brooks, was overheard to say at a local eatery. But get to the bottom of things, she did!*

"No, no, no." In the back of her mind, she could hear herself saying those words to Luke, in the dim light of the bar where she'd spotted Caitlin trying and failing to flirt with Jack. She thought that Caitlin was too far away to hear, although she'd been turning around on the bar stool and that must have been enough, because those were Jessica's words... but taken out of context. Jessica had been worried about Jack. And she had investigated him — though not anywhere near as intensely as Caitlin made it out to seem, and she'd never wanted to broadcast Jack's identity to the whole town. Caitlin had obviously done plenty of digging of her own.

Gently, Lily eased the newspaper from her hands. As

Lily began to read, she exclaimed, first in fury, then in horror. "Jess, I'm so sorry, I didn't think she'd stoop so low as to tangle you up in our feud."

"It's not about the feud. She just wants to get her hooks into Jack," Grant said.

"Why would Ed Stanton print this?" Lily asked

"Because it's news, and it's fact," Grant replied. "He can't hide things just because he knows the people involved, it's a kind of integrity."

"A very strange kind," Lily was inclined to argue, but Grant carried on.

"It's in *Ask Agatha's* column, too. Word must have gotten around the Post's news office. There's a whole article about how rude it is to invade people's privacy, and how Montrose Valley ought to be above petty gossip..." A rustle, as he took the paper from Lily to find the column again. "My favorite quote: '*loose lips drive perfectly wonderful people away.*'"

"Drive them away?" Jessica felt more tears filling her eyes which she swept aside angrily. She'd made this happen by her own suspicions, and no amount of apologizing or explaining was going to make it better. But that didn't mean she shouldn't try.

"I've got to go and talk to Jack — he might not have read this yet." She raced for the front door, grabbing her coat from the hook as she went.

"Do you want me to — " Lily began.

"I'm fine," Jessica barked, slamming the door behind her. This was her own mess. Lily wasn't the one who kept questioning who Jack really was or what he wanted here. Now, Jessica needed to clean it up.

But she wasn't the only one with a similar idea. When she reached the B&B, she froze in the middle of the sidewalk, shocked. A dozen people had gathered out front with takeaway coffees from the café in hand as a flimsy excuse. The way they all craned their necks made it obvious what they were really doing here and who they were looking for.

Jessica didn't recognize most of them — tourists, probably. But a couple familiar faces caught her attention, and she frowned. She was about to say something when the front door of the B&B opened and Miss Daisy strode out, arms folded over her apron. "If anyone would like a seat in the café," she called, gesturing next door. "There are spaces available. Otherwise, please keep the front porch here open and accessible to my *guests.*" She laid emphasis on those last two words, which was enough to convince the locals to scatter.

The tourists were slower to move, milling around and shuffling their feet, but still craning their necks for a glimpse through the front door as Miss Daisy closed it once more.

Bracing herself, Jessica wriggled through the traffic and surged up the front steps. She opened the front door, only to be confronted by Miss Daisy and a raised finger. "Unless you've a reservation — oh, Jessica, dear." She pressed her lips together, looking fretful, then shot a venomous look over Jessica's shoulder at the gathered gawkers. "Come inside, dear heart."

Miss Daisy led Jessica straight past reception to the cozy library. Jessica's pulse rang in her eardrums the whole walk over. She kept picturing Jack's face. The way he'd confided in her about his family, his struggles, and that kiss…had he felt the same as she had? That it had changed everything?

"I need to talk to Jack," she blurted, as soon as she and Miss Daisy were alone.

"I'm not certain that would be a good idea at the moment," Miss Daisy replied gently. "He told me he doesn't wish to entertain any visitors today."

She flinched. "It wasn't true, what Caitlin wrote. I mean, some of it, but she twisted everything. I was only trying to help Clara; I never wanted anyone to intrude into Jack's life. How could I have known about all that stuff written about him?"

"You couldn't have," Miss Daisy soothed. "None of us had any idea." She looked suddenly old, her face lined and drawn. "I just hope he isn't too badly shaken by this. And I'm awfully disappointed in how some in this town have handled the news." She narrowed her eyes at the door through which they'd come.

"If you see him, can you just… please tell him I'm sorry. I never meant to cause such a mess." Her lower lip quivered.

Miss Daisy reached over to pat the back of her hand with a sympathetic, worried expression. "If I see him, I'll let him know. But to be honest, I'm not sure if he plans to stay in town much longer."

Heart sinking, Jessica nodded and forced herself to stand. "I understand. Thanks anyway, Miss Daisy."

Jessica left to walk back to Lily's but paused to look over her shoulder, searching the B&B windows. But if Jack was up there, watching the road, she couldn't tell. There wasn't so much as a shadow moving in any of the rooms.

CHAPTER 25

Noonday sun painted the ceiling of Lily's guest bedroom a very different hue than the morning one. Jessica lay in bed staring at it, having feigned sleep when Lily crept upstairs to knock softly on the door and murmur that she'd made breakfast. Yesterday had gone by, she and Lily fretting between them, alternating between hope that Jack would call, and dreading someone ringing to say he'd left town.

She couldn't remember the last time she'd remained in bed this late. Maybe not since adolescence. Flashes of memories ran through her mind — Simon storming into her bedroom to wake her, informing her that their parents had left a whole list of chores and he refused to do them all by himself. The fights they used to get into seemed petty now, but also predictive, perhaps, of how their relationship devolved over the years.

Clearly, Simon still thought of Jessica as that little girl, shirking duty. And maybe she was. Maybe that was what all this dissatisfaction with her career path was about, or this yearning for a simpler life somewhere like Montrose.

Maybe she just wanted to run away from real adulthood, like Simon claimed, because she was still that teenage girl trying to escape reality.

Except... Lily and Grant weren't escaping reality. Neither were Lily's parents, or Luke, or Miss Daisy. Montrose was their reality. Just because they didn't have high-powered executive jobs, did that make them any less successful or grown-up?

Jessica kept her mind swirling back to those topics, because it was easier to think about her past than the mess with Jack. Every time she pictured that article in the newspaper, or imagined the trusting expression he wore at Christmas when he opened up to her about the pressure he was under, pain seared across her chest.

No wonder he refused to see her when she stopped by Miss Daisy's. Jessica wouldn't have wanted to either, if someone she'd trusted had gone behind her back like this.

She imagined barging into Miss Daisy's, trying to explain the disaster away — *I never meant for the news to get out; Caitlin made up those pull-quotes.* But the truth remained: she did go digging into Jack's past. A past he'd made very clear he did not want to raise. In the end, Jessica was the one who'd allowed his secrets to fall into the hands of someone like Caitlin Johnson. *Although he was the one who'd met with Caitlin...*she thought, then sighed. He wouldn't have known Caitlin was a reporter, would he?

The thought of facing the town now, after everyone had read that article, was too much. Jessica pulled the blankets over her head, groaning. Maybe she could change her train ticket, leave early. It was the 30th, she was due to leave tomorrow morning. How much would it cost to change her ticket?

Probably a bucketload, since half of the northeast planned to travel down to New York City in advance of the famous Times Square New Year's Eve celebration. People started lining up at dawn on the 31st, which was the only reason Jessica had been able to get tickets on a train that didn't reach the city until the evening.

She was still doing math on the likelihood of a ticket change when footsteps creaked up the stairs.

"Jessica?" Lily murmured from the other side of the attic door.

"She's not here," Jessica called. "She's currently evaporating from shame."

A stifled laugh from her friend, followed by a heavy sigh. "Luke called, he wanted to know if you were ok?"

"Tell him...tell him he's the best friend a girl could have."

"I can't," Lily said.

"Why?"

"Because I can't hear you through the door."

It was Jessica's turn to sigh. "Well, come in then."

She cried, she couldn't help it. Lily put her arms out and she broke into stupid heaving sobs.

"I'm going home tomorrow," she said, her voice cracking.

"He'll call. He's always called when he said he would." Lily tried reassurance.

"Until I trampled all over his life," Jessica replied. "Why should he call me? I'm just this horrible city girl. I don't trust anyone, I don't respect anyone's boundaries. Just pushing through life, oblivious to whatever anyone else wants."

"That's not true of you, or city people and you know it," Lily replied. "Come on, get dressed, we're going out."

"Where?" Jessica didn't move.

"Girl's lunch, my treat."

"Not in town," Jessica was adamant.

"No…" Lily sighed. "We'll go as far away as we can and you can wear a bag over your head if you want."

Jessica closed her eyes, then opened them and pushed back the covers. "OK, as long as it's a nice bag."

Lily grinned, then went to make hot chocolate while Jessica showered and dressed.

* * *

He didn't call. Not all that day and not the next. She packed her things into the canvas bag. Every action felt like she was fighting through molasses, her shoulders weighted, her hands fumbling to stuff her black dress in with the socks Luke had given her. Tears trickled down her cheeks, she dashed them away. *You've earned those,* she told herself harshly, then relented. She'd meant it for the best. Life, or fate, or whatever, was like this. She'd write him a letter when she got home, maybe he'd read it. Maybe…

Grant carried her bags to the car. Thor lay on her lap in the back, it wasn't far, only fifteen minutes. They drove through town, past the square, the Christmas tree still standing tall, but all the market stalls were gone. The place where Jack had stopped the runaway horse was now grimy with tire tracks. Miss Daisy's cafe looked busy, the windows were steamed up around the frames. The B&B looked quiet, as though everyone had gone home, or hadn't yet arrived for the big New Year's Eve unveiling that night.

"We'll see you come summer," Lily was saying. "We'll have picnics by the lake."

Grant frowned down at her. "Or if you can't get time off, we'll come to New York."

"So — picnics in the park!" Lily tried an upbeat note, then her face crumpled. "I'm going to miss you so much, Jess."

"Me too," was all Jessica could manage before her voice broke too.

They hugged, then Lily helped her climb into the train, shove her bags onto the luggage rack and waited as she sat down in her seat. Grant stayed on the platform, keeping Thor close to him.

"Call as soon as you can," Lily said, glancing out the window.

"He's not coming," her voice sounded weary.

"He might–"

The shrill note of the train's whistle cut her off.

"You'd best hurry or you'll be coming with me," Jessica warned.

"Ok, but I'm going to Miss Daisy's myself and talk with him!"

"No, Lily, it's his decision to make, and I guess he's made it."

Lily hesitated, then gave her one last hug and went back to join Grant and Thor. They all waved madly as the train pulled out, and then it was just Jessica, left alone with her thoughts.

The journey felt twice as long as it had coming. The carriage filled up and she leaned against the window, watching without seeing the world fly by. The journey felt interminable, her book just a blur of words, which she finally gave up trying to read. Could she have made it work with Luke? She'd done the right thing, she knew she had, but that question was going to eat away at her. And Jack? She thought of the grainy images of him and those beautiful women. He must have walked away from them. Why wouldn't he just walk away from her after what she'd done to him?

It was late evening when the train pulled into Grand Central Station. Back where she'd started — the same but totally different. She gazed up at the magnificent ceiling of the station. This was her life, accept it, get used to it, she told herself. She took a breath, straightened her shoulders and strode to join the crowds to make her way to the tall imposing office building she'd left two weeks earlier.

* * *

Ned gave her a tight grin as he glanced up from his cubicle. Frank frowned, he waited until she'd stowed her bag and powered up her computer before coming over.

"Late, Jessica, and you're way behind. There's a stack of codes," he nodded at the pile of printouts on the corner of her desk. "All of them have bugs. I need them working by ten, then we can run a system check before the big test at eleven."

"And I hope you had a great holiday too, Frank," she said.

He grumbled something inaudible and stalked off. Her phone rang, probably her mother. A frisson of guilt ran through her. She ignored it, reaching for the printouts to study in more detail. No-one in the workspace was talking, all she could hear was the rattling tap of keyboards. Dimmed lighting came from above, making it easier to see the screens, which glowed onto faces, intently staring into their monitors. Vermont could have been on a different planet.

She sighed, the red light blinked insistently on her phone. Damn it. She picked it up.

"He was there," Lily spoke breathlessly. *"I went straight round after the train left. I explained and he listened to me. I think he understands, I told him it wasn't just you, it was me too and we did it for the right reason, Jess. And I told him Caitlin had written the article…he said he's going to speak to Ed Stanton!"* She sounded excited. *"I told him he should have done that before, especially as he'd had drinks with Caitlin twice! Anyway, don't lose hope, Jess."*

She put the phone back in its cradle and bit her lip. Maybe it would make a difference…but even if he understood, it was down to his feelings for her. And whether he could bring himself to trust her…

She shook her head and turned her face to the screen, fingers beginning to fly.

CHAPTER 26

"What the?" Frank's voice broke the intense quiet. "I don't know who you are, but you'd better turn yourself around before I call security."

The low rumble of a man's voice answered him.

"She's busy, we're all busy," Frank snapped.

The voice replied, unhurried, unruffled.

Heads lifted, trying to see over the top of plain wooden cubicles. Jessica stopped typing, her fingers frozen over the keys.

"Now just you listen…" Frank's voice rose an octave.

Jessica let her hands drop. Slowly, she stood up. Her eyes sought him out. He seemed to realize as he locked onto her face, half lit by the glow from her screen. She whispered his name under her breath, then walked into the center aisle. People turned to stare, some half out of their chairs, craning for a better look.

"This is a cutting edge company, we have processes here that are market sensitive and I'm telling you to —" Frank carried on.

The man he was trying, and failing, to intimidate wasn't listening. He was staring down the aisle, hands dug into the pockets of his greatcoat. Sea-green eyes dark under lowered black brows.

"Jack?" Jessica's voice was hoarse.

"Jessica," he replied, his tone softening.

Frank spun round. "If this is some friend of yours, you tell him —"

"Jessica," Jack repeated. "May I take you out to celebrate the New Year?"

"What? Now, you just listen —" Frank tried again, he barely reached Jack's chin and was almost on tiptoe, glaring up at him.

Jack didn't seem to notice he was there. His eyes were fixed on Jessica.

"Right, I'm calling security," Frank turned on his heel to march back to his office.

"I'm a friend of Calum Mathieson," Jack said.

"What? You're…" Frank spun back around. "But…who *are* you?"

Jessica was quite aware that Calum Mathieson had founded, and owned, the company. So was everyone else, and murmurs began to fly around the room.

"Jessica?" Jack held his hand out.

She stared at him; it didn't seem possible. Then she walked towards him, putting her hands out, which she dropped again when she saw the astounded faces of her colleagues.

"Jack?" the smile on her lips trembled. "I thought…I thought you'd never forgive me."

"There was nothing to forgive, Jessica."

She reached him, placed his hands in his, feeling the strength and the warmth. "How did you get here?"

"Always so practical…" He smiled at her. "I flew on an airplane. That's what they're for."

Laughter rose in her throat.

"But who is he?" Frank demanded again, very loudly.

"He's Sir Jonathan Montgomery of Montgomery Hall, Chilcot, England," Jessica said without moving her eyes from Jack's face.

Gasps followed that. Frank's mouth opened and closed, goldfish like.

"And you may bid farewell to the future Lady Montgomery." Jack's glance flicked briefly to Frank.

Frank didn't say a word, his jaw had fallen and his eyes rounded to almost bulging.

"Shall we find your coat?" Jack asked Jessica.

"Yes, please." She smiled suddenly, a beaming smile that lit the room.

He turned, waiting as she fell into step beside him. She tucked her hand into the crook of his arm and together they walked towards the door.

"Goodbye Jessica," Ned said quietly when they reached his desk.

She stopped. "Goodbye, Ned," she replied and leaned down to kiss him on the cheek. "I hope you have a wonderful life."

"And you… my Lady," he said and let out a long sigh, before turning back to his computer screen.

EPILOGUE

"Rose pink, a simple cut, just sweeping the floor and short sleeves," Lily was leaning over a notepad, pen in hand.

"Dusky pink," Jessica reminded her.

"What's your Mom going to wear?"

They were in the kitchen of Lily's farmhouse. Snow still lay thick on the ground outside. Thor's gaze was fixed to the counter where a plate of home-baked cookies were cooling.

"Lilac, I think." Jessica wrinkled her brow. "She's been in a fluster since I introduced her to Jack and he formally asked for my hand." She grinned. "She thinks he's wonderful."

"I'm so happy you're having the wedding here." Lily picked up a cookie to see if it had cooled, then took a cautious bite from it. "Umm, I love peanut butter and chocolate chip…"

"We'll have a blessing later in England. Jack says there's a chapel next to the house. We can all fly over together."

Jessica took a sip of creamy coffee, looking over at Lily on the stool opposite.

"Clara won't be able to make it," Lily said. "Or at least I don't think she will, it's such a long journey."

"No, perhaps it better if she doesn't," Jessica replied. "But the contractors are due to start on High Meadow House at the beginning of next month. She'd be more comfortable if she were somewhere else."

"Bethany said she can stay at her place," Lily finished the cookie. "Oh darn, I daren't have another or I'll never fit into my dress."

"The dusky pink dress."

"The rose pink dress," Lily said, then laughed.

It was a month after Jack had proposed to Jessica and met her mother and Simon, and it had felt like a whirlwind ever since. Simon had been difficult to start with, until he checked up on Jack and found out he was a partner in a major hedge fund company. He'd actually become friendly towards Jack after that, and after his initial astonishment, had treated Jessica with slightly awed respect. She was trying to treat him like her big brother, her grown up big brother. It had put their relationship on a new track, and while relieved, she thought it was a shame it had taken her engagement to Jack to achieve it.

"Do people think we're taking over her house?" Jessica had worried about this.

"No, she's been telling anyone who listened that Jack is having the makeover done for his grandma, like the good grandson he is." Lily said.

"He so wanted to help her out, make the place comfortable and warm for her." Jessica shook her head. "I still can't believe it."

"Neither can I, and I wish we'd taken a camera to take the look on Caitlin's face when we handed her the wedding announcement."

Jessica grinned at that, then became serious. "I've hardly seen Luke."

"He's expanding the clinic now that he has a new partner…and he seems pretty keen on her too."

"Hum…" Jessica took another sip of coffee. "That would be something."

"Maybe another Montrose wedding!" Lily grinned.

"Maybe!" Jessica laughed. "I'm so glad you and Grant are coming to England with us. It's going to be intimidating, meeting all the people there."

"You'll be fine, they'll be polite and reserved and anyway you'll have that big old Manor house to hide away in, and it's not like you've decided on living there."

"No, I'd rather stay here. Jack would too…He loves England but he feels the pressure there. Montrose is so peaceful."

"But you can't move into High Meadows House with Clara until the house is finished. You all agreed on that," Lily reminded her.

"I know, and it will be wonderful. It was so kind of Clara to offer to share. I think it will work, we can take care of her. And my mother loves her. She's already chosen her bedroom so it looks like she's going to be spending her time in Montrose too." She laughed.

Lily shook her head, hands now wrapped around her coffee mug. "Who'd have thought a stupid newspaper article about hunting ghosts would have brought us to this."

Jessica nodded. "Yes…Lily, what do you think we saw that night?"

"I don't know, but it sure spooked Thor."

"You don't think it could have been that poor soldier from the civil war?"

Lily's blue eyes met Jessica's brown ones. "Or Joe?"

The telephone rang, making them both jump. Lily slid off her seat. "I expect that'll be Mrs O'Dowd about the flowers. Or Mr Gunter about the horse-drawn carriage."

"Or Miss Daisy about the cake," Jessica added, then returned to her thoughts. Whoever, or whatever was out in the back garden that night, it was part of Montrose. Just as she would be.

She sighed, it felt like she'd finally come home at last.

Coming Home for Christmas is the first book in the Montrose Valley romance series. There will be more!

Karen Baugh Menuhin is an established author with over a million book sales, mostly in Murder Mystery. These are set in England in the 1920s, are clean, quite complex and enjoyable.

Jo Baugh is a young Canadian/American author just starting out and loves writing about romance!

If you'd like to keep up to date with new releases, perhaps you'd like to join the Readers' Club? As a member, you'll receive the FREE audio short story, including the ebook itself, 'Heathcliff Lennox – France 1918' and access to the 'World of Lennox' page, where you can view portraits of Lennox, Swift, Greggs, Foggy, Tubbs, Persi and Tommy Jenkins. There are also 'inspirations' for the books, plus occasional newsletters with updates and free giveaways.

You can find the Heathcliff Lennox Readers Club, and more, at karenmenuhin.com. You can also follow me on Amazon for immediate updates on new releases, plus special deals, sales and free giveaways.

Here's the full Heathcliff Lennox series list. All the ebooks are on Amazon. Print books can be found on Amazon and online through your favourite book stores.

Book 1: Murder at Melrose Court
Book 2: The Black Cat Murders
Book 3: The Curse of Braeburn Castle
Book 4: Death in Damascus
Book 5: The Monks Hood Murders
Book 6: The Tomb of the Chatelaine
Book 7: The Mystery of Montague Morgan
Book 8: The Birdcage Murders
Book 9: A Wreath of Red Roses
Book 10: Murder at Ashton Steeple
Book 11: The Belvedere Murders
Book 12: The Twelve Saints of Christmas
Book 13: Valentine's Day Murder – ready for pre-order now

There are Audio versions of the Heathcliff Lennox series read by Sam Dewhurst-Phillips, who is superb. He 'acts' all the voices – it's just as if listening to a radio play.

The audio versions of Miss Busby Investigates are narrated by the amazing Corrie James and extremely popular. These can be found on Amazon, Audible and Apple Books.

Here's the list so far of the Miss Busby series.

Book 1: Murder at Little Minton
Book 2: Death of a Penniless Poet
Book 3: The Lord of Cold Compton – ready for pre-order now

A LITTLE ABOUT KAREN BAUGH MENUHIN

1920s, Cozy crime, Traditional Detectives, Downton Abbey – I love them! Along with my family, my dog and my cat.

At 60 I decided to write, I don't know why but suddenly the stories came pouring out, along with the characters. Eccentric Uncles, stalwart butlers, idiosyncratic servants, machinating Countesses, and the hapless Major Heathcliff Lennox. A whole world built itself upon the page and I just followed along.

Now, some years later I have reached number 1 in USA and sold over a million books. It's been a huge surprise, and goes to show that it's never too late to try something new.

I grew up in the military, often on RAF bases but preferring to be in the countryside when we could. I adore whodunnits, art and history of any description.

I have two amazing sons – Jonathan and Sam Baugh, and his wife, Wendy, and five grandchildren, Charlie, Joshua, Isabella-Rose, Scarlett and Hugo. My wonderful husband is Krov Menuhin, a retired film maker, US special forces veteran and eldest son of the violinist, Yehudi Menuhin. We live in the Cotswolds.

For more information you can contact me via my email address, karenmenuhinauthor@littledogpublishing.com

Karen Baugh Menuhin is a member of The Crime Writers Association, The Author's Guild, The Alliance of Independent Authors and The Society of Authors.

Printed in Great Britain
by Amazon